You and Me

KATIE CROSS

KCW

Chapter One

CORA

The smell of espresso drew me downstairs.

I ventured carefully. No cars populated the parking lot of the Frolicking Moose Coffee Shop, which meant that the customers had already cleared out. Deep darkness coated the mountain world, where a torrential snow storm loomed with promise.

Local chatter expected ninety inches of snow in the highest elevations, and potentially sixty in town. Five feet of snow in forty-eight hours. Hardly seemed real, though flakes already twirled down.

At least I'd have access to all the coffee.

Snow crunched under my boots as I hurried around the building and through the front door. Muted lights reflected the CLOSED sign as I slipped inside.

Leslie, the store manager, brightened when she saw me. Her bright-eyed gaze met mine with an unusual glint.

"Hello Cora!"

"Hey."

"I completely forgot you were cleaning tonight." Her gaze

slid to Maverick with a conspiratorial gleam. "Cora will be here cleaning . . ."

Her low drawl indicated . . . something. The hair on the back of my neck perked up.

Maverick, co-owner of the Frolicking Moose Coffee Shop, stood across the way. He ran the shop with Leslie's help and his wife, Bethany's, oversight. He leaned against the counter with both palms, eyebrows lifted with interest. Sooty eyelashes framed inquisitive eyes.

"How long will you be cleaning?" he asked.

"Depends on how good the music is on the radio tonight."

He chuckled, a deep, rolling thing. "My cousin Hawk was supposed to be here a few hours ago. He normally gets a ride share, but rented a car instead. We haven't heard from him. I expect him to show up soon. I was going to drive him to our house so he didn't get lost, but Bethany needs me now."

"I can give him directions."

"The GPS doesn't always take people on the right path." His gaze flitted outside. "And the weather is going to worsen. If he has a sedan rental car, he may not make it up my drive-way. I might have to come back for him if he arrives."

With his fingertips, he slid a piece of paper to me.

"Here are some written directions to get him to my place. Do you mind hanging out down here until he shows up?"

Leslie slipped around the counter, where she reached for a coat draped over a tabletop. Wrinkles occluded her brow as she peered outside, illuminated by shining headlights that drove into the parking lot.

Her husband, Tanner, whom she married only a few months ago, waved from inside the truck. Snow had already collected on the hood, like cotton ball puffs set in lines.

"Gotta go." Leslie flung her purse onto her shoulder. "With this storm, I fully expect to get stuck on top of the mountain for a week, so don't bother me." Leslie pointed to me, then Maverick, with her firmest mom-glare. "Be safe, both of you. Maverick, go home already. You're stressing your wife out."

Leslie stepped outside with a wave.

"What did you say your cousin's name was again?" I asked with a glance at the directions. Simply broken down and easy to read.

"Hawk Mercedy."

The name rang a bell, but I couldn't peg it.

"He's late thirties, dashing, and looks a bit like me."

Built like a refrigerator? I thought.

"He'll probably be wearing a baseball hat, if I had a guess, and shorts. Really chill guy. I can vouch for him."

My eyebrow lifted. "Did you say he'd be wearing shorts?"

"Texan."

"Does he visit often?"

Mav snorted. "No, almost never. I saw him a year ago, at our Mercedy family reunion. We've kept in touch with text messages since then. Of all my cousins, he's probably my favorite. Well, next to Noah. Hawk is . . . well . . ."

"He's what?"

His hesitation lasted a moment longer. He eyed me, as if weighing something out, then shook his head.

"He's . . . Hawk."

The dying energy of his response left much unstated. Not sure what to say, and ignoring the niggling feeling that told me I'd heard the name Hawk Mercedy before, I let it go.

Maverick continued to stare outside, drumming his fingertips on the counter.

"Okay," he declared through a breath. "I'll head home. If Hawk doesn't arrive within the hour, he probably won't come. Hopefully, he pulled off to wait out the storm somewhere in the middle of the canyon, or stayed at the airport and forgot to call."

"I'll hang around down here for a couple of hours, just in case."

"Thanks, Cora. Appreciate your help. "

Maverick's truck disappeared into the maelstrom of a storm, leaving me alone in the shop. Snowflakes twirled like frozen confetti, thickening the cold. I headed for the back hallway. A bin of cleaning supplies rattled as I pulled it out and set it on the closest table.

The sooner I finished cleaning the shop, the faster I could return to my painting. *The* painting. Like an itch, it impatiently waited for me to make it the current pinnacle of my career.

Tonight, I would take a cleaning break, then answer the call of the oils. Not only would it be my greatest work to date, but it would yield the largest commission.

A commission I had *big* plans for.

I plugged my phone into the speakers, cranked up the nineties pop music, and grabbed a spray bottle of organic lemon cleaner. With any luck, Hawk would stay lost and I could return to my slice of heaven-on-earth upstairs during snowmageddon.

Somehow, that seemed far too simple.

/ Chapter Two

HAWK

White stuff.

Gross.

Nose wrinkled, I peered out on a snowy picture. Pineville lay in quiet isolation, little more than an abandoned mountain town. I'd only been here once, and barely recognized it now that it lay under a blanket of rapidly accumulating snow.

No cars.

Not even a streetlight.

So much friggin' ice.

Blerg.

The heat blasted at full speed through my little rental car. Somehow, I'd finagled down a slippery highway that, I assumed, closed just behind me. If the flashing lights and amassed highway patrol cars and lowering bars meant anything.

Close call.

With great reluctance, I peered out the window and to the ground. How many inches had already fallen? Three? Four, at least. Enough to chill my ankles and swamp my toes.

Siiiiick.

Why had I worn sandals?

Why had I rented a car instead of paying for a driver?

Ah, right. Conspicuousness. The novelty of fading into life without drawing attention held too deep of a draw. At home, I couldn't be just another person. Here, I could fade into obscurity.

Or so I hoped.

Besides, I needed all the practice I could get with disappearing into life, even if only for a night. What with the whole live-like-a-normal-person thing I had planned for a vague time in the future. When one hoped for an entire life overhaul, one had to make it happen.

A step at a time.

Cursing under my breath, I readjusted my baseball cap and reached for my backpack. Better to get the cold walk into the shop over with. Maverick would probably have boots I could borrow for the drive to his house. With any luck, the storm would disappear and I'd be on my plane, Texas bound, tomorrow evening.

Snow brushed along the back of my neck as I shoved the door open, slipped a backpack strap over my shoulder, and stepped into the cold. A hiss of breath through my teeth accompanied the bone-chilling hug around my bare ankles.

Lead a multi-billion dollar empire.

Can't figure out how to dress myself.

The car door slammed, spilling more snow on the packed ground, as I quickly skittered up wooden stairs and onto a creaky porch. Ice crystals accumulated in the spaces between my toes. Sweet misery. Who could stand this?

Halfway across the snowy scape, I paused.

Inside, a woman stood in the middle of the coffee shop, clutching a mop. Music blared through the windows. Eyes closed, head tilted back, she belted out a pop song from the nineties like her life depended on it.

Hello.

Locks of auburn hair, mixed with tones of black and a lighter red, danced around a soft face. She swung into a spiral, laughing when she nearly tripped over her own feet. She wore a pair of old sweatpants littered with stains. A black, long-sleeved shirt ran from shoulder to wrist.

Snow melted beneath my toes as I regarded her, struck by something I couldn't put my finger on.

First, did people *still* listen to this music?

Second, who enjoyed it with such abandon?

A quick scan pegged her in her late twenties. Curved in all the right places, with a gentleness about her facial expression. I shuffled forward the final steps, reached for the door, and rapped on it. The pulsing music must have hidden the sound, because she continued to whirl with her mop.

I lifted my hand to knock again, but waited.

On a lower strain of music, she grabbed a chair and stacked it on top of a table. Clad in socks, she slid to the next one. The mop accompanied her, loosely held. A smile threatened at the corners of my lips, but I pushed it back. No, I didn't want her to think I laughed at her.

More firmly, and during a break between songs, I rapped on the door.

Her head popped up, hair swaying around her jaw. Azure eyes widened slightly as she stared at me. Seeming to recover, she scrambled forward, flipped the lock, and pulled it open.

"Hey."

Her bright smile welcomed me inside without a hint of embarrassment or rebuff or irritation.

"Hey. I'm Hawk." I stuck out a hand as she closed the door in a gust of flurries. "I'm Maverick's cousin."

She accepted the handshake with a smile. "Good to meet you. I've been waiting for you to show up. I'm Cora."

"Cora."

Her grin widened. "You got it."

Her voice had a lyrical, flowing quality to it. Husky. Thick, too. Like she'd just woken up. I struggled to focus on the words instead of the sound. My backpack dropped lower on my arm.

"You have been waiting for me?"

"Maverick had to go home." She twirled around, headed back to her mop with lithe movements. "Bethany was calling for some help, I think. Sick kids, or something? He left you directions on the counter if you want to drive to his cabin tonight."

The word *cabin* fell into the air.

She leaned back, glancing behind me to the spot where I'd parked a four-door commuter car. Her eyes slid back to my legs with basketball shorts and flip-flops.

Amusement quirked her lips into another full smile.

"Might not be the best idea with a city-boy ride to take you there," she drawled. "The mountain switchbacks will eat you up in a second."

She turned back to her work.

Bothered more than I wanted to admit, I dug my phone out of my pocket, found Maverick's name, and called. Five rings later, it dropped to voicemail. I closed out of the call, and sent a quick text.

Hawk: Just made it to the coffee shop. Everything all right over there?

No immediate response followed.

I glanced up. Cora set the last chair on top of a table,

humming under her breath. She must have lowered her music because it didn't peal through the shop anymore. The limp, graying mop followed her across the room, like a toy tugged by a child.

I pulled my baseball hat off, scrubbed my hand through my hair, then replaced it. "He uh . . . didn't answer."

Cora glanced up, then quickly away. "Might be in a dead spot. Want some coffee or tea while you're waiting?"

"Are you a barista here?"

Further amusement lined her voice. "Not really. I clean at night, but I can warm water and sling coffee grounds or tea bags around. They have some killer croissants in the fridge too, if you're hungry. If this storm dumps even part of what they're predicting, you'll have lots of chances to eat them."

The impression that she found great amusement in everything left a strange sensation under my skin.

"Ah, I'm good, thanks."

Her humming picked back up. A faint, trilling little ditty that ran in time with a slow ballad. She disappeared into a back room with the mop. I stared at my phone, mind blank.

Pull it together, Hawk. Focus. You have a problem. You are a solution finder. Why isn't your brain working?

Cora strolled by, mop-free. The faint scent of lemon followed. I drew in a deep breath, let it out.

Did I just . . . *smell* her?

Gah.

The mountain air had me all fuddled.

Instead of doing something productive to solve this dilemma, I stared at my phone and thought about the way this woman smelled. As if willing the phone to ring would make Maverick call me sooner.

Irritated, I shoved the phone into my pocket and moved to my backpack.

"Mind if I hook up to the Wi-Fi?"

From behind the counter, she waved a hand toward a sign on the wall with the password. She lifted a coffee mug that said *Adulthood is straight up the worst hood I've ever lived in* to her lips to have a sip. A piece of paper lay on the counter in front of her. Her eyes darted around, reading it.

Turning my gaze away, I pulled my computer out, set it on a tall table not cluttered with chairs. Once I connected, I immediately regretted it.

Emails flooded my inbox. Messages popped up on my chat threads. The same would be on my phone, but I'd stopped those notifications while driving and hadn't checked.

My heart sank into my stomach.

THIS IS YOUR BOARD MEETING REMINDER, HAWK.
M. Ventures Acquires Losing Business
The Winds of Change at M. Ventures.

Alerts and text messages continued down the screen. I ignored all of them, slammed my computer shut, and shoved it back in the bag.

Nope.

Not ready to tackle that hellhole yet.

My phone vibrated in my pocket. I yanked it out.

Nicola: You made it safe, bro?

Hawk: Just at the coffee shop, trying to track down Maverick. Stupid amount of snow outside. I might need the chopper tomorrow.

Nicola: Say the word and I'll send it. We need to talk

when you can. Some developments with the new acquisition.

Hawk: Bad developments?

Nicola: Not from my purview.

I scowled. My sister, Nicola, the Chief Operating Officer of my company, M. Ventures, had a strange way of seeing the business world that rarely made sense to anyone but her until it was too late. Then, her genius usually came through on a lucky chance.

Hawk: I'll be in touch. Plan on 4:00.

Nicola: Now that you successfully closed a deal with the local hospital, aren't you hanging out with Mav until your flight?

Hawk: There is no vacation, Nic.

When I set my phone back down, Cora drew my gaze. She stood a few paces away, peering at me with interest. Instead of a blush or withdrawal, she held my equally curious stare.

"Anything I can do to help?" she asked. "You look stressed."

"Drive me to Mav's with a truck that has winter tires and four-wheel drive? Better yet, back to the airport."

Another beaming smile broke her lips. "I left my fairy godmother's wand upstairs tonight. Maybe in the morning."

Her levity loosened the tension in my chest. If I had to wait around for Maverick, her company wouldn't be so bad.

"Does it always snow this much?" I asked, hooking a thumb over my shoulder. The urge to make small talk wasn't usually one I indulged in. The intimacy of being the only person here with her necessitated it.

Not to mention an unidentifiable . . . something . . . about her. Her voice, so amused and quick and easy, made me want to hear more. A melody I couldn't get enough of.

She shrugged. "Dunno."

"You're not from here?"

"Nah. Just here to do some work stuff for a while." A jerk of her head motioned above. "I rent the loft from Mav and Bethany. They needed help with cleaning in the evenings—having a hard time staffing it, I guess—so I offered my services."

"How long will you be here for?"

"Until I finish a work project. Another six weeks or so?"

"Where will you go then?"

"Dunno!"

I nodded, intrigued by the details-at-large. *Work stuff* and *offered to help* and *dunno*. I couldn't peg her. Bright pink socks under old sweatpants covered in paint, yet a charmingly fast smile, could mean anything. A sense of impermanence filled her words.

"Interesting."

Cora set the mug off to the side. "Well, you're stuck here until Maverick calls, right?"

"Ah . . . yes."

She opened her mouth to say something, but a phone buzzed. The rattling sound sent a hiccup through my thoughts. I reached for my cell, but it wasn't mine that rang. Before I could process it, Cora had her phone pressed to her ear.

"Hey Bethany."

Cora's dark blue eyes lifted to mine. I watched her, wary, as her lips dropped. Her expression crumbled.

"Oh, I see. He's all right? Of course. Right. Yes. Totally fine. We'll figure something out for the night. Will do."

A sinking sensation dropped my heart into my stomach when Cora tucked the phone into her pocket.

"Maverick was just about home when he stopped to help a little old lady into her snowy driveway near them at the top of the mountain. She made it inside her garage, thankfully, but he slid off the side of the road on his way home. He's stuck. Benjamin has a friend with a winch, but he can't get there until the morning. Mav walked home and is safe, but can't go anywhere now."

"That means?"

Her teeth sank into her bottom lip before she said, "I'm pretty sure that means you're sleeping here tonight."

All the air left my chest in a long breath.

"Oh."

Her hands dropped to the end of her shirt, which she toyed with. The tips of her fingers had telltale signs of paint. A sapphire hue—black too? My thoughts strayed as I tried to imagine why a woman cleaning a coffee shop had paint on her fingertips. Artist, maybe.

Forcefully, I pulled my brain back to heel. Wherever my head frolicked now, it needed to be elsewhere. Namely, deep in problem-solving mode. I had sixty-some odd inches of snow coming my way, and a board meeting I had to attend in less than 48 hours.

Prospects didn't look great.

"Right."

Off came my hat. I scratched my scalp and gazed around. Cold coffee shop in the mountains with a historic snowstorm outside. That wasn't a problem—at least I had somewhere to crash.

The board meeting, on the other hand . . .

"Could be worse," Cora said in a bright chirp. "At least

you're not stuck in the car outside. There might be a blow-up mattress upstairs. You can sleep on it down here. I'll lend you a pillow, if you're nice."

Cora stepped out from around the counter, all business now. Her pert nose tilted up slightly as she walked my way.

What, exactly, did *she* think of this situation?

Did she care if some rando, big-city guy—who showed up in a historic blizzard with flip-flops and shorts—slept in the coffee shop below her house?

I held up a hand.

"Oh, no. I can't ask for your pillow or any of that. I can sleep in the car. It's got a full tank of gas. I can turn the heat on and off."

Cora stopped me short with a delighted laugh.

"Don't be ridiculous. You're wearing *shorts*. There's no way I can let you even walk out there."

I opened my mouth to protest, but stopped.

Really, could I say no?

Hardly.

"Ah . . . thanks."

Her eyes sparkled as she reached for a coat. "Leslie put all the display food away before she left, so you can raid the fridge and freezer if you want something to eat. You can work a microwave, right?"

"Believe it or not, I dress myself every day."

A pointed glance at my shorts caused me to lift my hands in surrender.

"Fair!" I said, laughing. "Fair."

She giggled again. A sound I enjoyed hearing far too much. "Wonderful. I'll be back in a few minutes."

Cora disappeared into the chilly night air.

The moment she left, a buzz jangled at my thigh. I glanced down. Ten missed calls, thirteen text messages, none of them from Maverick. I frowned. He must be digging himself out, still.

While horrendous music played in the background, I lowered to a chair and sped through the awaiting messages. They'd only quadruple if I didn't deal with them now, then set my boundary with the people at work, and eventually go to sleep. I'd figure this mess out tomorrow.

Several minutes bled by while I answered rapid-fire, ignored the missed calls to check emails, and skimmed the text messages from Nic.

Hawk: What's the update on that trending new virus?

Nicola: The case report details South America as the initial location of the illness. It's far from an epidemic yet, just something to be aware of.

Hawk: What's the death rate?

Nicola: 15% chance across the board, most from dehydration. Some from cardiac complications. Advanced-level telemonitoring is a must across all age ranges.

Hawk: We'll have more information at the board meeting?

Dots populated across my screen as I waited for Nicola's reply, already knowing what she'd say. When it came, it still didn't make me feel any better.

Nicola: Of course I will. Do you really think you'll leave in time? I saw the weather. It's . . . pretty intense.

Hawk: If you have to extract me by helicopter, I'll be

there. I'm a two-something hour flight away by private jet. Texas isn't that far. Take care of the rest of the chatter on the team messages for tonight, will you? I'll field interference from here over email.

With that, I shoved the phone back into my pocket. Nicola would waylay the rest of the fires for now. None of them threatened to destroy anything.

In the meantime, I had to find a way home.

Chapter Three

CORA

Light flooded the loft when I flipped the switch on, welcomed by the smell of linseed oil and turpentine.

A gigantic canvas, six feet wide and four feet tall, sat propped against the far wall. Twirling snowflakes punctuated the windows behind it, dancing by in ever-thickening clouds.

A mountain scene, taken straight from the behemoths surrounding Pineville, emerged from the layers. Such an enormous area had been a real pain to work with at times, but as I sank into the details of the ridges, the rills, the pines, the true magic of the scene manifested.

Six weeks left, and I'd finish.

A thrill zipped through me at the sight of it. A glade nestled at the edge of two rocky spines awaited tomorrow. Such minuscule detail work, combined with several shades of various colors, utterly excited my inner challenger.

Hue, shading, color, paint on the palette. My world.

Thoughts of Hawk cluttered my mind as I dug into the closet in search of a blow-up mattress. Maverick hadn't been kidding. He resembled Hawk in sheer *size*. Broad shoulders.

Sculpted arms. Hawk had darker skin—brown where Maverick was currently winter pale.

Every time Hawk reached for his hat, his thick forearms flexed, which drew my gaze to his powerful hands. Hands I very much wanted to hold mine. When he revealed that quiet grin?

I.

Wanted.

To.

Die.

A hanger dropped out of the air and slammed onto the top of my head. I scowled. Rubbing the sore spot, I backed out of the closet where a blow-up mattress did not exist. My phone vibrated. I glanced at it, did a double take, then snatched it off the table.

Mav: Can you talk?

I hit *call* and pressed it to my ear. He answered half a ring later. "So," his deep voice drawled. "What do you think of Hawk?"

Laughing, I leaned against the wall. "You have a real damsel in distress on your hands, Mav."

"Not me, *you*."

I'll take him anyday, I thought.

Mav continued.

"Before I speak to Hawk about this situation, I wanted to make sure you are okay with him sleeping downstairs. I mean, you have a separate entrance that's locked in two places to keep you safe, but still. If you're not comfortable, say the word and I'll tell Hawk to sleep in his car. He'll do it, for what it's worth."

I felt my answer out. Did Hawk strike me as a frightening type? Someone to fear? Not at all. I normally had a solid feel on this sort of situation, and nothing about Hawk rang alarm bells.

Except for his intensely attractive looks and that smoky gaze.

"Oh, it doesn't bother me."

"You sure? I mean, he's a stud. If you have to be trapped with anyone, you could do worse."

Mav had *that* right. Lovely Hawk, with his dark gaze hidden beneath a baseball cap. He had a careful wariness about him. Not mistrusting, but calculating. As if he created probabilities and statistics in his head.

Flip-flops and shorts in the mountains in January?

What a puppy.

"Totally sure," I said firmly. "Besides, he'll be sleeping in the shop and can't get into the loft, so I'll be safe. I appreciate the concern, and it's totally fine."

A long exhalation of relief followed. "Thanks for being flexible, Cora. There will be no driving down the mountain before a plow arrives. I predict no movement tomorrow, considering the expected inches. Think you can throw some food at him and make sure he stays warm?"

"You bet."

"Thanks. I'll text you updates, but will try to get down there as soon as I can. I know he had a narrow window of time in which to be here. Bethany called to see if there was any availability, but the hotel was already full with other stranded people. They've already closed the highway, too, even though plows are out."

"Sounds good. I thought I had a blow-up mattress, but I don't."

"Throw him a blanket, or something. He'll probably work through the night, anyway. Show him where the food is and he'll figure it out. Thanks, Cora."

"No problem."

A yawn distorted his reply. "All right, we'll see you tomorrow, with any luck."

"You really think so?"

He laughed. "Not a chance. This snow is moving in, parking for a while, then taking off when it wants. Hawk doesn't have a prayer of getting out of here in the next three days. Help yourself to the food and coffee. Someone should eat it if we can't sell it."

* * *

After more rummaging and no blow up mattress appeared, I gave up the search. Grabbing my best pillow and three warm blankets, I headed back down the spiral stairs.

Hawk sat at the edge of a chair, elbows propped on his knees. He glared at his phone, brows crashed together. A hint of a text message was visible over his shoulder as I stepped by.

He glanced up, eyed the blankets, and set the phone aside.

"Sorry." I grimaced. "I can't find a mattress."

Hawk shrugged those rippling shoulders that made my stomach catch.

"No problem."

His easy agreement startled me. I set the pillow and blankets down on the counter. "I could bring my couch cushions down?"

"Nah, it'll be fine. I used to sleep on the floor all the time."

"Really?"

He nodded with a vague slant. My desire to probe deeper into that story almost compelled me to ask more, but the late night prevented me. My brother, Cade, would say, *Chill out, Cora. You freak people out when you interrogate them. Your curiosity is going to get you into trouble.*

My enthusiasm dampened with the reminder. Hawk was a temporary stranger. Someone moving through. Fascinating he might be, but like all things that glittered, he, too, would disappear.

I patted the top of the pillow, sensing it was time for me to slip away.

"Well, is there anything else I can get you?"

The trailing question caught his attention. He stood up.

I swallowed.

Up close, I could better see his features. Powerful jaw. Broad cheeks, with a firm brow and a slightly dimpled chin. A hoodie cut across his wide shoulders. Snow clung to strands of dark brown hair, which topped his head in tight curls.

"I appreciate the help, Cora. I can figure out my way around down here."

"Sounds good."

With a tug, I pulled my jacket more tightly around me, avoided his eyes, and slipped back into the storm. As I hurried back to the loft, I tried not to imagine his eyes on my back.

Chapter Four

HAWK

My phone screen illuminated my face in a glare of white light that I really should turn off.

The buzz of travel, driving through snow, and knowing that I might not fly out tomorrow afternoon, as planned, had my adrenaline spiking.

Hawk: Your furnace is busted.

The text to Maverick immediately showed he read it. Three dots popped up.

Maverick: Impossible. I just bought it a few years ago with the remodel. You're being a wimp.

Hawk: It's 59 degrees in here. Icicles have formed on my nose hairs.

Maverick: Your nose hairs are too gross for water.

Hawk: Your hospitality is worse.

Maverick: We aren't Texans. We don't keep the heat at eighty overnight when no one is there. The thermostat is on the wall by the tables, to the left of the big window, you baby.

I grinned. The ribbing with Mav—who had always been my favorite cousin, though we'd never been close—eased some of my tension. A cocoon of blankets kept me warm. On the far wall, a glowing square caught my gaze. I *could* walk over there and turn up the heat.

Or I could stay in this exact spot, where the warmth finally permeated through all the blankets.

Decisions.

Cora drew my thought power instead. The repressed curiosity in her gaze had me wondering what questions she wanted to ask. I could *feel* them, though many people had queries about my life.

How did you make your first billion?
Was this a family inheritance?
How can I be stupid rich like you?
I have this idea . . .

Deal with my father, I always wanted to say, *and you can have all the billions.*

My lips curled up. I'd known Cora for all of fifteen minutes before she left, yet I couldn't stop thinking about her. The ruffles of red in her hair, like a gradient palette. Normally, I preferred the quiet. Tonight, I wished she had stayed. I had questions. She had questions.

The night was young.

Did she know about the empire behind me?

I hoped not.

Her auburn hair.

Messy hands.

Subdued clothes, with a wispy-like style that reminded me

of an artist. A laid-back, mountain bohemian flair. She'd hinted at a job, but withheld the juicy details. Painting, or something creative, I'd wager.

With a grimace, I turned onto my side. My arms pressed into the hard floor, but the pillow remained fluffy under my head. I closed my eyes, breathed deeply. A floral scent filled my head and soul.

Lavender.

Cora.

She'd given me her pillow. A gesture that felt . . . tender . . . on a night that had been so frustrating. Guilt bubbled in her gaze when she broke the news of no mattress. Had she offered a couch or a place to sleep up in her loft, I would have refused it.

That wouldn't have felt safe for her.

Plus, the last thing I wanted was a scandal. Headlines led to issues with the company. Quiet settlements were then made to get the lies to stop. Negative press drew Tate's attention, too, and anything that drew my father closer was something to avoid.

Pathetic, really. A sweet soul like Cora seemed too good a person to pull a manipulative stunt like others had before. Yet, my lawyers held the proof of what a fool I had been in the past. Still, I wondered . . .

Snow had never been my forte, but I couldn't deny the charm of the drifting flakes, so calm, as they descended. Especially now that I wasn't driving in it. My eyes closed and my body unwound.

Nothing I could do tonight. Tomorrow, I'd fix this situation and leave. Couldn't afford to be a fool.

Not with the brewing storms that M. Ventures faced.

* * *

Blearily, I rubbed the heel of my hand into my eyes to stop them from closing. Hot sandpaper lay beneath my tired lids.

8:00 in the morning.

Had I already been awake for four hours? I still had thirty emails left. The most critical messages were resolved before the rest of the world awakened, at least. If nothing else, the internet held through the gusty winds and ludicrous snow drifts outside.

Three feet and counting.

At the table, as far from the snowy windows as I could manage, papers cluttered the surface. A half-filled coffee cup and a few pens lay scattered, too. My computer glowed. All the lights on forced me to stay awake.

Coffee escorted me back to life, but that edge faded too quickly. I stood, headed toward the counter to refill a fourth time, when a vague figure in the window stopped me.

I paused halfway.

A bundled-up person stood there with a shovel. Cora. A fluffy, turquoise coat buttoned tight all the way past her hips. With a creamy hat and matching mittens, she resembled a little girl about to hop in the giant drifts. Hints of auburn hair peeked out from beneath the knitted cap. A bright scarf flopped around her neck as she fought her way through, snow piled to her waist as she battled the mounds with a shovel.

I set my mug down, heading for the door.

Bitter air swept past as I leaned outside. Snow tumbled across my bare toes, shockingly cold. I sucked in a sharp breath through my teeth, then regretted it when my mouth held the chill.

"You're up early," I called.

Cora's head peeked around the corner near the door. She'd waded through almost half of the porch. None of her tracks from the night before were visible in the thick snowfall. Loads of it dropped from the roof, toppling to greater piles. Much more of this, and we wouldn't be able to see the street.

"I thought I'd get ahead of the snow while I could."

"Need some help?"

To my consternation, she laughed. "With flip-flops? No thanks, I got this."

Another shovel, propped near the door, drew my gaze. I grabbed it, stepped more fully into the brisk morning, and attacked from my side. A few minutes outside wouldn't cause any damage except chattering teeth.

No way she'd do dirty work alone.

She glanced up, beamed, and continued. Flurries trailed off the shovel as she shoved it into the parking lot.

"Did you sleep well last night?" I asked.

"Like the dead. You?"

"Fine."

She quirked an eyebrow. "Even on the cold, hard floor?"

"Wasn't that bad."

She laughed. "Glad to hear it. Any changes in the weather updates?"

I peered out. Hints of what must have been a plow showed on the road, but rapidly disappeared beneath layers. No other lights illuminated the bank, the grocery store, or any other buildings. Silence reigned over forgotten mountains.

"I've been checking every hour," I called. Or every fifteen minutes, but she didn't need to know that. "Not a lot of updates. The storm is likely to continue through the day. The mountains have accumulated somewhere like four-and-a-half feet, or something crazy like that."

"Impressive, but there's more to go." Her nose wrinkled. "*Lots* more to go, if yesterday's report was true."

Images of a boardroom filled my mind.

"Indeed."

"Let's just hope the power holds."

"Excuse me?"

She shrugged. "With snow like this, who knows? It's the mountains. Shouldn't count on anything."

Her laissez-faire attitude struck me as undeniably insane. "What would we do for heat?"

"Ah, we'd figure something out."

Sultry ideas underlined the thought.

Grateful for the bitter chill for the first time, I turned my attention back to the waiting piles. Ten minutes later, we clomped inside. The cold had revived me more thoroughly than the coffee, though my bare toes prickled. I breathed deep, grateful for arctic blasts *and* warm coffee shops, as snow melted off my calves.

Delicately, Cora stepped out of rubber boots and left them on the rug. She shivered off the rest of the snow, tossing her coat on a rack. Her bright eyes and reddened cheeks charmed me. A deep emerald shirt with a wide neck dropped partly off one shoulder, revealing a hint of skin.

I looked away.

"It will definitely keep dumping out there," she said, oblivious to my attention. "There's three feet already. Isn't it wonderful?"

"Gross."

Her giggle startled me. She headed around the counter, filling the bland area with prisms of rainbows and light. Suddenly, the shop had texture and depth.

"Maverick said to throw food and coffee at you this morning." She tossed a hand to the table where I camped. "Looks like you've already done that."

"I'm a good scavenger."

"The croissants are top-notch."

"Coffee is still warm, if you want it."

"Yes." She reached for the pot, eyes wide. "Yes, I do."

On the table, my phone buzzed. I glanced at it, saw Nicola's name, and snatched it off the top. A quick silence and shove into my pocket followed. Bringing work into the coffee shop with Cora here felt . . . wrong.

She selected a mug off the wall that said *I heart kittens*. No adorable splotches of paint on her reddened fingertips today, just loose hair on her shoulders, a tousle to her eyes. Disappointing to have her so put together. She had fascinating imperfection last night.

While she rooted through the fridge, I blithely cleaned up the paperwork, closed my computer. Unfinished business remained. Problems I had no reason to turn my back on, yet I couldn't pull myself from the layered tones of chestnut and burgundy in her hair. The messy illumination of her smile.

"So," she drawled, a coffee cup perched near her lips. "You're stuck here for the day. What're you gonna do with it?"

Dozens of ideas ran through my mind, all of them boring as cardboard. Meeting prep. Discussions with Nicola. Emails. Contracts.

"Coffee, I think."

"Good man."

"You?"

She waved a hand. "With weather like this? The possibilities are endless. Snow angels. Coffee and carbs. A winter wonderland nineties dance off. Shoveling, for sure."

The low-spoken amusement in her husky voice sent heat through my gut.

This girl . . .

She studied me over the top of her coffee mug and sipped. I fought not to look at her full lips by motioning outside with a tilt of my head.

"The highway between here and Jackson City is closed, so . . ."

The implication trailed away.

Hilarity lifted her eyebrows. The uncharacteristic feeling

of not knowing what to say swept over me. Attempts to reply led to greater tongue-tied fervor. I couldn't even *speak* around her.

Cora set her mug down with a serious mien.

"Then it sounds like you're stuck with me. So, once I carb up, we have things to do."

Why did my breath catch?

My curiosity spike?

Challenge lingered in her eyes when I licked my lips.

"Things to do?"

A grin split her face.

"Shall we start with truth or dare?"

Chapter Five

CORA

Sweet Hawk.

He stared at me with enormous eyes, a slightly wrinkled space between his brows, as if he couldn't quite figure me out.

A baseball hat lay on the table, leaving adorably mussed hair behind. Lines cut across his shirt, and tension lingered around the edges of his eyes, as if he hadn't slept well.

Who could blame him?

Part of me wanted to pull him into my arms and give him a hug. Not only to see if his coiled arms were really as tense as they appeared, but mostly because he looked like he needed one.

"Truth or dare?" he repeated slowly.

I motioned to his empty coffee mug and opened my hand. "C'mon, gimme your cup. I'll pour you some more, and we'll start. If you're this surprised at the mere suggestion, you'll need all the help you can get."

With great hesitation, he obeyed.

I suppressed a smile at his unsure movements, like he moved through water, or didn't understand.

Already, with just a few sips of caffeination, the tendrils of life seeped into my bloodstream. With both mugs in hand, I headed for my favorite table in front of a sprawling window.

Snowy mountains butted up against the sky, dropping to the sapphire lake. White swaths of snow, like shorn cotton, hid the road, water, civilization. The fluffy flakes twirled in the wind like scattered sand.

Hawk and I held the whole world in our palms.

"Please," I said blithely, patting the chair across from mine. "Tell me you've played Truth or Dare before."

"I have."

He lingered until settling across from me. Tension radiated off him in waves. Pulled-back shoulders. Clenched jaw. Wary gaze. The transformation from a snowy Texan dork with flip-flops to this pillar of marble startled me.

"Are you all right?" I asked.

"Fine."

"You don't seem fine. You seem terrified. Does the idea of Truth or Dare frighten you?"

He blinked several times. My penchant to say exactly what was on my mind had been a problem before, but not one I apologized for. Life was too short to guess at what other people thought.

I had a feeling Hawk would appreciate it . . . when he picked his brain up from the floor.

With a shake of his head, he came back to life. "Frightened? No, I'm not afraid."

"Right."

His gaze tapered to slashes. "I'm not."

I rolled my lips together to quell a smile. "Then you can start. Truth or dare?"

"Dare."

I hooted. "Oh, ho. A man after my heart. Hmm . . ." My fingertips drummed along the warm coffee mug. My gaze slid around the room, then stopped on the far side. Neatly stacked paperwork and a computer perched in the middle of a table.

Inspiration struck.

His air of authority and low-level suave smiles that didn't quite reach his eyes spoke of a business executive. Clearly, he'd been up for several hours. Presumably working.

Sweet sassy molassy, I'd found it.

"I dare you not to open your computer again today."

His lips parted. A slight hitch of breath accompanied it. A sip of coffee hid the thrill I felt knowing I'd taken him by surprise. Truth or Dare was only fun when you could unseat the other person with deep truths or unexpected challenges.

Hawk had been easier than expected.

"My computer?"

"Yes."

He opened his mouth, then closed it again. I enjoyed the trouble which clouded those clear, suspicious eyes. Moments of silence passed. His jaw tightened before he met my gaze with equal parts challenge and irritation.

"Accepted."

"You have until midnight."

"What happens if I open it?"

"Then you lose Truth or Dare!" I cried, laughing. "All your integrity will melt away and the stars will conspire against you and I will emerge as the victor. You definitely don't want that. The stars can be relentless and I'm hopelessly arrogant when I win. Ask my brother, Cade."

A flicker of amusement appeared from the depths of deepest irritation. "Well," he murmured in a rolling way, "we can't have that, can we?"

My lips pressed in a slow smile as he leaned forward, long fingers wrapping around the coffee mug. He motioned toward me with a wave.

"Truth or Dare, Cora?"

The sound of my name on his lips sent a shiver all the way down my spine.

"Truth."

His lips quirked.

"What's your boyfriend's name?"

An incredulous laugh took me by surprise. Boyfriend? Was he . . . that is . . . He sipped his coffee, a daunting challenge in that loaded gaze.

Well, fair.

I'd found his weak spot, he found mine.

I leaned back in my chair, unduly discomfited now. Not by the question. Few questions bothered me. I valued frankness too much to play that way. The undertone he brought into the situation, on the other hand . .
.

Hawk made a statement without saying anything.

A current of energy swelled between us. I didn't mind all that much. Perhaps *that* is what I didn't want to admit: I wanted him to ask such a bold question and then *do* something with my answer.

Hawk, the man I just met.

Didn't know.

Couldn't puzzle together.

Equal parts defiant, I tilted my chin up ever-so-slightly. "There isn't a boyfriend."

The deep growl in his throat sent heat shooting into my stomach. "Hmmm. Men are idiots."

"Truth or dare?"

He tensed again, studied me, then eased slightly.

"Dare."

"Are you afraid of truth?"

A slight pause gave him away as uncertain, but he continued as if it hadn't happened.

"No."

"Then I dare you to let me have your phone for the rest of the day."

His eyes widened. Another charge bolted through me.

Hello, second weak spot.

Though I knew nothing about Hawk's career or business or whatever he worked on so obsessively with his screens, I knew I wanted to see him away from it. Find Hawk without all . . . that garbage.

This time, I didn't smile, too serious for levity. Today would be an unprecedented opportunity to discover one of the most bewitching men I'd ever met. A man who, by all appearances, might be one of the most breathtaking, complicated people I'd run across.

Ever.

Cade's warning about my curiosity be damned.

"My phone?" he rasped.

I nodded.

"All day?"

"I'll return it at midnight. With your computer," I tacked on, for good measure.

He paled. A protective hand went to his pocket, where the phone hid. I held out an open palm, and waited.

Emotions rotated through his eyes. Consternation, irritation, fright, and finally, a stone-cold resolution. He reached down, pulled it from his pocket, and slipped it into my palm.

Shock ripped through me like lightning.

"You're going to do it?" I whispered.

His eyes slammed into mine.

"Cora, I'm all yours."

Those words should be kept under lock and key. My heart galloped in my chest. He stated them with such a clear resolution. The tips of his fingers brushed my palm as he surrendered the phone.

A shiver rippled through my body.

The phone felt like a live wire as I clutched it, breathless. He'd given me more than resolution to a challenge. Deeper promises lingered beneath the surface. I just didn't know what they meant.

Heat rose to my cheeks as I curled my arm to my chest. A smile appeared, as sheepish as I felt.

"Then today we play. No phones. No computers."

He lifted a finger. "Ah ah. It's your turn. I've gone twice, now you choose. Truth or Dare?"

My stomach smoldered when I read the ultimatum in his gaze. The obstinacy in his stare. He wanted me to take the dare. With electricity crackling like this, I knew what he'd say. I licked my lips. His attention dropped, jaw tightened, eyes returned to mine. Heat smoldered. My whisper sounded like a wild question turned loose, whipping free.

"Dare."

Victory tainted his smile. He braced both arms on the table, leaned into them.

"Kiss me, Cora."

The bottom dropped out of my stomach. A nest of butterflies replaced it. Expected or not, the request stole my breath.

A flux of insecurities trapped me.

"What if you don't like it?"

The vulnerable question softened the hard angles of his face. He reached over, put a warm hand on top of mine. His fingers squeezed, heavy and reassuring.

"Not going to be a problem."

The smell of cream and coffee lingered in the air when I leaned closer. My head whirled, dizzy with the sensation of being near him. The contours of his full eyelashes, the wrinkles along the edges of his eyes that hinted at smiles.

A breath away, I paused. His rich heat caressed my cheek.

"Hawk?"

"Yes?"

Words fled. I didn't know what I wanted to say. *I've never kissed a man I don't know*, waited on the edge of my lips. I bit back, *I've never felt this way before.*

I closed my eyes, tilted my head, and sealed my lips against his. A soft pillow to fall against. His hand lifted, touched the sensitive skin just under my jaw. The mellow kiss was a tentative approach on both sides. Warmth seared by circumstance.

My body bloomed like an inferno.

I deepened the kiss.

His hand cupped my neck, then he pulled away. He paused, breath flowing across my face. My eyes blinked open to see him staring at me.

Reality returned.

Coffee shop.

Stranger.

Buckets on buckets of snow.

I jerked back, cleared my throat.

"Done," I whispered, and dropped my gaze.

His touch slipped away, lost heat. Hawk stared out the window. His angular jaw, broad shoulders, and general air of tension, created a stunning portrait. My fingers itched to bring him alive on the page as I committed his image to memory.

A cosmic shift had occurred.

In the last ten seconds, he jolted my world. I stood in a new place, a different sphere. A line in the ground existed between me and the old Cora. Whatever happened here, I'd never go back.

The irrefutable sensation that everything had just changed sank my bones to the floor.

You and me, I thought.

I didn't need to say it.

Chapter Six

HAWK

Whether Cora had mercy on me, or desired a moment to herself, I didn't know. She padded across the floor to set her coffee mug in the sink, leaving me in a sinkhole of gratitude.

My heart needed a breather.

The space where she'd been sitting, hot as a sun and twice as dazzling, opened my soul like a cracked nut. For several seconds, the room felt as if it would collapse. The world wheeled around, funneling me to that exact kiss. I rubbed my hand over my face.

What the hell?

Blood pumped through my body like I'd finished a set of sprints. A new squat PR. Something difficult and agonizing and life changing and . . .

Cora rattled me. The dare had been a stupid whim. A self-sabotaging attempt to clear the air, to see if I'd imagined the intensity and sparks. I'd spent all of an hour in Cora's presence and something in me already couldn't let go.

Was this desperation?

A rush of hormones?

Or inevitability?

The way I responded in the next several minutes would set the tone for the rest of the day. One that I had just guaranteed would be hers, in no unequivocal terms. Lawsuits happened for far less.

No.

Couldn't go down that sticky trap.

Cora didn't know who I was or what I represented. She'd have taken advantage of it during Truth or Dare, something I worried she planned at the outset. The game could have been her way of understanding the details I didn't give to the public.

Nope.

It had been a harmless, fun, flirty way to pass the time. When had I last done that?

Too long ago. Cora didn't know who I really was, and I wouldn't tell her. She'd gifted me anonymity and the chance to unfold an entire day with a woman that lit firecrackers under my skin.

Without the wall of . . . life . . . that lurked on the other side.

The surge of panic I felt when surrendering my computer and phone faded in the memory of that kiss. Not an extravagant or shocking kiss. Simple, and too fast for my liking. Her touch had sizzled along my skin, indulging a space too empty . . .

This wasn't fair to her. She didn't know what it would mean to involve herself with me. Billions of unknowns lurked at my back. The most frightening of them?

Tate.

My ruthless sabotaging do-it-my-way father.

I had to make this less unfair, so I stood all at once. Cora worked her way across the shop with two water bottles. Seeing me move, she paused. Uncertainty permeated her ruffled forehead. I closed the distance and put my hands on her shoulders. She tilted her head back.

Words rushed out of me.

"Can I . . ."

. . . try that again? Prove that I'm not insane? Duplicate whatever sparks distract me every second in your presence?

"Yes," she whispered.

I pushed a lock of hair out of her eyes, which peered so far into mine she'd find the hidden recesses. Routine. Drudgery.

Tate.

The terror simmering below.

Her lashes fluttered. I dropped closer, hesitated. One hand lingered on her neck, the other wrapped around her from behind. Water bottles dropped to the floor as she collapsed into my chest, hands on my shoulders.

Our lips crashed, colliding like stars. Magic infused again, infinitely deeper. Coiled with apprehension and disbelief and the thirst to never, ever, let this go. Thrumming lightning in my hands.

Firepower.

Cora's kiss.

All the same.

My head swam when I pulled away. Cora blinked sluggishly. She reached up, touched my cheek. I leaned into her fingers.

"Hawk?"

"Yes?"

"Do you feel it too?"

"Yes."

"Have you before?"

"No."

"It's not just me?"

"No."

Breath shaky, she leaned into me. I accepted her weight,

tightened my arms. The otherworldly hum thrived. We stood in the middle of the shop until she tilted her head back. Questions filled her eyes.

"We'll only have today, Cora. That's all I can promise. One day where I'll be here with you. That's it."

Curiosity deepened.

"Why?"

"It's how it has to be."

Her expression darkened. "Then what?"

"I can't make promises, so I won't. I have today. Can you sign up for that?"

Her hand trailed across my shoulder, down my arms. Goosebumps rose on her arms when she stepped back.

"Today?"

"Yes."

"Just today?"

"Yes."

"Okay."

I paused, certain I misunderstood. "Okay?"

She nodded. Our fingers intertwined. I tugged her near again, hooking a silky strand of hair behind her ear.

"If it's only one day of magic," she said, "that's better than none."

A smile surprised me. "I agree. What do you want to do on this perfect, snowy day that belongs to the two of us? No one to interrupt. Nowhere to go. My computer and phone are in your care."

Clouds built in her suddenly sharp gaze.

"I won't sleep with you. That's not—"

A finger to her lips stopped the fears.

"Not on my mind. Let's not cheapen whatever this is between us, all right? I'm not asking for it."

Relief turned her to putty in my hands. Her forthright

penchant for bringing all the questions out of hiding and into the air eased the tension.

"Come to the loft!" she said with a bright gasp. "I want to show you something."

* * *

Snow melted in between my toes when I followed her up a spiral staircase on the other side of the coffee shop, through a different door, and to the attic loft. She radiated a mixture of excitement and terror.

"No one has seen it yet in person," she said in a nervous, babbling sort of way. "I always keep it covered with a sheet. Except for Cade. He says older brothers get to see all of them first, so I let him. I'm . . . I hope you like it."

I trailed behind her, curious about her relationship with her brother, until we stopped at a wooden door at the top of the stairs.

She flung it open.

A quiet, low-toned attic loft unrolled. The smell of something sharp—was it turpentine? Oil?—drifted past. Colors of muted gray and mustard yellow and burnt orange mixed with the cloudy day outside. Cora advanced, then whirled around with her usual larger-than-life smile. Her hair twirled around her neck, then settled in burnished strands of umber and sienna.

"Welcome to my workshop."

Canvases filled nearly every wall. Some were propped against the floor, others hung. Blankets hid two of them. Curled tubes of oil paint, easels, palettes, and glass jars cluttered the far side of the room, near a six-foot-something canvas that occupied the entire wall.

I pulled in a breath.

"Whoa."

She sank her teeth into her bottom lip, eyes bouncing between me and the masterpiece. A half squeal followed.

"You like it?"

I stepped forward, stunned. A sprawling mountain scene —mostly done—opened over the white canvas. Sharp rocks, boulders highlighted by carefully toned colors. A snowy clime, desperate with a sense of escape. Inhospitable, gloomy, and stark in its rendition.

There was something drawing about how far away it felt, yet she painted it so close. Facets of changing granite lay obvious in the color, the clashes of bold blue against black that shadowed the cold.

Evergreen trees and flowing clouds occupied the foggy, moody scene. The painting stood at least six feet tall, four feet wide. A behemoth of a job, with details painted from left to right, and only a quarter of it remaining. Ghosts of color outlined other areas, mere slashes that revealed a greater story hidden underneath it all. The skeleton of greatness.

Smaller paintings scattered the room. Some appeared to be practiced, accidental, spurts of a fit of imagination. Scopes of color, a swash of green that might have been a baby tree, taken to granular detail. Tiny insights into this massive work in progress.

"Do I like it?" I murmured, finally able to use words. "Cora, I'm speechless."

She turned to face it. "It's my biggest commissioned piece so far. A woman named Carlotta hired me. She lives in Jackson City. She has an enormous house that she wants to decorate with a massive gallery-piece no one else has. Something that reflects the world she lives in, here, in the mountains."

"Are you doing this from another picture? An existing mountain?"

"No."

"From your mind?"

Hesitantly, she nodded.

The cut of shadows, mixing of colors, spoke to far deeper expertise than her humble response.

"You just . . . came up with this?"

"Well, yes." She folded her arms over her chest. "I study real life. It comes to me in pieces. I spend time driving around and hiking through some of the snow and the mountains. Carlotta hired me in the fall. I moved here at the end of the month, had Thanksgiving with Cade, then got to work. Around the time I finish, my lease will be up."

"Then what?"

She shrugged. "Don't know, yet. I have some ideas I'm working around to get my work into galleries. This is a sizable piece that my client will be quite proud of. I'm hoping to leverage her position in society to get an exhibition. Maybe see if this can hang in a local art store for a month, with some of my smaller works, before she takes it home. Could help me get other commissions."

"Do you want to stay here?"

She smiled quietly. "I think so? I like being close to Cade."

"Wise idea to leverage a contact from one commission to find others," I murmured. "Network connections are every-thing in business."

I stepped closer, drawn to the nuts and bolts of the artistry. Behemoth companies like mine, at their core, also reduced to details. Flow charts. Rules. Lines. Money became numbers that moved from one place to another. An exchange of energy, not necessarily dollars in the hand. Such untold wealth lost the same power when one viewed it as numbers.

Which made the elemental nature of her work even more fascinating.

Without systems, rules, a guide, how did she take some-thing vague in her mind and create it for others to understand on the canvas?

To *feel?*

Swirls of color trailed along the edges of the swarthiest mountain, creating ridges. Swaths of trees with speckles of snow on branches half the size of my pinky nail and shadows underneath that made them leap off the page.

When the air in the room changed, I realized I'd been staring at it, lost in thought, for a long time. I stepped back. Cora watched me with a funny expression on her face.

"I'm . . . amazed, Cora."

That demure smile I loved returned instantly.

"Thanks. I'm proud of it."

"Do you have others?"

"Scads." She waved a hand around the room. "I'm always painting something. Drawing, too. I sketch more than I paint, but those rarely go to commission. Something else that I plan to change once I can find gallery slots."

"Which do you like more?"

"Oh, how do I choose? Painting is so much more dramatic for customers, where drawing is more intimate. Some view sketches as *cheaper* art, even though it can be just as bold. I need a better footing before I can really make money from the charcoal stuff, but I love to do it."

She pointed to a portrait of streaked colors. Yellow, intermixed with orange, white. Shades of black lurked around the left and bottom edges, blending to brown. Like an explosion of light in a dark room, revealing secrets.

"That one was a random idea I had while sitting in a movie theater with Cade a few weeks ago. I had the thought that *sunshine can never live with the darkness.* And . . . I don't know. It popped into my head."

"It's magnificent. Looks like quaking aspens in the fall."

"Thanks. Made me think of my mom," she added in a way that shielded me from asking more. Her humble acceptance was heartfelt.

Cora cleared her throat, stepped back a little. "Sketching, art. It . . . helps the world make sense."

"How so?"

Her arm waved, encompassing the painting. "Art is just . . . layers. When you break something down to a picture, a single image, you get to the grainy core. You find the bottom layer, the most important, and build up from there. You figure out the essence before you know the image. It's all depth and perception. Everything about it eventually makes sense."

Get to the grainy core.

Is that what happened here?

"It's just like people," she added. "We're all layers. When you understand what's beneath, you can create the entire picture."

Notepads and spiral bound books were stacked on top of a table not far away. The rest of the loft held a similar state of dishabille and warmth. Flannel shirts hung over the back of chairs. A frumpy couch sat near the fireplace on the far side, a bed close to the kitchen area. The windows peered out on the lake, an unending vista of snow that ringed mountains on the far side.

Imposing buggers, too.

"How long have you been painting?"

"Since I could hold a brush."

"That long?"

She reached for a mustard-yellow jacket flung across the back of a chair and twirled it onto her shoulders. It hung loosely over her shirt. She grabbed the edges, folding it across. With so many windows in this room, cold tinted the air.

"Cade says I used to fill up the dining room table with watercolor paintings as a kid."

"Is Cade older or younger?"

"Seven years older."

I set my hands on my hips, studying the other paintings

along the wall. Many of them were mostly lines. Simplistic explorations of structure—a jaw, a neck, a bunch of red hair gathered into a messy bun at the top of an unfinished head. Some paintings had areas filled with colors, others abandoned to be nothing more than a snowy canvas.

Studying her work felt far safer than meeting her eyes.

"Have you always sold paintings?"

"More over the last several years than before." She chewed on her bottom lip as she shuffled a couple of stacked canvases around, allowing me to see a few in the back. A baby raccoon emerged next to a young deer.

"It took a while to build a clientele and a reputation, but now things move more steadily. This commission will help. Carlotta has a lot of art-loving friends and the local connections that I mentioned."

"Networking is power," I murmured, an echo that gave me something to say when words fled.

"Yes," she said, with a minor note of surprise. "That's what Cade told me."

Memories of art galleries, awkward dates, and forced smiles flitted through my mind. Social requirements subjected me to my fair share of art galleries and study of all that world brought.

None of those art pieces had me excited, though. Not like her pictures. Half finished, but certain.

Boldly imperfect.

"Will you miss the painting when you're done?" I pivoted to face her again. Her musing expression dropped.

"No. I'm happy for it to go into the world to make other people smile. That's what it's all about, right? Art helps us escape. Remember. Through pictures, we can imagine things we never thought possible."

"Thank you for showing me this."

She beamed. "I appreciate you dealing with my tour. Cade says I can be insufferable."

She laughed it off, but I sensed an underlying tension in the admittance. I shook my head, eyes on one of the closed notebooks she hadn't opened up. My fingers itched to see the images on the paper.

"No," I murmured. "Not insufferable at all."

"Well," she drawled with a coy smile, "that's not the only reason I brought you up here. I'm starving and there are only so many cold or microwave-warmed croissants a girl can eat. You want some pancakes?"

* * *

Halfway through breakfast preparations, Cora pulled her jacket back off and tied it around her waist. With her hair swaying round her neck, her feet bare, and the cold snow falling outside in torrential flakes, she painted a cozy picture.

Her charm had no ceiling.

The words *Linkin Park* scrawled across the front of her shirt in white, lightning-like letters. I leaned back, an arm sprawled over the back of one of her chairs, and gestured to the words.

"Declare yourself, ma'am," I said, in continuation of another one of her ridiculous games she proposed we play. "Do you actually like Linkin Park, or are you just trying to ride the wave of cool shirts?"

She lifted an imperious eyebrow. "I happen to be a staunch fan, thank you very much. Yourself?"

"*Numb* is my favorite song."

Her lips twitched. "Predictable."

"Yours?"

"*In the End.*"

"Dark." I laughed. "At least you know the band."

She put a hand on her chest with an imperious hip cock. "Please. I have class."

"I pegged you as more of a Spice Girls type."

She illuminated like a Christmas tree. "I love the Spice Girls!"

"I saw that coming."

She sent a wry look my way that made me laugh again, then beckoned for me with a curl of her fingers into her palm. Unable to resist the invitation, I obeyed. She shoved a spatula into my hand.

"Babysit the pancakes, please. I have bacon to sizzle. Then declare yourself, sir: how much caffeine do you drink every day?"

I snorted, accepting the spatula. "Way too much."

"Coffee?"

"Energy drinks, but I won't say no to coffee when I have the chance."

"How about tea?"

My nose wrinkled. "Hot brown water? No thanks."

Her laugh pealed through the room.

Several quiet moments of kitchen bustle followed. I attempted to not destroy all the pancakes while she dumped bacon into another pan. Heat filtered from the range, filling the air. Fog clouded the closest window, which hid the storm outside. The sun had risen somewhere behind the mat of snow, but the world continued in a grayish miasma.

"Declare yourself, ma'am: peanut butter on scrambled eggs. Yes or no?"

Cora recoiled, nose scrunched.

"What?"

"You heard me."

She laughed. "Peanut butter on scrambled eggs? That's gross."

"It's not."

The smell of golden pancakes bubbled from the pan, mingling with the delicious zip of butter and maple syrup. Two plates clattered as she withdrew them from a cabinet nearby, setting them on the counter near me.

"Definitely no peanut butter on my eggs."

"Ketchup?"

"Salsa." She cut a hand through the air. "I'm a strict salsa-only girl with my eggs. Be careful."

"Disagree."

She smirked. "Fine," she called grandly. "You may disagree. Declare yourself, sir: smooth peanut butter or chunky?"

"Smooth."

"Wrong! Chunky is so much better."

"False."

"Agree to disagree."

"Fine," I said with fake reluctance. "You eat your chunky, I'll have my smooth on eggs, and we'll both be happy."

She radiated another smile.

My heart tangled all up in it.

After dropping a sloppy cupful of pancake batter onto the hot pan, I leaned against the counter, spatula in hand. A stack of pancakes collected on the plate nearest me, and my mouth watered as the smell of bacon drifted through the air.

"Declare yourself, ma'am: do you want to have children one day?"

Cora paused, a hand halfway to a pile of forks. She spun to face me with a hidden laugh.

"Going for the big guns, are you?"

I shrugged, not sure I understood my compulsion to know her so thoroughly. To hear every word that she had to say, every thought in her head. I felt drunk on Cora, ready to soak her up.

"Just a question. Doesn't have to mean anything."

The silverware clattered in her hands as I flipped the

bubbling pancake over, gratified to see golden brown. Maybe if I kept up the charade that I knew what I was doing, Cora wouldn't ever suspect that I never made my own breakfast.

Or, for that matter, ate breakfast.

"I suppose I want kids," she mused. "I know Cade does. He's always talking about having a family, raising kids, sunsets on the porch, and that kind of thing. He's a cowboy and a romantic at heart."

"I didn't ask about Cade."

"Are you always this bold?"

"Yes."

She giggled with half-hearted awkwardness. "I'm eighty percent certain I'll have kids. I want to do better with my family."

A host of unsaid things lingered behind those words. I had to stop more questions from barreling out, alerted by the pain in her voice.

"Declare yourself, sir!" she called. "Are you a big money spender, or do you hoard it away like a miser?"

"Miser," I countered instantly.

"Really?"

A finished pancake flipped through the air in a twist right before I caught it, then thrust the plate out to her. She grinned, accepting it, then waited for my response. My hope that she would forget the question died instantly.

Nope, she wouldn't let this one go.

"I don't have a lot of things that I want to buy. I have the necessities, and I don't spend a lot of time at my place, anyway."

Place because *penthouse* sounded so pretentious.

Curiosity lifted her voice. "Where do you spend your time? Work?"

"Yeah. I'm at work a lot."

"Do you like your job?"

She must have seen my hesitation, because reluctance flashed through her now-wooden smile. With a sweeping gesture, I took the pancakes back.

"That, my lady, is another question for a different time. For now, shall we pancake? I'm starving."

Chapter Seven

CORA

Hawk reminded me of an open book. Everything on the page before me was clear, no questions or vacancies. The truth laid bare. But other pages lay behind what I could glimpse, yet not read. He'd handpicked the area of his life I could safely view without diving deeper. More waited back there to explore.

Those stolid, velvet eyes prevented me from turning the page, however.

Any mention of career or work made his arms tense, his body clam up, and a distant expression steal across his face. Whatever he hid in the boxes of his mind around *career* couldn't be pleasant.

I curled my knees into my chest, my elbow propped on the back of the couch, while he unraveled a story about his favorite place to eat waffles. Sparse details came—no name, specific location, or anything like that—but his rapture over the food was genuine enough. From basic details, I could tell he must live in a big city.

He sat close enough to touch, but far enough that we didn't. A residual cup of tea lay in my hands, warding off a constant chill the furnace didn't banish.

Outside, there was ever more snow.

"Those waffles sound delicious," I said, realizing that only half my attention had been on him. The rest of it?

Those luscious lips.

A wry smile told me I hadn't fooled him. Heat warmed my face. He reached out, touched my cheek with the back of his knuckles. I fell into the movement, startled by how much it meant.

He was distant one breath, all-in the next. I couldn't help ruminating over the fact that he and I had only known each other a few hours.

Somehow, time didn't matter.

Whatever live wire hummed between us *mattered*.

"Are you going to tell me what you do for a living?" I asked. "Or are you hiding from it for our day?"

A stricken look crossed his features. I reached over, put a hand on his arm. The muscles tightened, then relaxed beneath my fingertips.

"You can hide from it here, if that's what you need. I just want to know if that's what you're doing."

A flash of something appeared, then faded.

"I'm hiding from it, not hiding it from you. If I don't have to think about what comes after today, that would be . . . restorative."

"All right. Then let's hide from it. What do you say to a movie?"

He beamed, and the joy in it startled me. When he gave me that side of himself, it changed everything about his demeanor. My breath escaped in a hiccup and shudder that rippled through every blood vein.

"I would love to watch a movie with you." He leaned closer, trapped my wrist in his fingers. "Will you sit by me?"

I nodded and scooted closer. Tentatively, he stretched an arm along the back of the couch. Throwing caution to the wind, I pulled myself to his side, snuggled against his shoulder. With a long exhale, he dropped his firm arm around me. My stomach melted in a puddle. Such strength in the move. Power.

Navigating with my remote, I pulled up a movie list, selected a comedy at the top, and tried not to think about his heat. The easy slide into cuddling that we both accepted while ignoring reality.

Like a paintbrush along canvas, Hawk molded to my side. He made a few quips at the beginning, but by the twenty minute mark, he quieted. I glanced up, delighted to find his dark lashes heavy on his cheeks. The gentle whisper of his breath sang in my ear, steady. He'd slumped farther into the couch, his fingers loose against my arm.

Carefully, I extracted myself from his grip. He didn't stir from sleep as I leaned to the side, studying him. The movie flickered on while I crept across the room, snatched my favorite notebook and pencil, and returned.

I lowered back to the couch, though not at his side. With the snow falling, and the unbroken monotone of the movie in the background, I let the pencil fly across the page. Maybe if I sketched Hawk, he'd make more sense.

His head tilted away from me, which cut a fascinating angle from his jaw, along the neck, the back of his head, where his dark hair curled so tightly. A sweet, vulnerable figure. I'd never forget it.

My hand soared across the page, releasing the frenetic buildup since we met last night.

Layers.

Information.

Parts of Hawk came together. I replayed our interactions as I mapped out the arc of his shoulder, the way it rounded down slightly. Shaded the hollow of his cheek, the hints of stubble that darkened his face. Everything showed up on the page, though he turned away from me.

So close.

Yet far.

He wasn't mine, not really. Was unlikely to be mine if I were honest with myself, and I always was. He had his secrets; I had mine. Acceptance allowed us to skirt those lines. After today, we'd part. I understood this.

By the time the movie finished, so had my sketch. I closed it before I could survey it too closely, because I didn't want to intimately understand any of this. I set it back on the coffee table.

Hawk stirred and drew in a deep breath when I returned to his side. His arm tightened around my shoulders like it had never left. He leaned over and pulled me to him. Tucked in between him and the couch cushions, I could finally relax. My harried fingers were satisfied.

Full of delicious breakfast, and the sharp tang of his aftershave, I slipped to sleep in Hawk's arms.

* * *

Darkness, quiet, and a chill woke me.

I startled awake, my eyes flying open. A heavy weight at my side groaned. Under my hand, rippling muscles and a deep, throaty moan followed.

Hawk.

Oh, right.

Hawk.

"Hullo," he murmured. His rumbly voice made my stomach catch. I straightened. The TV was off. The lights, too. Only a vague glow from the storm clouds brightened outside. My nose, nipped by the cold, woke me fully.

"Oh, no," I whispered.

His eyes batted open. His sleepy gaze took a moment to focus on me. When it did, a mixture of delight and concern lingered there.

"What's wrong?"

"The power."

I shoved off the couch and hurried to the wall, shivering. Indeed, it felt as if the heater hadn't been on for a while. A quick glance at the clock revealed it was past noon. We'd been asleep for hours on the couch.

"Uh oh."

Hawk stood, rubbing his arms. Wrinkles lined his face as he passed a hand over his eyes.

"Power is out?"

"Looks like it."

He frowned, peering outside. Snow continued to fall. I grabbed my phone off the counter, but no messages had come through from Maverick or Bethany.

"Well." I turned to face him. "I guess we can pack on some clothes and snuggle under blankets for a while."

His flat expression replied.

My enthusiasm dampened. With no fireplace for heat, our options were severely limited. The Frolicking Moose didn't have a generator. Maverick had a sleeping bag or two stashed away in the closet out in the hall, but not much else.

"They'll probably get it back on pretty fast, right?" he asked.

"I hope so."

A dubious glance outside didn't bring me comfort. The snow continued with relentless drive. If a power line had fallen, who knew how long it would take for crews to get it back together? The snow would barricade them on every side. I pulled my arms in with a shiver. If I had to, I could hike my way to Cade's ranch, but that would take all day in a storm like this.

This lovely day had taken a slightly-sinister turn.

Hawk stepped closer, crowding me, and put his hands on my arms. I tilted my head back when he tucked some hair out of my eyes. He studied my expression.

"We'll be fine," he said.

"Yeah."

Amusement lifted his lips. "If nothing else, we always have body heat."

A laugh caught me by surprise. I let it go, relieved to have the tension in my chest unwinding. Though I barely knew him, I couldn't help but feel glad he was here. Alone, this could be far more concerning.

Hesitation stole over me. Hawk and I barely knew each other. The comfort I drew from his presence should have terrified me. Too fast, too soon, right? The sense of living in a bubble, one destined to break, kept the fears tucked aside for now. At some moment in the not-too-distant future, I'd grapple with all the things that made little sense.

For now, I belonged here.

Minutes later, we returned to the couch, shrouded in blankets. I bundled up with sweats, socks, and a long-sleeved shirt under my flannel jacket while Hawk grabbed his bag from the shop and brought it upstairs. An armful of food accompanied him. He dumped it on the table with a ceremonious cry.

"So," I drawled, reaching into my pocket. "Since we have no movies to watch, I want to propose a game."

"I'm noticing a trend."

"That I love games?"

"Very much so."

"I do!" I brightened. "Games. Are. The. Best. This is a little different. A newer version of Truth or Dare."

His eyebrow lifted. Last time we'd played Truth or Dare, it led right to the steamiest kiss of my life.

Both of us found renewed interest.

"I'm listening."

"We play a card game." I pulled my favorite deck of cards free. "You pull a card off the top of the deck. If it's red, you get to ask the other person a question. If it's black, they ask you."

Heat smoldered in his eyes when he looked at me. A smile curled my lips as I read the memory there. The smoking-hot kiss that still curled my toes when I thought about it made me want to draw all the reds, then beg him to kiss me again.

"This is not a dare game," I drawled. "This is a get-to-know-you game."

He turned away, smiling to himself.

"I see."

"But . . . not just *any* kind of get-to-know-you-game. You have to ask proper questions. The deep ones. This is not *what is your favorite color*? This is a dive into the things you've never told anyone."

Several seconds of deliberation passed before he slowly said, "Okay."

"Okay?"

A firm nod punctuated his response.

I set the deck on the couch between us, if only to help suppress the desire I had to curl up against his side. It seemed all-too-easy to picture me pressed into his arms again, tucked under his protective warmth.

Yet . . .

Hawk reached out, drawing off the first card in a bold move. A smile deepened when he deftly flipped the card around. A red two. I chuckled, brow high, as he stared, hard in thought, at my wall.

What would those stormy eyes seek?

"What keeps you up at night?"

My breath hitched. He turned, glanced at me. Challenge lingered in the shadows of expectation. I sorted through a dozen replies, suddenly hating myself for doing this. Though

I'd sought to get to know him better, I should have known he'd ask me the perfect question.

"My Mom."

The hard edges of his face softened slightly. I drew in a deep breath, let it out. Technically, I *had* answered the question, but . . .

"She's homeless. Lives under a bridge or wanders through some ditches in Florida, depending on the season."

Shock passed quickly through his eyes, though he tried to hide it. I met his gaze, a sinking weight in my stomach.

"She has a lot of mental health issues, and no matter how much Cade and I try to help her, she resists. We've done everything we can, but . . . she just doesn't want us in her life. No matter what we do, she always finds her way back."

"Drugs?"

"Among other things."

His warm hand clasped mine. The heat gathered in his palm gave me the courage I needed to finish the story.

"It's something we've always battled, so it's not a new war. At some point, I just had to draw a line in my mind. Stop picturing her as my mom. Understand that this person isn't who she really is, but instead an addiction and mental health challenge gone undefeated. Still, I think about her at night and wonder."

He squeezed my hand. "Thanks for telling me."

I tossed the gravity of the answer aside and reached for the card deck with a smile. He gifted me with a similar one that made my stomach flutter, escorting the shadows out the door.

I flipped the top card over.

Red five.

Hawk exhaled hard. "After what you just gave, go easy on me." I laughed, unable to help it. His fake fear had a charming quality.

"Are you ever lonely?"

His eyes cut over to mine instantly. "Lonely?"

I pulled my knees into my chest and canted my body to face him better. I propped my elbow up on the back of the couch as I tightened the blanket around my shoulders.

"Yeah. Lonely. Are you ever lonely?"

He sat like a rigid board again. Arms by his side, feet on the floor.

"I think everyone gets lonely."

The silence waited.

Finally, he sighed. "Yes, I get lonely, and I hate it. My . . . place is quiet after work. I speak to people all day, but feel like I never really say anything. Sometimes, a little more noise would be nice."

"What do you do again?"

His neck snapped straight up, like a ramrod ran down his back.

"Ah . . . corporate management stuff."

"Huh."

"It's not as exciting as it seems."

Something stiffened his tone. That note of anxiety compelled me to nudge the deck his way. The small motion might save him from whatever frightening things rippled through his mind, though I had so many more questions.

If he didn't want to talk about his career, that was fine. Whatever we had going on here didn't have to require that much. Besides, Maverick could tell me later, after Hawk left. Because Hawk *would* leave.

He drew another card.

Ace of spades.

My lips twitched as he sighed dramatically. I leaned back, laughing. "I'll lob you a slightly-easier one. What's your favorite breakfast cereal?"

"The one with the rainbow marshmallows."

"Oooh, nice choice."

The top of the deck slipped to the side as I reached for a card and drew a four of diamonds. Relief became visible on his face. This time, he met my eyes. A deep curiosity lurked in the recesses.

"Tell me about Cade."

Warmth flooded me at the sound of his name. "Cade? He's my hero. Well, he's my older brother." I tossed the card onto the face-up pile and picked at a loose string on the quilt. "You know a little about my mom, so you can guess that things weren't all that easy growing up."

Hawk's sober expression startled me. He watched me so intensely, with such concern, that I almost lost track of my thoughts. A hand reached out, settled on my knee. I inched closer, but Hawk hooked a hand around the back of my knee and pulled me in. His heat, his smell, wrapped around me. This close, I could see the flecks in his eyes.

He nodded, a sign to keep going.

"The day that Cade turned eighteen, he packed up our stuff. We didn't have much in the first place, but he shoved it all into a really crappy old truck he'd bargained off a farmer for a couple hundred bucks and took me away. A ranch on the outskirts of town needed some help, and he'd been working for them in the summers. They let me and Cade stay there in a room above their garage."

"If he was eighteen, you were . . . eleven?"

I nodded.

"Do you remember all of it?"

"Yeah."

The memories flashed through my head in intervals all the time. Bouncing down the road at Cade's side. The tilt of his cowboy hat, the steel in his jaw, as the dirt billowed behind the truck. He'd raced like the devil himself chased us.

"Your mom?"

I shrugged. "For all that I know, she didn't try to find us.

At least, not hard. We went back home several times, but she became slippery. Eventually, the landlord evicted her from the hellhole we once lived in. She wandered the streets. Cade somehow tracked her to Florida, and we tried to help her."

"You must be close with your brother."

"Very."

"Does he live here?"

"Works as a ranch hand in a place just outside of town. That's how I found out about the Frolicking Moose and could stay close to him to work on this painting."

"I assume he's a protective older brother?"

"Very."

Before an awkward quiet could fill the space between us, Hawk tossed the card deck aside. He reached up. The touch of his hand on my jaw, so gentle on the sensitive skin, made my breath hitch. I swallowed, peering fast into his gaze.

His breath hit my cheek like a silky caress. A smoky fire lurked in him.

"Cora?" he whispered. "I shouldn't feel this way. Not in so short a time. Shouldn't feel like I want to keep you safe from the pain in your eyes, from the cold storm. Like I don't want to leave whatever little bubble we have here. I've never felt this —whatever it is. It's terrifying, yet the most exciting thing that's ever happened to me."

My heart slowed to a gentle squeeze.

"Me too."

His hand slipped up my jaw, fingers in my hair. The heat of his palm on the shell of my ear sent a shiver down my neck.

"Thanks for telling me about your family. You're . . . incredibly brave."

I snorted delicately. "No, that's Cade. He raised me. An eighteen-year-old raising his eleven-year-old sister in a small room over a garage? A miracle. I don't know what I would have done without him. I might have . . . he could have left, you know? But he didn't. He . . . saved me."

"He's clearly brave, but that doesn't diminish your courage, either."

Hawk closed the distance between us. Our lips lingered, a tantalizing breath away, so close his heat intoxicated me. I closed my eyes, held my breath. The moment clung to us, mystifying and magical. My heart thudded so hard it shook my chest.

Finally, he pressed his lips to mine again.

The same zip filtered through my body, this time languid. An easy tantalization. The sound of him pulling in a sharp breath sent butterflies through my stomach. I tilted my head, deepened the kiss. Passion curled my stomach into knots.

Hawk didn't dissolve into the sensation. He didn't sweep me away into more of the same, though I wanted it. He pulled back. A hand slipped across my forehead, drawing my hair out of my eyes.

"We're not here just for your magnetic kisses, all right? I just . . . can't help myself around you. It's . . . unsettling."

Concern brewed in his eyes, mirroring the same questions I held onto so tightly.

Was this real?

I placed my hand on his, leaned into it. "I understand."

A smile twitched across his lips. "Think there's a chance the power will come back on tonight?"

I laughed.

"Not even a little."

Chapter Eight

HAWK

The darkness settled like a wool blanket over the evening. With no power, everything landed in utter black.

Snow piled ever higher. Before daylight faded, the flakes thinned into greater spaces, but continued with restless zeal. I lay on Cora's bed, staring at the ceiling, one arm propped beneath my head.

She lay next to me, tucked into a sleeping bag. A pink knitted cap peeked out of her cocoon and her wispy breaths breathed a soothing soundtrack. The scent of lavender drifted toward me whenever she shifted, which wasn't often. She'd fallen into a hard and fast sleep.

Somewhere on the wall, her clock would likely say it was close to ten.

The day whirled before my eyes. Her fast smiles, hearty giggle that came so often. Never had I met someone that laughed so much. Stupid little games that delighted her left me feeling drunk and giddy.

Never had I ever.

The thought that Cora might have been stuck here alone, in the dark and the cold, sent a knot into my stomach. She would have been fine, of course. No damsel-in-distress lay in all those optimistic folds of life.

For me, however, our chance encounter seemed a narrow miss.

I could have *not* come to Pineville after scouting out the hospital in Jackson City and speaking with the CEO about onboarding our patient medical records software. Could have ditched the trip and never showed up. Might not have met Cora, this dazzling, blinding star.

What if?

Yet, if I hadn't, I'd never know what I missed. Would never know that a person existed who could flip my world upside down like a snow globe. The slippery, nebulous nature of this entire situation flummoxed me.

Her regular breathing reassured me she remained asleep, so I slipped off the bed, padded over to the wall where she'd ditched both of our phones in a basket. Close enough to midnight.

No sound came from the bed as I sat on the edge of the couch and touched the screen.

Nausea welled in my throat.

35 text messages.

115 emails.

42 missed calls.

Nicola was going to murder me.

I scrolled through the text message list with mounting dread. I clicked on Nicola's name and prayed the call went through. Nicola's wry voice picked up a second later.

"Long time no—"

"I know, I know."

My whisper caught her attention. Her tone dropped.

"What's wrong?"

"I'm in the middle of a friggin' snowstorm that's dumped

something close to four feet, and the power has been out for half the day."

"Oh. Well, you're calling me now, so at least you survived. I wondered if you died and it would be easier for me to be promoted to CEO after all."

Her relentless laissez-faire attitude at life—did nothing rattle Nicola?—caused me to roll my eyes.

"I'm sorry about the delay."

"In what?"

"Returning calls."

"I didn't call you."

Puzzled, I glanced down. My brow furrowed as I thumbed through the list of missed names. Indeed, not a single one from Nicola. Other members of our leadership team, but not Nicola. Six times from our Managing Director, Salvatore.

Maybe the cold numbed my brain. I pressed the phone back to my ear and rubbed my fingers over my eyes.

"Sorry, I thought I saw you on that list."

"Salvatore probably did. Rakesh had a bunch of questions too."

"They'll be unbearable after this."

She chuckled. "Please, you insult me. I talked them down when you didn't answer. It's fine. Hawk, I've got this. You told me what to do. I did it. When no one had a response from you, I figured an avalanche fell, or something equally devastating."

"Thanks. I think. I'll explain it all later."

"Why are you whispering?"

"Someone else is asleep."

Interest piqued her tone. "Oooh, tell, tell! Who is it?"

"Doesn't matter. Update me on what you know."

Nicola skimmed through a laser-fast rundown of developments that made my chest ache. While not ideal, none of the talking points wreaked havoc. Still, I needed to be at that board meeting the next day.

I stood, moved to the window, and peered through the shuttered blinds. Not enough light existed in the world to see much, but a general lessening of snow fall seemed obvious.

"We'll cover that question in the board meeting tomorrow," I said as she finished a summary from the Chief Technology Officer.

"Sorry, Hawk. You know I love to handle hurricanes myself, but that particular issue is beyond the power you've given me. If you want me to step into CEO and represent you with the board . . ."

"No, I'll be there."

A dubious pause stretched between us. I pulled the phone away to eye the battery, then pressed it back.

50%.

"The meeting is at 10:00 am," she finally said.

"I know."

"How are you going to be there?"

"Send me a chopper."

Bewilderment filled her voice.

"What?"

"A chopper is a small hovercraft that moves easily through the air. Can drop into areas that planes can't, and are easier to charter than others. You know?"

"Hawk, a *chopper* in the mountains after four feet of snow? Please tell me you're kidding."

"Find one farther out, away from the storm. Pay them whatever they want. The snow is lessening here and there's a place behind the Frolicking Moose where they can land, in the lake bed."

"There's also four feet of snow."

"I'll wade through it."

"But . . ."

"Nicola, do you want the position of CEO? You *need* me there at the board meeting? You want me to back you against Tate when I turn the position to you?"

A pause.

Then a firm, "You know I do."

"Then impress me. Make this happen. Get me back there in the morning, even if it's 4:00 am and I have to hike through five feet of snow to get to a helicopter that picks me up in a basket, all right? I *must* be at that board meeting at 10:00."

Annoyance, but determination, hardened her voice.

"Fine. Yet again, I'll prove myself Master of the Multiverse that is your corporation."

The call ended. I glanced at Cora's sleeping form. The glittery world we'd lived under ebbed. All levity, amazement, curled away. Not the raw, teeming mass of my feelings for Cora, however. Not the horrendously terrifying emotions she stirred up from a cavern long dormant.

A sleeping dragon.

That's all I'd ever been.

I rubbed a hand over my face. This wouldn't be easy, but it was time to get back to reality.

* * *

Hawk: Sorry for the early text. I'm heading out.

Maverick: It's 4:30 in the morning. HOW are you heading out?

Hawk: Why are you awake?

Maverick: I have children.

Hawk: Right. Chopper coming. Have meetings later in the morning.

Maverick: Can't say I'm surprised. Travel safe.

Hawk: Check on Cora, okay?

Maverick: Why do I need to check on Cora? What happened?

Maverick: Hawk?

Maverick: Hello?

Maverick: What did you do?

Chapter Nine

CORA

A dull, distant sound stirred me from restless dreams of shifting icicles. Frozen swirls of snow, drawing intricate patterns on windows that faded into darkness, then grew light again. Amongst them moved a quiet figure.

Hawk.

My eyes flew open. The dream broke.

I sat straight up, blinking. The cold room hadn't warmed. No lights on. Sunlight streamed through the window, falling on the floor. My warm sleeping bag slipped down my torso as I sat up. An empty bed lay at my side.

"Hawk?"

No sign of life.

Had he made a coffee run downstairs, maybe?

No. We had no power to make coffee.

I frowned.

Something about the silence felt percussive. Strange. Off-kilter. As if leached from the room, leaving a gaping hole. I pulled my knees to my chest, shoved the sleeping bag off. The cool floor startled me further out of sleep, despite the heavy socks wrapping my toes.

"Hawk?"

No bags.

No flip-flops.

I rushed to the window, but there was nothing to see. Without confirmation, I already knew what had happened.

Hawk wasn't here.

I grabbed my jacket off the back of the couch as I passed, intent on going outside. I twirled it around my shoulders, then stopped. A flutter of white drifted to the cushion.

Frowning, I reached for a piece of paper with a scrawl across the front.

Cora,

The sunshine can never live with the darkness.

—Hawk

* * *

The sound of creaking doors, bright voices, closing cupboards, and the enticing aroma of fresh coffee drew me out of the loft two days later.

Boots over bare feet, I ventured into the coffee shop, where Bethany and Maverick stood behind the counter. Bethany beamed, her bright blue eyes crinkling at the corners. A heavy sweater protected her torso from the bone-chilling cold that remained in the storm's wake.

She spread her arms.

"You're alive!"

"Very much so! A sleeping bag kept me warm enough through the night, but I was glad when the power was restored that afternoon."

Her eyes widened. "Me too. I'm glad you were okay.

Thanks for texting us updates. We had a fireplace, so we were all set. Give your brother our appreciation for bringing his front loader and clearing our parking lot. That was so kind."

"The plows left a five-foot berm from the road that you would never have been able to get over," I said with a wry smile. "He was happy to help."

Indeed, watching Cade roll up in the front-loader with ear muffs, bright red cheeks, and a wave, had made me laugh for the first time since Hawk left without saying goodbye.

A hero in a tractor.

That was my brother.

Maverick had both hands resting on the counter. He peered at me with something like concern, but I avoided his gaze.

"Wow, does it feel good to be out of that house!" Bethany let out a long breath and reached for a mug. "Just three days, but it felt like so much longer."

"Three days with small kids," Maverick uttered.

She giggled. "Took us forever to shovel out. By the way, thanks for keeping this place cleared! We weren't expecting you to shovel the porch."

"My pleasure."

"When did Hawk leave?" Maverick asked.

"Ah . . . sometime in the morning after the snow stopped?"

I think, I added silently.

"Did he stay down here?"

"One night, yeah. He slept upstairs with a sleeping bag the second night, when it was so cold."

"Oh, that's nice of you." Surprise brightened Bethany's tone. "Was he good company?"

"Yes."

Unbearably good.

"One never knows with Hawk," Maverick drawled. "He's completely predictable . . . until he's not."

His eyes pressed on me. I wouldn't be able to avoid his attention for much longer without greater suspicion. Aggravated at myself, I met his gaze. This wasn't me. I wasn't the girl that avoided reality. That avoided *anything*. I always faced the world head-on.

Sensibile.

Grounded.

All the things my mom never managed to be.

Maverick lifted an inquiring eyebrow. In the depths of his question, I sensed that he knew. Something, at least, though I couldn't fathom what Hawk would have told him.

Because I didn't know Hawk.

Not really.

"Fine!" I cried, hands propped on my hips. "Fine, I'll tell you. Hawk . . . changed everything."

Bethany froze, the mug halfway to her mouth. Her eyes widened.

Maverick frowned. "What do you mean?"

The story rolled out, one sordid detail at a time. I skipped how deeply Hawk's kiss had affected me, satisfying them instead with *it was the best kiss of my life* and ending with the note he left behind.

When I finished with a breathy, "And that's the story. I don't even have his phone number."

Maverick hung his head.

Bethany stared. "Sweet baby pineapple," she whispered. "You have a crush on Hawk."

I closed my eyes, but refused to be humiliated. No, we had a lovely day together. I met a fascinating man I'd never forget, remembered what the zing of a crush could feel like.

Of course, Cade would have . . . so much to say about this.

"I didn't mean it to be anything more than a fun day

together. We made that clear from the start and we agreed. That's fine. I knew he would leave. But I just . . . didn't expect him to duck away without saying a word."

Bethany shot Maverick a knowing look. "Boy," she murmured, "do I know how that heartache feels."

He smiled ruefully.

"I don't even know *how* he got out of here," I continued. "The plows hadn't been out. There was a trail to the lake bed that *someone* walked, but that makes little sense. The rental car disappeared yesterday without anyone explaining how or when or who took it."

"Chopper came for him." Maverick straightened again. "The company chopper, maybe. Or a hired one. They might have a chopper closer than Texas, with all his holdings."

Company chopper.

Holdings.

"I'm sorry?"

Bethany put a hand on Maverick's arm, but kept her fastidious gaze on me. Her whisper carried across the room. "She doesn't know?"

"Apparently not."

The back of my neck prickled. "Know what?"

Her ice-blue eyes held such warmth when she set her coffee aside. "Who Hawk is, I mean. I'm not trying to talk over you."

A tickling sensation crept up the back of my throat.

"What does that mean?"

Maverick reached for his jacket, hanging on the wall not far away. He grabbed something out of the pocket—a rolled magazine—and dropped it onto the counter in front of me. I stared at it, uncomprehending.

A headline scrawled across the top.

THE BASEBALL CAP BILLIONAIRE.

My fingers trembled as I reached for it. A picture of Hawk filled the front in profile. He sat on the stairs of a massive downtown building, forearms on his knees. Blurred-out people buzzed behind him.

He stared out, profile illuminated by a setting sun in the background. On top of his head, a baseball hat. The image didn't show his eyes, which proved to be my only saving grace.

My lips could barely form the words.

"Billionaire?"

"Hawk is the CEO of M. Ventures, which is a parent company of a *lot* of companies in the SaaS space, which is fancy terminology for *Software as a Service*. He deals mostly with hospital-oriented work: medical records, billing, and customer support. The subsidiaries of M. Ventures run communication. Recently, his sister Nicola pioneered a big branch into telehealth. It's picking up steam, slowly."

Maverick rolled his lips together, watched me closely. The only reply I could muster slipped out like a lost word.

"Oh."

"He's pretty private about it," Bethany said. "Hawk started M. Ventures on his own years ago. Rumors that he might take a few years off have been swirling, but he hasn't confirmed." Bethany shrugged. "Not to us, anyway. Not that he knows us well. I've only met him once, but he knows Mav better. Hawk's brother, Noah, is closer to the family."

I tore my eyes off the front cover.

"So he's a billionaire, or his company is?"

"Both," Mav said.

"Oh."

"A lot of wealthy people fly under the radar, which is what he's always wanted, but he's single. Young. He created this empire in a handful of years. The media always pushes him into the limelight. He's . . . not what you'd expect, and he likes being that way. It's why they call him the baseball cap billionaire. Most of the time, you'll find him in jeans and a hat."

Dozens of puzzle pieces slid together. His unwillingness to speak about his career. The hesitation around details, desire to hide, and inability to commit to anything.

I set the magazine back down.

"I see."

"You gave him a gift, Cora," Bethany said. "A place to fall. Anonymity, even for a day. I'm sorry that he escaped without saying goodbye, but I can't say that I'm surprised."

"Thanks for . . . for telling me."

Mav nodded at the magazine. "I had a hunch and brought that for you. Read it. It's one of the . . . kinder articles."

"Kinder?"

"Hawk has a lot going on right now. Shifting pieces in what assets M. Ventures holds, moving leadership, and . . . a potential for something else, I think. He's been unclear when I ask about it, but it has something to do with Nicola personally spending millions of dollars to acquire physical assets without a clear motivation for their use."

"What physical assets?"

"Warehouses." His brow furrowed. "A bunch of them. A failing medical device company that's been dying out after their CEO died and left his idiot nephew at the helm. Stuff that doesn't puzzle together. She hasn't declared an intent for purchasing these companies yet, just their warehouses, and people in the business world are curious. It's generated publicity Hawk hasn't cared for. Regardless, take the magazine. It might answer some questions."

Against my inner will, my fingers curled around the papers.

"Thanks."

"Anything we can do to help?" Bethany asked. The

compassion in her gaze would have been my undoing if I didn't have something to hold.

"No. I'm honestly fine. No promises given, none expected. I crushed on him harder than I thought possible, and I think it startled me. More than anything, I felt disappointed that he left without saying goodbye."

"You had honest feelings," Bethany said. "Sounds like Hawk did too."

"Then he ran." Maverick's annoyed mutter made me feel slightly better, though I wasn't sure why.

Bethany reached out, put a hand on his wrist.

"To him, it wasn't running. I believe he felt he was doing the right thing by sparing Cora whatever attention would land on her by being in the spotlight with him. Whatever his motivations, I believe Hawk had the right intentions."

"Let me know if you want me there if you tell Cade," Maverick said with a laugh. "Knowing him, you might need someone to restrain him from going after Hawk."

* * *

A warm loft awaited.

I closed the door, strode across the room, threw myself onto the couch, and flipped the magazine open. A quick skim of the featured article—Hawk, which I still couldn't wrap my mind around—yielded several phrases and words that I understood well enough.

Sort of.

Bachelor.

Corporate holdings.

SaaS offerings.

Multi-billion dollar growth.

Delayed inheritance.

A second, third, and fourth perusal cleared some of the

smoke away, but sparked more questions. I switched to my phone, pulled up a browser. Searches of his name yielded further information, but the picture of who Hawk truly was had become more opaque. My thumb hovered over the *Images* tab on the screen, but I navigated past.

No.

I didn't want to see him.

An hour later, I tossed my phone to the other side of the couch, covered my eyes with my hands, and let out a long breath. The prickling fireworks that had exploded under my lips replayed.

His tenderness.

Heat.

Burning gaze.

He never had been mine. While it made me sad, I also believed in fate. We crashed into each other for a reason, if only to learn exactly what was possible between us. Nothing would change that.

My heart felt like a burning coal. I reached for my sketchbook. In seconds, I had a pencil in hand and fingers working quickly across the page. His image, still bright in my mind, poured out of me into half-formed sketches.

I recalled the curve of his jaw, the shell of his ear. The brim of his hat, hiding his face. A bump of nose, a swoop of cheek. Black curly hair near his ears, wispy at his crown. Everything.

Everything but his eyes. His dark soul-windows, framed by thick lashes, eluded me.

Page one.

Page two.

Page ten.

The sketches clustered at the front of the notebook, growing in number, until my emotions ebbed. The easing intensity allowed me to focus on what I actually felt. To burrow under my own layers, see the beating heart beneath.

Attraction.

Connection.

Plain and simple. Hawk and I had formed a bond in a single day. Tentative, fragile, but real. When all was unburied, *that* remained.

The pencil flowed. Now I could bring the full picture together. I worked, shading, swirling, swooping, until the final image of Hawk filled the page.

He stood at the window, arms folded over his firm chest, staring out. From the angle where I had studied his pose, I could just see his nose, the contours of his profile. No hat meant his hair skewed around the edges in an ebony halo.

So casual.

So *not* the man in the magazine.

Once finished, I stared at it, eyes wide. My breath came faster than it should have. I let it ease out of me in long, tremulous shudders. The pencil dropped back onto the table. I set the picture of Hawk next to it, propped it up so it stared at me.

"Thank you, Hawk. You taught me what was possible. I wish you well on your adventures."

Then I pitched it into the garbage.

With a sigh, I sank into the couch. The pillows and cushions held me like a blanket of warm cotton. I attempted to force thoughts of Hawk from my mind and closed my eyes.

Rest was a long time coming.

Chapter Ten

HAWK

One Month Later

The sound of Nicola's voice made my molars grind.

"Seriously, Hawk. What *is* this picture?"

With a scowl, I snatched my phone back.

Nicola stood across from my desk, dressed in a sharp pencil skirt of deep mauve, her hair pulled halfway out of her face. The rest hung down her back in long waves. Not exactly the sleek bob or shiny, sharp cut the way most corporate women in our building wore, but that had always been Nicola.

She pushed subtle boundaries with an iron fist and a delighted grin.

"That," I muttered, shoving my phone into my pocket, "is none of your business. Can we turn back to the important stuff now?"

The picture I'd taken of one of Cora's paintings before I left disappeared with it. Nicola didn't need to know where it originated, though I'd told her about Cora.

Nicola tapped a finger on the top of my desk as I turned back to the review of assets. Her silence could have woken the dead. I braced myself, thoroughly distracted from the list of numbers on the right-hand side.

"Is it a sun?" she asked, head tilted. "There's yellow and white—"

"No," I ground out. "The picture is not of the sun. It's a painting, if you must know. One of my friends created it."

"A flower? The darkness around the edges looks like—"

"Don't worry about it."

Cora drifted through my head for the first time in . . . an hour. Thirty days separated us. Thirty miserable, loathsome days in which time was supposed to make this easier, and it only worsened.

The simmering brevity of our connection—only twenty-four hours strong—plagued me. The hope of forgetting her as a memory to sigh over later dwindled with every day that passed.

Nicola let out a breath.

More silence.

I braced myself.

A second later, she broke the fragile air. "Where did you take the picture? There's no painting like that in any of the local gal—"

"Nicola!"

Two hands shot up, palms to me. "Fine. Fine. Just asking. Oh!" Her eyes widened. "Is it from Cora, back in Pineville?"

I shot her a glare.

She pressed her lips together, hiding a smile.

"Look," I muttered, finished with this conversation. "I still don't see why you're championing that we acquire this warehouse and fading company for twenty million when there's loose applicability to our current line of work."

"Alessandra has cleared it." She ticked an eyebrow higher. "If you don't, you know I will. This is M. Venture's last chance."

Her smug words annoyed me. Alessandra, the Chief Financial Officer of M. Ventures, and I, had met over lunch regarding this deal. If M. Ventures didn't purchase this failing company for pennies compared to what we had, Nicola would dig into her personal coffers—inherited blood money, I called it—and buy it herself. With a rising virus from South America knocking on our borders, M. Ventures might have to prepare for the worst by being versatile.

If Nicola owned assets we later needed, I'd regret not acquiring them myself. She'd charge M. Ventures an exorbitant amount of money to use them. Practically extortion, but not really. Cut throat, but that was Nicola too.

I loved her for it.

"Fine," I muttered. "Finalize it. Clear the employees, secure what's there. Come up with a plan for the space and . . . leave it on my desk so we can forget it. The media blitz about it has faded from your last personal purchase."

Nicola folded her hands in front of her. "I can do that right now. Ready for your update from South America?"

"Yes."

But no.

Nicola rolled her eyes, as if she could read my mind. "Case count continues to grow. Further investigation reveals a virus that's spreading. Several countries down there are struggling to keep up with enough hospital supplies."

My hand paused halfway to my closest pen. I lifted my gaze to meet hers.

"Really?"

"Of utmost importance in the care of this virus? Telemetry monitoring. Cardiac arrhythmias are prevalent. High incidence of stroke and heart attack is clear."

No clear connection between the assets Nicola gained and the virus appeared, but I felt the circling logic of her thoughts.

"Land the plane, Nicola."

Her usually pert lips were half-cocked now, an imminent sign of a win.

"They have reported two cases of the virus in Europe, one in Canada, three in Africa, and two in Asia. If this blows up to a global scale, all countries will require many things."

Understanding dawned.

"Advanced tele monitoring systems."

"Not to mention supplies to support a greater number of heart attack victims." Two fingers popped up on her hand. "M. Ventures—and myself in a few cases—have just acquired, at the cheapest possible rate, ten different facilities outfitted for medical device manufacturing utilizing a sterile process."

Tingling broke out across my shoulders.

She smirked.

"Schematics are already underway. I have a meeting with each warehouse manager scheduled tomorrow morning, and I think you should be there. With a little tightening up, we can have all ten warehouses spitting out the needed devices in two weeks." She leaned forward. "That, *brother*, is why I purchased them."

"What if the epidemic doesn't happen?"

"Then we count ourselves lucky that the world avoided a frightening situation and we outfit the warehouses, anyway. My telehealth branch continues to flourish. We can recoup the cash flow loss quickly."

Her use of *my telehealth branch* wasn't lost on me.

Ramifications calculated in my mind like a whirring computer algorithm. Should the worst happen, Nicola had not only given M. Ventures an edge over the competition, but enabled us to help the world without the frustration of delays.

Brilliant.

Pride filled my voice as I leaned back.

"Well done, Nicola."

Her wry smile told me all that I needed to know. The

swirling rumors about her *failed venture* and *hopeful press into medical devices that will only waylay M. Ventures bottom line* delighted her.

Nicola loved nothing more than people who underestimated her. Tate commanded front and center for that show.

"Let's just see how it plays out," she said, distracted by her phone. "I'm ready for every scenario."

With a nod, I conceded.

"Fine. Finalize this contract by tomorrow morning for our outreach team, and plan for me with the warehouse managers. I approve the individualized list of assets. James will keep me apprised of the situation in South America as part of our daily routine from here on out."

"About time you use your assistant," she muttered.

As nonchalantly as possible, I said, "I'm scheduling a dinner meeting with Tate in a few weeks. I'll mention your brilliance then."

She froze.

Her cold eyes met mine.

"You what?"

"I'm going to have to tell him eventually, Nicola. He knows I'm looking for an exit strategy, and he knows that I consider you first in line to take over."

She scowled.

"Don't breathe a word about the acquisition of warehouses to him until something firm happens in South America," she snapped. "I won't be made a fool in front of Tate again."

"He'll know either way."

"But not directly. I can deal with that. With any luck, we'll avoid this whole tragedy. I don't want him throwing a failure in my face."

"It's not a failure if the global market shifts away from your prediction, Nicola."

"It is to Tate. If I want the position of CEO, I can't be wrong. You know that, Hawk. He gives you more space because you are his son, but as his daughter, I have zero margin for error."

Her scowl dissipated into a familiar mask. Business, easy box to slide back into. Shove all the rest somewhere else, where she could forget about it.

"Enough about him." She nodded to me. "Who are you taking to the gala?"

I reared back. "Gala?"

Nicola's expression deadpanned. "Are you serious, Hawk?"

My mind blanked. Although I should have understood exactly what she meant, I didn't. Over the past four weeks I had been in this exact scenario repeatedly. The edge of annoyance in her eyes meant she noticed.

Hawk Mercedy didn't drop details.

No, he did *not.*

Until now.

"The Gentle Hearts Gala for women's heart health awareness. It's run by the Minutemen Health System of hospitals. *Our biggest client, you dolt.*"

A swear word lingered on the tip of my tongue. Of course. How had I forgotten? The Minutemen had a network of almost 3,000 hospitals that we served through our technology. Our biggest client to date across the US.

The gala was hosted by three famous chefs, would have gargantuan, intricate cakes on display for auction, and have several Hollywood types in attendance.

No press.

No media within the inner doors.

That meant I could arrive alone, then meet a date inside and never have said date subjected to the media or Tate. It would be low key, for such a hyped-up gala, but littered with expectations.

I ran a hand through my hair.

"Right. *That* gala."

Nicola's lips twitched. Wisely, she showed no further signs of amusement. Instead, she stared at me with an expression that said *don't-be-an-idiot*.

I glared.

"Might I remind you," she drawled, "that you've taken Shanice, Monica, and Heui-Ling with you twice now to social events? Each one several weeks apart, and obviously there was nothing in between those times. Still, you're fresh out of dates and . . ."

"This gala matters," I muttered.

"A helluva lot."

The wry glib of her tone would have been funny if this whole situation didn't feel so desperate. I tapped my teeth together, lost in thought.

Really, there was no question.

I wanted Cora there.

Yet, I had no grounds to make that ask.

Nicola's heels sank into the soft plush of a new rug some interior designer had laid out. She edged closer to the door.

"If you don't call your girl from the mountains and arrange for her to come, then I will. Trust me, the request won't be as good from me."

On any other day, I would have acted ignorant. Pretended not to know what she meant when reality painted an obvious picture. Today, I didn't have the energy. I'd spent most of it attempting to pretend that Cora didn't exist.

Nicola paused in the doorway.

"When you're miserable, the entire office suffers. If you don't want to lose staff, do something about it, all right?"

She disappeared.

I stared at her retreating form with a sigh.

Well.

Time to grovel.

* * *

"Hello?"

The sound of Cora's voice stalled my entire brain. One moment I paced across my office, palms sweaty, filled with the grim determination to get this done. The next, my brain fell out the bottom of my skull.

Her bright greeting brought a dozen memories rushing back. The ones I'd tried so valiantly to lock away.

"Hello?"

"Cora?"

Dead air met my ears.

"Cora?"

"Hawk?"

"Uh . . . yeah, it's me."

I held my breath, heart thudding so loud she must have heard it. Did it sound like a helicopter rotor to her? The way my chest shook with each beat felt like it.

"Uh . . . I . . . hi."

"Sorry to surprise you." Why was I sweaty? "I just . . . I've been thinking about you and wanted to see how you're doing."

"Really?"

The disbelief and hesitation cut deep. I winced, though I deserved that and more. Like a lowlife, I'd slunk out of her loft, too cowardly to say goodbye and thank her for the beautiful day that had to end.

"Yeah, really. You're surprised?"

"Definitely."

"I'm sorry. That's my fault."

A heavy exhalation followed. Despite my attempts at the latter, I tried not to picture her frustration. Her wrinkled brow. She'd been so happy. So full of levity, the image almost didn't coalesce.

After a long quiet, she asked, "So . . . what's up?"

"Can you switch to video?"

"You want to video chat?"

"I want to see you."

Another long hesitation sent my heart into my throat. Until I'd said the words, I didn't realize how true they rang, or how much I yearned to remember the snowstorm that changed my life.

"I don't think that's a great idea, Hawk."

"I know."

"I don't look . . . presentable."

"Oh. Is that why it's not a good idea?"

"Yeah."

"Not because you don't want to see my ugly mug?"

A giggle broke some of the strain. "Nothing about your mug is ugly. No, I'm just . . . it's so embarrassing."

"You'll be beautiful no matter what. It would mean a lot."

"No, really. I—"

"Stop, Cora. It doesn't matter."

An aggravated growl followed. "Fine," she muttered. "But I warned you."

I pulled my phone away, hit the video button. When a picture came together from her side, I burst out laughing.

Her glare burned through the phone.

"I warned you."

A splotch of dark green paint smeared her forehead. Messy hair drooped away from her face in a ponytail that stuck out of the top of her head like a fountain. An equally disheveled flannel shirt covered her shoulders.

Sputtering with laughter, I asked, "What happened?"

Despite her glare, a flicker of amusement lingered in the deepest depths of those eyes.

"I had an argument with my rug and my palette, that's all. Doesn't matter. I was just trying to clean it off when you called and . . . here we are. It's still smeared across my face and I need to get it off ASAP."

She set her chin on her palm in a pointed refusal to clean it off while we spoke. Instead, she lifted a piece of muffin to her lips and chomped. Questions remained, but I took mercy on her and set them aside. Seeing her again, the laughter hidden amidst the peeved annoyance, sent a bolt of energy through me.

One I hadn't felt in weeks.

No, ever.

"Do you want to take care of that?" I asked, grinning widely.

"Yes."

"Are you going to?"

"When we're off the phone."

"Will it stain your skin?"

"Probably."

"Cora, go clean it off."

With a roll of her eyes, she set the phone done. "Fine. Give me a minute."

Amusement rumbled through me when, five minutes later, she picked the phone back up. A reddened—but paint free—forehead returned with her.

"Now," I drawled, grateful to have her back. "Shall we begin again? Did I interrupt anything except you falling all over yourself?"

"You did." She held up half a muffin, then a cup of coffee. "But it's fine. I just . . . I thought I'd never hear from you again. Combined with the paint, it creates an interesting morning."

The phone settled, as if she'd set it against something.

"Well, I didn't really say goodbye, nor set realistic expectations for anything else to happen. I'm sorry, Cora. You deserve so much better."

The peevishness slipped out of her eyes.

"No, you didn't set expectations, and yes I do, but . . . we're all human, Hawk. I get it."

Underneath one eye, a shadowed part, darker than the rest, drew my gaze. A terrible thought darkened my mood and set my teeth on edge.

"Are you . . . do you have a black eye?"

Her gaze tapered. "What?"

"Your left eye. It's—"

She reached up, laughed. The giggle sent another shock-wave through me.

"It's just charcoal, from some sketches. No one has hit me."

Relief slowed my strides. What had I been thinking? How had I walked—no, waded through almost five feet of snow to a spot where the helicopter could land—away?

"Why did you really call Hawk?"

"I miss you."

Her lips tugged down, then flattened. For a second, she gazed away. All I could see was the lovely column of her throat, pulled taut. A tense jaw. She played with the lobe of her ear.

"I . . . I'd be lying if I didn't say that I missed you, too."

Unable to help it, I laughed. "But you don't *want* to say it, do you?"

She gave a short-lived smile. "No."

"Secretly, you're glad I called."

Like a crumbling landslide, she nodded. All levity faded. Through the phone, I felt her intense scrutiny. Saw the thump of her heartbeat in her throat. Could sense that she felt as desperate, wild, and out-of-control as me.

Ah, comfort.

I hadn't imagined it.

"Why didn't you tell me, Hawk?"

I sighed.

She knew. Of course she knew. Never had I expected her to *not* figure out that I was a very wealthy man with a high-level business under my command. A tiny part of me had hoped that she didn't discover the full picture yet.

That Hawk Mercedy, removed from all this, could remain with her.

"Because it would have changed everything."

Only a quick beat of time passed.

"Yeah, it would have."

Clearly, she'd thought this through, which gave me a moment of relief.

"So . . ." she drawled. The remaining slice of muffin lay between two fingers, just within the screen. She nibbled a piece of the top but didn't tear her gaze from the phone. "You are calling because you missed me and . . ."

"Does there have to be something else?"

"No, but there is."

"How can you tell?"

"Because . . . "

"Because you know I'm a billionaire with a giant company that walked away from the best day of my life and wouldn't call unless I wanted something?"

Her lack of immediate denial burned.

Finally, she nodded.

"Yes."

"Ouch, but deserved. You're right, there is something I want to ask of you. But it's a selfish ask on my part and tied into my original purpose for calling. I missed you, wanted to see you, and also invite you to a high-level gala."

She blinked.

"Pardon?"

"A charity gala. It's a closed-media affair once you get inside, but open outside of that. My plan is to go inside separately, to avoid the press and the mess they make of everything. Then we'd be able to spend the night together. You could . . . meet some of my people. I like most of them."

Shock lifted the register of her voice.

"Me?"

"Yes. You."

"Me? The girl who had green paint smeared on her forehead and muffin crumbs on her chin when you called?"

"Is that so hard to believe?"

"Well, sort of. You don't even know me."

"Yes, I do."

The firm assertion stole her reply. Her open mouth closed again, lips pressed together. She licked her lips.

Panic made my heart race.

I couldn't lose her. This increasingly heady breath of fresh air she provided wouldn't be enough. Now was the time to pull out all the stops. The time to show her exactly what I could be for her. To show up the way my cash resources allowed me—with excitement, glam, and massive amounts of *wow*.

I attempted to ease my thumping heart.

"The gala is in a week. You could stay at my place, get comfortable. We'll buy you a dress and new shoes."

"I don't know, Hawk."

"Can you take a break from your painting?"

"Well . . . yes. I'm technically early. I should finish it in a week or two, but . . ."

"Great. Then a chopper will descend at the lake bed behind the Frolicking Moose in two hours. From there, it will take you to the airport in Jackson City. The company jet is already en route. They'll have dinner, wine, dessert, whatever you want, so don't worry about eating before you go. My driver, Diego, will pick you up. I'll see you in about five hours, when you arrive at my penthouse."

"Hawk, I . . . I don't know what to say. I can't—"

"I want to do this for you, Cora. Please. Pack nothing. I'll have whatever you need available here. Nicola's already on it. Well, maybe bring a toothbrush if you're picky about that. I'm completing a few important things at work, then I'll head home and see you there."

She didn't breathe a word.

"See you soon."

I clicked *end* before I lost all courage. Emotionally spent, I leaned my head into my hands. At least that was over. Later this evening, she'd arrive and all the angst of the last thirty days could dissipate.

"Coward," I muttered.

Then I shoved back to my feet to finish my work.

And prepare for Cora.

CORA

Shock locked me into a daze.

Had he just . . .

But I . . .

Finally, I let the phone fall to my lap. After several moments of filtering through what just happened, I forced myself to pick the phone back up, dial the passcode, and navigate to the call list. My return call went unanswered once.

Twice.

Four times.

Cora: Hawk, please answer. I want to talk.

I dropped the phone in my basket, retreated to the bathroom, and returned seven minutes later with an even cleaner face and jittery nerves.

No response.

Cora: Hawk, call me, please? Let's talk.

A quick sweep, straightening of the room. After burning six minutes puttering around, I returned to the phone.

No reply.

Scowling, I shoved it on the charger and set it aside. Such an extravagant act of caring wasn't my thing. Kind, but I wasn't the girl swept away by a fancy offer and ridiculous gesture. Not when a clearly troubled foundation lay beneath it all.

Hawk and I stood on the thin ice of a single day.

Brittle.

Cracked.

Ready to fail.

One. Day.

He couldn't pull a billionaire stunt and make everything safe with money. Not all that glittered was gold, and this reeked of something I didn't like, but couldn't peg.

Fine.

Two could play this game.

I shoved into my snow boots, jerked a jacket on, and headed outside. As I stepped up to the main porch of the Frolicking Moose, wandering past still-frozen piles of snow from the giant storm, the sound of Dahlia's laugh filtered out. Bells tinkled on the door when I stepped inside.

Leslie glanced up from where she sat in her usual corner booth. She brightened.

"Hey girl!"

Her face fell when I didn't respond with my usual bubbly smile. She straightened up, spine locked.

"What's wrong? Are you all right?"

Dahlia's smile faded from behind the counter. Her fiancé, Bastian, lurked in the far corner. He glanced at her first, then me, then back to her. Seeing concern there, he straightened.

"Fine," I said, breathless. "Just . . . can you do me a favor?"

"Anything."

The words stuck in my throat at first. I cleared it, barely squeaking them out. "There's going to be a chopper landing behind the Frolicking Moose in a couple of hours. Will you . . . ah . . . tell them I said no?"

Dahlia's mouth dropped.

Leslie tilted her head to the side.

Bastian blinked.

Slowly, Leslie stood. One hand remained on the table as she studied me, gaze tapered.

"Why do I have a feeling this has something to do with Hawk?" she murmured. "It has Mercedy written all over it."

I couldn't admit it. The sound of his voice, the bright smile, lay too fresh in my mind. If I questioned my response too long, I'd never go through with it. Never tell him *no* when my heart so desperately wanted to say *yes*.

He deserved a *no* tonight because he didn't listen. Didn't give me a chance to protest. Hawk struck me as the kind of guy that required drastically clear communication.

Well, he had the right girl for that.

"Please?" I pleaded. "Just tell them I'm not coming."

Leslie hesitated again, then nodded.

"Of course."

"I'll be upstairs when they land. I won't come down. Tell them to leave me alone. Don't let them knock or—"

"I will." Bastian stood. "I'll take care of it."

I nodded once. "Thank you."

Curiosity glittered in Bastian's eyes as I hurried out of the shop and returned to the back door. The moment I slid the lock home upstairs, I felt better.

I did it.

Line drawn in the sand.

Now, I wanted to vomit.

Chapter Twelve

HAWK

A gleeful anticipation compelled me to work more attentively than I had for weeks. Contracts finalized. Paperwork reviewed. Emails discussed. My pending to-do list whittled down in near-record time. Apparently, I should have plunged into a lovesick fervor sooner than this.

My office door creaked open. James, my assistant, peered through the crack in the door.

"Hey, Hawk?"

"Yeah?" I shoved to my feet, grabbed my baseball hat on the side of the desk. "I'm just heading home. I'll have to deal with whatever—"

"Ah . . . phone call for you. You'll want to take this."

The wary look in his eyes grabbed my attention. The phone on my desk blinked an obnoxious green. With a scowl, I reached over, pressed the button, and picked up the phone.

"Hawk."

"Mr. Mercedy, this is Tanner with Mountain Helicopter Rentals. Forgive me, but the woman you wanted me to pick up refused to come."

"I'm sorry?"

"She sent a man out, said to go back. She didn't want the ride. What do you want me to do?"

"Are you still in Pineville?"

"Yes." Hesitation stole over his next response. "But, ah, I will not get my butt kicked over this contract. The guy who came out was pretty firm."

A simmering frustration rippled through me. Whatever man Cora sent out must not be all too nice about his message. Probably wasn't Maverick, because he would have called me.

"I see."

"So?"

Several moments passed before I said, "Well, if she won't come, that's her decision. You may return, Tanner."

"Thank you."

The call ended. I chewed on my bottom lip, awash with disbelief, more than irritation. She refused? I'd offered her . . . everything. The whole affair. The chopper, the jet, the clothing. These were things I loved to give, to share. Experiences that most people thrilled to experience.

"What the . . ."

Nicola piped up from the doorway. "You're an idiot!"

I glanced up with steep reluctance. Whatever Nicola had to say about this situation would come with a hearty sense of gloating.

With a wave of my hand, I motioned for her to enter the room. She leaned against the doorframe, barefoot on the hardwood floor, with a stack of papers in her arms.

"Go home, put on your baseball hat, and fly out there yourself. Clearly, she wants something a step above the royal treatment, all right? By some miracle, this woman might actually defy all odds and want *you* and your oblivious self."

The note of hilarity lessened the inherent insult hidden in her sisterly words.

"Is that what this is?"

"I hope so."

"Are there people that . . . I mean . . ."

"That don't care about wealth?"

I shrugged, helpless.

Nicola straightened. "Believe it or not, yes. Otherwise I won't like her as much as I'm hoping to. Don't be a fool, Hawk. Some girls don't care about billions of dollars in bank accounts. You met her on a snowy day and played stupid games with her, right? Go do that now. Her priorities are actually on point."

Nicola disappeared. I tried to summon some regret for telling her what happened between me and Cora, but couldn't drudge it up.

Instead, I leaned my palms on the desk and let out a long exhale.

Well.

That had been unexpected.

And utterly refreshing.

I looped my backpack off the back of the chair, reached for my keys in the top drawer. Plans hurried through my mind as I shoved my phone into my pocket.

Nicola stood with James behind his desk as I zipped past. "Contact the jet," I called. "Tell them to reroute back to here and then wait at the airport until I arrive. I'll want to leave immediately."

Nicola saluted.

"Good luck, boss brother. And do nothing else really stupid."

Chapter Thirteen

CORA

An old, flaky painting of a trout leaping out of a lake, ripples of water spreading out beneath it, captivated my gaze.

Nothing about the portrait had me transfixed. The greens were subdued and molded into each other. Umber brown turned to sienna too soon, leaving a squelched, muddy appearance. Rather, the too-bright sunset behind it provided a point I could safely stare at, letting my thoughts run wild in the background.

Snippets of articles featuring Hawk filtered in and out of my mind.

Baseball Cap Billionaire. Goodwill-focused initiatives. Multi-billion dollar wealth.

Refused.

Denied.

I closed my eyes with a suppressed groan.

What had I been thinking? I'd turned away from an extremely generous offer to sweep me into a world of glitz and glam. Despite all stoic outward appearances, I cringed deeply. Part of me *wanted* to be that girl.

I couldn't.

Dependable, down-to-earth Cade spoke too loudly in my brain and I knew I'd never be that girl.

The clatter of a plate and cup on the table in front of me drew my gaze. Dahlia stood there, concern apparent in her features. A plate lowered down, filled with my favorite raspberry-stuffed croissant.

"You all right?"

I straightened with a sigh. Yet again, Hawk commandeered my thoughts for too long.

"No."

A plethora of papers scattered the table, on top of a gridded notebook that mapped out my monthly expenses. Tucked underneath all the paper layers was an envelope with cash for grocery shopping this month.

How much farther from Hawk's life could mine be?

I should budget before I slip over to the grocery store to get my weekly allotment of groceries. One envelope at the back —the thickest—called to me.

Cade's ranch fund.

I'd need to run it to the bank and put all that cash into savings. An event that gave me a thrill each time. Watching the dollars ratchet higher with each passing month filled me with a deep satisfaction.

Of course, Cade would kill me if he knew I'd been squirreling funds away to help him purchase his own place instead of running other people's ranches. As long as he worked with animals, he'd be happy anywhere.

Instead of focusing on goals and artistic stretching and how to leverage what I had to get into more galleria slots, Hawk distracted me.

Eternally.

Dahlia lowered to the seat across from me, propped her chin in her hand. Her wide eyes, dark as melted chocolate and twice as warm, waited with silent invitation.

I slapped a hand on top of a small spiral calendar.

"I shouldn't have refused."

Dahlia blew a raspberry, leaned back. With a wave of her hand, she dismissed my comment.

"Stop, you did great. The man needed a solid refusal to teach him what's *real*. He's a Mercedy. They're . . . stubborn."

"You've never met Hawk."

She recoiled. "Doesn't mean I don't track him! Of course I know about Hawk. Between Benjamin and Hawk, the Mercedy name stays pretty warm in the tabloids, and I am *all* over those."

"It could have been so fun to ride in a chopper."

"Maybe."

"The complete experience. Ride in a corporate jet. New clothes. Ritzy gala. I'm an idiot!"

"Nah. You're a woman who knows what she wants long term, who doesn't give that up for one gala, and that is a powerful thing."

My poor inner child yearned for the glamor of corporate jets, getting ferried away to big cities, escorted around by a private driver, only to land in Hawk's lap. Of all the gorgeous, broken men . . .

But what Dahlia said hit far deeper.

She was right.

Lovely, but not what I wanted.

"What if . . ."

I never hear from him again. The unfinished thought occupied all the free space in my mind. What a stupid idea. I'd already resigned myself to *not* hearing from him ever again before his phone call and lived my life just fine afterward.

Why did it bother me so much now?

Ah, his voice.

The dismissal of his impact on my life had been easier

before I heard his voice again, and understood that he had also missed me.

Hawk Mercedy sought *me* out.

Gamechanger.

Dahlia didn't comment, giving me space to spiral out of control in my mind, like a flagellating star whipping around in the night sky.

"Something amazing compelled you to give the chance up. Let's get back to that, because you need to re-anchor, girl-friend. Remind yourself why."

"As much as I want it to be, even for a short time, giving into that control is not who I am. That's not . . . it's not the relationship I want. I don't want him to buy my attention. I want a firm foundation of trust before we go into the blitz of a rich lifestyle."

"You're not saying no to wealth?"

"Wealth is whatever." I shrugged. "I'm saying *no* to hiding behind it at the start of something that could be life changing."

"What's the best thing here? If you don't want his money, what *do* you want?"

"Him."

The response came so instantly I covered my mouth with my hands. The truth of it had a startling effect.

Dahlia smirked.

"Girl," she drawled. "You've got it *bad*."

The one day I had Hawk, I *knew* I had him. Looking back —and after reading an embarrassing number of articles about him—I could read between the jagged lines. Hawk had been himself with me at the shop. His real self. The one that I doubted many saw.

Would he give that side of himself again when real life intruded?

Could he be *that* Hawk and *this* Hawk?

"Without question, Hawk is better than the wealth," she said. "I'd take Bastian wrapped up in a garbage bag and nothing to his name, and it would be enough. Hang onto that truth, okay? Use it as your north star to guide you. The ball is in his court now. If he does nothing, you have your answer."

I leaned my forehead into my hands.

"True."

Dahlia chuckled under her breath, squeezed my shoulder with a hand, and left. I vaguely registered her boots crossing the shop. The smack of her laying a kiss on Bastian followed, and I tried not to burn with jealousy.

Resigned, I turned back to the books and numbers, relieved to have something else to fall into. I grabbed my pen, forced my brain back to the page, and set thoughts of Hawk aside. Despite all attempts to clear him from my mind, he never drifted far.

Reservations aside, Dahlia's speech helped.

Eggs, milk, bread, and other necessities awaited. With a grimace, I added *tampons* and *Midol* and *more chocolate than is good for me* to the list.

Like life wasn't dramatic enough already . . .

After several minutes of blessed silence where my brain went back to an almost-full functioning status, I set the notebook and grid paper down with a sigh. Grocery list mapped out. Money set aside for Cade.

Time to adult.

As I shoved the envelopes and paperwork into my bag, the bells on the door clinked. I tossed an idle glance up, then froze.

A pair of cowboy boots, well-worn jeans, a white shirt, a long-sleeved black jacket, and aviator glasses stood in the doorway. My heart skipped a beat. I'd know those shoulders, that baseball-cap topped head, from anywhere.

Hawk reached up, removed his glasses, and faced me.

My blood turned to slush.

We locked in a tight gaze. His expression remained as implacable and difficult-to-read as smoke. I held my breath.

"Hawk?"

"Hey, Cora."

The easy rumble of his voice simultaneously irked me and whipped my heart away. Who did he think he was? Hadn't I made my position *very* clear?

The door whispered to a close when he advanced, throwing a nod to Dahlia behind the counter. Her eyes widened, but her lips sealed as she shuffled blindly to the drive-through window. Bastian watched through a hooded gaze from where he sat in the corner, arms bent, shoulders tense.

Hawk paused, motioned to the seat on the other side of my booth.

"May I?"

I nodded, pulled my backpack onto my lap, and wrapped my arms around it.

Hawk set his sunglasses on the table. My heart twisted with a sickening sensation. Hawk drew in a breath. I let mine out, dizzy from holding it.

"Can we talk?" he asked.

I nodded.

His gaze slipped to Dahlia, then back.

"Somewhere else?"

Another nod.

The edges of his lips twitched in a half smile. A welcome sign that he wasn't livid with me, at least. Did men like Hawk throw temper tantrums? Did being a billionaire or CEO make him liable to fits of rage when things didn't go the way he wanted?

He could rage all he wanted.

My boundary remained.

I mentally rolled my eyes. No *wonder* he didn't want to tell me about his wealthy life. The moment I knew about this angle, assumptions about him—dumb ones—had followed. Assumptions *and* questions.

"Upstairs." I heard myself speak in a raspy voice, but it all felt disconnected. "We can talk up there in private."

"How about I take you to dinner? There's a place across the street that looks good, and I'm starving."

His immediate counter startled me, mostly because of the offer. Time with just me and Hawk sounded better than the bustle of a restaurant, but I accepted with a nod. I stood, tossed my backpack onto my shoulder, and followed him out.

Chapter Fourteen

HAWK

Cora's stiff spine, closed lips, told me just how badly I'd screwed this up. We crossed the street without another word. She didn't fight me, but she looked far from eager to see me again.

Okay.

Didn't blame her. The trip over here had prepared me for taking the full weight of what I sent her way. In my desire to get her close to me again, I tried to take away her choice and *make* the connection happen.

Idiotic.

A table waited for us at the Italian restaurant. I guided her to it, motioned to the waitress I'd talked to earlier with a wave, and sat across from her. The server, a woman named Tani, slipped over with two menus and water. The ice clanked against the glass as I reached for it.

"Take your time," Tani said with a wave. She headed for another table across the store. Cora glanced around, taking it in, before facing me fully. Her wide-eyed expression didn't waver. I sensed a wave of truth about to come.

She didn't disappoint.

"Let's get this over with. Are you angry?" she asked.

"No."

"Upset?"

"Also, no."

An eyebrow lifted higher. "Frustrated?"

"With myself."

Her lips parted in a shocked breath. "Oh?"

I shrugged. "I should have known that you weren't the shock-and-awe type. Though . . . I guess that's a weird way to put it. I wanted to do something nice, but it came across as too much. I get it. To be fair, I haven't dated a woman who didn't like those things, so I just . . . didn't know. I should have. I'm sorry if it was insulting or presumptuous. I should have asked if you wanted to come. Should have given you a chance to refuse. It was a sincere attempt to do something nice."

"Why didn't you answer when I tried to call and text?"

"I dove into work, ignored everything else. Honestly, I didn't want to think about you refusing. I should have communicated better."

By a small degree, she softened. "It's not that those things wouldn't be great, or even fun. I'd just . . . I'd rather do them with you than without. What's the point if you're not there?"

The question stole my breath.

What's the point if you're not there?

No one had ever asked that before.

Replies bobbled in and out of my mind. Yet again, she'd stolen my brain. Made it almost impossible to know what to say. Such raw sincerity deserved an equally honest reply. I just . . . didn't know how.

Now that I was with her . . . I wasn't sure what to do.

Tani returned. We gave our orders, then remained in the silence after she disappeared. Fresh, twisted breadsticks lay on the table, their buttery surfaces gleaming. I reached for one, peeling the hot bread apart.

Cora traced a picture on the tabletop with her fingernail, and glanced at me with renewed hesitation.

"So . . . why did you come, Hawk?"

My name on her lips sent a shiver through my jaded soul. I leaned back with a smile, eager to turn this a bit more casual now that I had given the apology. My hands spread in an open gesture.

"To take you on a date."

"Really?" She laughed. "How do you know what I like to eat?"

"Lucky guess. Also, Pineville is painfully lacking in places to eat."

She laughed, then sobered. Her brow wrinkled. "Oh, do you have to leave soon?"

"Tomorrow afternoon."

"Not tonight?"

"I took the rest of the day and the morning off."

"I see."

Ropes of anxiety curled in my chest at the thought of leaving for a full day. Nicola wanted me there to visit the warehouse managers of the newest acquisitions. I didn't need to glance at the clock to know she met with them right now.

I brushed it off.

M. Ventures would survive.

Besides, I had to get used to it. I already actively planned my exit strategy, and Nicola could handle the day-to-day for less than 48 hours. Nothing tonight would require my immediate presence. One evening was not a big deal against the grand schema of life.

Still . . . it hadn't been easy.

For the first time since my return, her shoulders pulled back. Intrigue brightened her tone to the normal blitz of joy I'd dreamed of for four weeks. She wrapped her fingers together and leaned onto her elbows.

An eyebrow lifted as she whispered, "What are your plans for our date?"

Feed you. Return to your place. Ravish you with kisses that will make your head spin.

Instead, I reached into my pocket, extracted a card deck, and tossed it onto the table between us. Shock filled her widening eyes.

"A game?"

I chuckled. "A game. This time, I came up with it."

She motioned to the cards with a wave, new eagerness infusing her eyes.

"Well Casanova? Explain yourself."

Chapter Fifteen

CORA

Hawk's brow lifted as he set the cards more fully in front of me. The stack spread out, moved by the pressure from his fingertips.

"Same sort of game, different rules. If you draw a red card, you ask me a question. Any question. If you draw a black card, you ask me a question. Any question."

I laughed.

"So I get to ask you fifty-two questions?"

His smile echoed with tenderness when he said, "Yes."

An admission lingered in the words. A heartfelt understanding that he held back so much when we spent the day together, walked the fringes of each other's world, then parted. I stared at the cards, drowning with questions. He gave me permission to break the silence. He offered what I wanted more than anything.

Transparency.

Hawk leaned back, finger in the air. "Only rule is that you have until the close of the deck. Once you run out of cards, the game is over."

"Does the game repeat, but with me answering the questions instead?"

"Only if you're willing."

I flipped the top card over. Two of spades.

Our gaze met.

"Are you hoping that I'll still attend the gala with you after this big romantic gesture?"

His lips puckered slightly. He hesitated, then nodded. "Yes, because I want to spend time with you, but it's not why I came."

Another card.

Seven of hearts.

"Then why did you come?"

"I missed you and I messed up. I wanted to make it right."

A curl of heat warmed my belly.

Jack of clubs.

"Did you really wade through almost five feet of snow to a chopper in the middle of the lakebed in order to get away from me?"

His lips twitched, but he revealed no amusement.

"Not to run from you, but to return to something far less thrilling. But . . . yes. Four feet of snow, in flip-flops and shorts." He shivered. "Sweet misery. I'll never do that again."

I grinned.

Weirdo.

Next card: ace of diamonds.

"How many siblings do you have?"

"Four."

The three of clubs.

"Which one are you?"

"Oldest."

I tossed another card off the top of the deck, but didn't pay attention to which one it was. It didn't matter. The intensity that thrummed between us like a live wire had returned, and it required all my focus.

So quickly this had become a microcosm of the snowstorm. A replay bottled up in an Italian restaurant. As deep as before, with the vibrant layers that only time could give.

"What's your favorite vacation spot?"

The skin between his brows wrinkled. He stared at the cards, then at me, before slowly answering.

"Once, when we were little, my Mom took us to a cabin in the Virginia mountains. Totally off the grid. Nice little place. No one knew it was there. Friend of a friend owned it, or something. We had a great time. No TV, just playing. Campfires. Food. That kind of thing. I think that was my favorite."

For the first time, I felt his sincerity through the rawness of his words. Yet again, the sense that *this* was Hawk overcame me. I tapped on the edge of the next card, flopping it onto its back.

Four of spades.

"What's your favorite food?"

His brittle stare hardened. He leaned forward, swamping me with a spicy aftershave and sweet mint.

"Why aren't you asking?" he whispered.

I knew what he meant. A billion elephants stood in the room, but not between us. Maybe he thought his money meant something in this situation. He couldn't be more wrong. I mimicked his intensity as I lowered my voice.

"I'm the one asking questions."

He reached up, placed a hand over mine.

"Ask it, Cora."

The heat of his hand radiated like an envelope of fire. I swallowed the building pressure in my throat.

"I'm asking the questions that matter most, Hawk. You don't get to control what I value."

His frown deepened.

I straightened, tapped the card. "Food, sir. What is your favorite?"

Troubled now, he answered with a distracted, "Nachos. There's a place down the road from my penthouse that has these nachos with white cheese and shredded BBQ chicken. They're to die for."

"I want in!"

He nodded, a brief glint returning. "Come with me. I'll buy you all the gooey nacho goodness you want."

My breath caught. Subterranean meaning floated under those words, something I couldn't hope to understand, but couldn't wait to figure out. The heat in his gaze bore testimony. Ten more cards peeled away while we waited for our meals, each question more ridiculous—and important—than the last.

Stuffed animals as a kid?

Ever been snorkeling?

Does he like rain better than snow?

How often does he scrub his bathroom sink?

Finally, a plate of eggplant parmesan appeared in front of me, and fettuccine for him. I swept the cards up, set them aside.

"Now," I drawled. "Is it my turn to answer?"

He reached for a fork, and I sensed a challenge in his eyes.

"If you're ready."

"No cards needed."

"Do you enjoy the nightlife scene? Clubs, bars, etc?"

Although I'd prepared for unexpected questions, that one took me by surprise. I cut into the edge of my eggplant parm with the side of my fork while I thought it through.

"I used to," I admitted. "When I was younger, late night dancing was more thrilling and exciting. I could have fun doing that now and then. Not all the time, however."

His nose wrinkled.

"I hate it."

Unable to help it, I laughed. "I can see that."

Hawk smiled, wiping the disgusted expression from his face. The muscles along his neck flexed as he chewed and swallowed his first bite, eyes momentarily closed with enjoyment. Unable to help myself, I stared.

What a handsome man.

With a clearing of my throat, I glanced at my plate before he caught me in blatant admiration. Maybe it wouldn't be the worst thing if he understood just how much he affected me.

Really, how could he *not* know?

"Did you tell your brother about me?" he asked.

I reached for my water with a laugh.

"No."

"That . . . is a good thing?"

"Yes. At least for now. Cade is a little overprotective."

"With your history," he murmured, "I can understand why."

"I'll tell him when there's a need to tell him."

"Got it."

"Anything else?"

Hawk hesitated, jaw tense, then met my gaze. "Why doesn't it matter that I never told you who I was? That I . . . left billions of secrets between us?"

The haunted expression in his eyes trapped me. I reached out, put my fingers on his arm.

"Because it's you I'm interested in, Hawk. Not the money. If you lost all of it tomorrow, it wouldn't change anything for me. So why talk about it? There are far more fascinating facets about you than that one, if you ask me."

"It's a huge part of my life."

"But it is *not* your life, nor you."

He blinked, clearly startled. "I don't know what to say. I've never had it not matter before, Cora."

"You say you never had another woman refuse your posh attempt at impressing either, so I hope you see now that you're in for a different kind of ride."

He chuckled. "I think I see that."

"It's you and me, Hawk. I guess you could say that we've been different from day one."

Chapter Sixteen

HAWK

Piles of snow flanked either side of the road when we walked back to the Frolicking Moose. Stalwart remnants of the storm that felt like lifetimes ago. Stubborn statues to time.

The urge to hold her hand as we crossed the street made my fingers itch. I kept them tucked into my pocket and tried to ignore the sensation of something missing. The lower floor of the Frolicking Moose lay in darkness by the time we circled around the back, her backpack on her shoulder.

At the door to the spiral staircase that led upstairs, Cora paused. She met my gaze.

"Thanks."

"Can I see you before I leave tomorrow?"

"I'd like that. Call me in the morning? We can plan time together."

Hints of lavender drifted toward me when she pressed a kiss to my cheek, then turned away. I stood outside, bemused, until the door closed and she disappeared up the stairs.

* * *

Cartoons and a crying baby greeted me at Maverick's house.

Warm lights hung above a table cluttered with bottles, toys, and burp cloths. Bethany stood amid the chaos in a pair of heels, her ice-blue eyes startlingly at ease in such pandemonium. A designer bag hung from her left elbow, while her right held onto a baby with a snotty face.

"I know you don't like your nose wiped," she sang, "but it's going to happen anyway, sister-girl."

A squawk of protest followed.

"Make yourself at home, Hawk," she called over her shoulder with a smile. "We're just wrestling havoc, as usual. Don't mind us."

I held up a hand.

Maverick waved from behind the stove, where several somethings bubbled in pans. The smell of cheese sauce filled the air. Shane, their oldest boy, occupied himself with a pile of green sand in a box on the floor as Bethany navigated around the busy table, daughter in arms.

A game show played in the background, interrupting the steady ambience with cheers and buzzers.

"Hawk!" Mav called. "Glad you made it this time. Pull up a seat. I will have macaroni and cheese straight from the oven —none of that powdered cheese garbage—in about ten minutes. Salad and grilled chicken on the side."

Bethany pulled a downy, pink blanket off the back of a chair and tucked it against the chest of their little girl, Baylee. Baylee gripped it and snuggled into her mama, brow scrunched in a powerful glare of distrust as she peered at me.

"What brings you to town?" Bethany asked, reaching for an envelope on top of a tottering pile. With tantamount talent, she kept Baylee in her arms as she stepped out of her heels and nudged them to the side with a foot.

"I came to see Cora."

Bethany's eyebrow lifted. "Oh?"

"Yep."

Though he stood with his back to me, I could feel Maverick's smirk.

The awkward quiet remained for an agonizing three seconds before Baylee broke it with a shriek. Never had I been so grateful for a wrathful child in my life.

Bethany excused herself with another smile and headed down the hall, walking silently on a thick carpet littered with toys. Baylee screamed against her shoulder the whole way. Mav glanced back, chortled, and reached into a hot oven with two mitts.

"Not a word," I muttered.

He laughed harder.

Forty minutes later, scattered remnants of golden macaroni and cheese, a few slices of cheesecake, and quiet remained. Shane retreated to watch a cartoon. Bethany murmured from Baylee's room in the back, singing a lullaby.

Maverick set aside a fork. One eyebrow tilted high as he regarded me.

"Sooo . . ."

I shook my head. "Not a word about Cora."

He held up two hands. "You're the defensive one, coz. I never even mentioned her."

My mouth opened to explain, but closed. This whole situation made no sense. A deep connection from day one that couldn't be real that we replicated our second time together, a full month apart. Everything happened as intensely as before.

No, worse.

I'd stayed away for weeks because it couldn't possibly have been true. The humming tension that felt so good it hurt. The connection that dove deep as time. We'd spent less than twenty-four hours with each other, at most, and part of me clicked into place every time she smiled.

I rolled my head on my shoulders and sighed.

"Look, I just . . ."

"You're about to hand off to Nicola," Mav said, a finger in the air. "You're CEO at the company, and you have five big things about to happen, including a potential acquisition. Nicola is kicking butt, except for the minor question of why she gobbled up a multi-million dollar medical device company that went into the toilet."

"She has her reasons."

"And I can't wait to hear what they are. The point is this, Hawk: You're in a fantastic position to, I don't know, have a *life* or something."

"Nicola isn't a guarantee."

He chortled. "Yes, she is. She'll run that company better than you, because she actually knows how to turn work off. You don't. Your work-life balance has always sucked. You run hard. Too hard."

Unable to contradict, I gave in with a nod. Nicola set better boundaries than I did, and without apologies. It slowed her progression into higher positions, but left her a better candidate once she arrived.

I would have been mildly jealous if I wasn't so ready to claw myself out of there.

"Maybe."

Mav snorted. "C'mon, don't give me that bull. You're scared."

"Shut the—"

"Children!"

"I wouldn't say it!"

"You planned on having a life, which is why you wanted out of the C-suite party. You texted me about your exit strategy, which is almost ready to put into place. Yet, you haven't tipped it over. Now, life has presented itself to you and you're running."

"I've known her for two days, Mav."

"At least a month."

"We've spent less than two days in each other's company."

He shrugged.

"I never said marriage. I said *life*. As in doing things. Taking risks that aren't financial. Spontaneous stuff like showing up unexpectedly in a mountain town to take a girl on a date after she boldly rejected your much bigger advance. That's *life*, brother."

Annoyance crawled through me. "News already spread, eh?"

Mav spread his hands. "It's life in the mountains. I knew before the helicopter left, empty, what was going on."

"I'm afraid that this . . . thing with Cora can't be real." I leaned forward, arms on the table, and readjusted my hat. "It's too strong to last."

"Give the girl a chance, Hawk. No, more than that, give her time. Date her. See if it holds. If it doesn't? Bummer. If it does? Welcome. This life is messy and so loud and out of control and the best thing that's ever happened to me."

Maverick's stare slammed into me like a jackhammer. He was right. I'd never chased the dream of family and kids, but seeing the effortless and liquid love between Mav and Bethany, I couldn't help but wonder if I might have missed out.

"What about Tate?" I asked, brows high.

Mav would remember.

His expression sobered. After a pause, he said, "He's not going to sabotage anything that's real, Hawk. I know he's frightened other women off so you're free to focus, or marry whatever girl he picks for you, but Cora is real. I don't think Tate will scare her."

Fear simmered in my gut, anyway. I didn't want Cora hurt like some of the others. Her goodness is exactly what Tate would exploit, attempt to destroy.

Just like my younger brother, Noah.

"Is it fair of me to date her?"

Mav snorted. "Would you ask that if you weren't a billionaire?"

"No."

"Then stop asking it. Stop being a billionaire. Just be Hawk."

Those words swirled through my mind in a storm. I nodded, rapped my knuckles once on the table. "All right. Time. Dating. I can do that."

"Finally, he talks sense." Mav leaned back in his chair, then tilted his head toward the screen. "So, you got time to watch the game together?"

"I've got five bucks on the underdog."

He shoved his chair back. "You're on."

Chapter Seventeen

CORA

Pancakes bubbled on my stovetop the next morning. Somehow, the throwback to our first breakfast felt just right.

Hints of vanilla and apricot twirled through the air from my teacup, invigorating me. My favorite white tea brew pirouetted inside. With every sip, I felt warmer. Outside, flurries spit out from a slate sky.

Hawk stood at the window, staring out, with a coffee cup in one hand. He'd been here for almost an hour and we said little in all that time. The silence wasn't a burden. Instead, he seemed to enjoy sitting back, watching me scrape and dot oil paint across the canvas. He alternated between appreciative throat noises and quiet rapture.

Until he sat on the couch, computer on his lap, and didn't make a single sound while I switched to making pancakes, I hadn't realized how much being around Hawk settled the urgency to ask the most important question.

Could intensity cohabitate?

Just because we had a deep connection that bordered on being spiritual, didn't mean we could work around each other in the same space. I wanted to live life with Hawk, not around him.

Sometimes, that arithmetic didn't work out.

With a spatula, I peered at the golden underside of the pancake closest to me.

"Are you sad to return today?"

"Only to be leaving you."

His raw honesty delighted me. I straightened, glanced over my shoulder with a little smile. "I'm glad you came."

He met my gaze.

"Me too."

A buzz from the counter drew my attention to his phone. With a sigh, he reached for it. Wrinkles marred his brow as he thumbed through a message.

I sent ready pancakes flying onto the plate with a flick of my wrist, then turned the stovetop off. Pats of butter oozed down the browning tops, melting over the sides, as I set the short stack on the table in front of his spot.

"Have a seat. Breakfast is ready."

Hawk frowned at the phone screen, his coffee set aside on a marble coaster. Light from outside cut a sharp silhouette around him as I lowered into a chair.

"Hawk?"

He blinked, met my gaze. "I need to go home. Now."

"What's wrong?"

Wordlessly, he crossed the room, passed his phone to me. Words in a text message conversation between him and Nicola filled the screen.

Nicola: Update just came from our contacts in the health department. The virus spread across the border into the US. Cases were just identified in Florida.

Hawk: How many?

Nicola: Five confirmed. They were at an amusement park before being diagnosed.

Hawk: So the count is about to grow higher.

Nicola: Extremely. Better get home, Hawk. It's go time. The warehouses I purchased are clearing as we speak in preparation for tele monitoring. The CDC is going to make an announcement soon, and I have people reaching out to our hospitals in Florida with preparation guidelines, starting with cardiologists.

Hawk: Send the jet. I'll drive up the canyon.

Nicola: Don't insult me. The chopper is already on the way to you. Mav said he'd arrange for someone to take your rental car back.

Hawk stood with both hands on the back of his chair and watched me take it in. I passed the phone back to him.

"There's a virus in Florida?"

"The media kept it pretty low key so far, but now that cases are spreading, it's about to go wild."

"Spreading like . . . globally?"

He nodded. "Nicola's been tracking it for a bit. We try to keep ahead of things like this so the different divisions of M. Ventures can anticipate support, needs, and pivots for the hospitals we serve. South America contained it after the initial shock of a new virus being discovered. The past few weeks it's been simmering. Cases popped up in various places in South America, and are now spreading. The number of heart attacks and heart failures have increased. There are loads of complications from the virus."

"Now it's here?"

He pursed his lips. "Yes. It's here."

Ice flowed through me from the top of my head all the way to my toes. "What are the nasty details that make you look so concerned?"

He lowered into the chair across from me. "It strikes fast, and the cardiac health implications are concerning. The origins are uncertain so far. Some scientists speculate it came from the depths of the Amazon, but we're not sure."

"Is it causing heart attacks?"

"Among other things. It presents as a chest cold. Most people survive that with little difficulty, and then the complications follow. Populations have shown higher death rates from conditions like stroke, heart attack, and arrhythmias. Unfortunately, we're not sure how it spreads yet, which is why it's scary."

"Why isn't anyone talking about this?" I asked with a nod to his phone. "This is a big deal."

"It could be. It isn't yet. With proper preparation, we could hold it off until more is discovered and understood."

"Could it be global?"

He nodded.

I sat back in my chair, eyes wide.

"My business provides support for large hospital corporations in a lot of ways. The warehouses Nicola spoke about? She wants to turn them into manufacturing centers for more cardiac equipment. If we act now, we can provide support to a lot of hurting health care systems and the people that rely on them."

"That's amazing, Hawk."

"Unfortunate, more than anything. I wish we didn't have to worry about this."

His teeth sank into his bottom lip. I had to tear myself away from the sight of his very-normal dubiety.

"We've all but confirmed a new virus is on the way and

now it's finally crossed into the US," he continued, speaking more to himself now. "We've been setting up for the possibility, and now we need to converge, make these things happen."

I leaned back, rubbed my arm with my hand. "Gracious, yes, Hawk. You need to go back. Nicola says she needs you. Why are you waiting? The chopper will be here soon."

A trying smile appeared on his lips. The knowledge that he had to leave me and whatever hummed between us again, brought me deep sadness. The mounting issues that were about to manifest, however, wiped out all complaints.

Hawk reached out, hand on my arm. "Were you serious when you said you wanted to ride in a chopper and a private jet, but with me?"

"Yes."

"Then, why don't you come? The potential pandemic hasn't happened yet. There's a chance that we can quarantine those who are infected and learn what happens. The country, at large, doesn't realize what's stewing under the surface. That means the gala is going to still happen, and is more important than ever from a support standpoint. If you're willing, I'd like to show you my world."

"Really?"

"Really." He squeezed my arm. "I might be busy while I get these things in motion, but if you're patient, I'd like you to come with me."

With a squeal, I threw myself across the table and wrapped my arms around him. He laughed, hand heavy on the spot at the middle of my back. I pulled away.

"Let me pack a bag."

He braced his hands on the table, gazed over at the wall where my painting awaited.

"What about that?"

"I'll take a break."

"But you have a deadline to finish. I don't—"

"It'll be fine. Like I said, it's early yet."

"Are you sure?"

"I'm not passing this chance up, Hawk. I want to go on an adventure with you, okay? Let's do it!"

* * *

Hastily eaten pancake remnants were scraped into the garbage, plates rinsed, bags packed. Leslie promised to lock my place up when she left and cover the cleaning at night.

Within thirty minutes, we stood near each other in a snowy field. Hawk held onto my arm with a hand, aviators shielding his gaze from the descending flakes. One moment I studied his profile, memorizing the lines, and the next I watched a helicopter descend on the lakebed.

Snow pelted me in the face like razor-sharp needles. I turned away, arm lifted, until it settled gently on the ground. At a sign from the pilot, Hawk put an arm around my shoulders and guided me forward. We ducked, rotors thudding overhead as we climbed inside the open door.

A woman with her hair in a bun, sitting in the back, outfitted me with headphones, a microphone, and strapped me into a seat. The overwhelming noise and immediate chaos took my breath away as we lifted into the air.

My stomach somersaulted. I clutched my backpack filled with charcoal pencils and drawing paper to my chest like a child's security blanket.

The snowy world disappeared.

Every breath felt unstable, like an avalanche, as Hawk, the pilot, and the woman spoke back and forth. He laughed, at ease in the sky in a small metal basket. Their staticky, tinny voices filled my mind as I carefully peered out the side window. Cotton-puff mountains peeled away in lines and ripples to the horizon.

A warm hand squeezed my fingers.

"You good?"

I turned to find Hawk peering at me with concern. The thought that this experience was a natural part of his life made my throat choke.

"This is really cool!" I cried.

Relief permeated his smile. "It's not a very long ride. They'll drop us at the airport, where the jet will land. Should be a quick transition. We can talk more easily then."

I gave him a thumbs up, then turned to study the ruched ruffles of the mountains. My fingers itched to sketch it out on a pad. To create, with charcoal and paper, a memory that would never leave. The aerial view on the same landscape drove deep into my heart of hearts. An adventure with Hawk at my side stirred my soul.

There was a certain novelty to being scooped up by a helicopter, swept to a private jet, and whisked away to big-money Texas. Nothing in my life had ever given me such a thrill. Of greater excitement, however, was Hawk sitting next to me.

Alone, this would have felt empty.

He simmered in the background, a quiet question. His life awaited. Now, I would have the chance to peel back the mask, test whether I truly understood the man hiding back there.

Chapter Eighteen

HAWK

For having her plans turned upside down in the matter of thirty minutes, loading into a helicopter from a snowy field, then scuttling into a private jet while I made far too many phone calls, Cora appeared shockingly nonplussed.

In fact, she bounced up and down with an electric giggle every few seconds.

Rapid-fire updates streamed from Nicola and other board members as I gripped Cora's hand and led her from chopper to plane, phone against my ear. Wind snaked through my hair, attempting to uproot my cap. The snow blitzed around, jostling us as we hurried up the metal stairs and into the warm interior.

"I'll call back when airborne," I said to Nicola. "Give me twenty."

A familiar white jet awaited, complete with two sections. A back room with individual chairs and wide desks for workstations. The forward area, with a meeting table and ten chairs that surrounded it. Lamps, pillows, and blankets gave it a cozy feel for cross-country travel, though nothing could erase *corporate* from the manicured, pristine layout.

"Choose any seat." I nudged her ahead of me. "I'll sit next to you. Terrance will bring some food by, if you're hungry. He's flying with us today."

Though I listened for strain in her voice when she replied, I found none.

"Thanks! This is gorgeous."

She lowered her backpack to a seat in the middle, but remained standing. Terrance, the attendant, smiled as he appeared with drinks, introduced himself to Cora, and glided to the fridge.

She requested a green tea, asked Terrance about facets of his life I'd never contemplated, then continued her calm perusal when the captain called for departure. I waylaid two calls, turned my phone to airplane mode, and shoved it in my pocket.

While the plane taxied to the runway, I tugged her into a chair near mine. We clipped into the seatbelts. I wrapped my fingers around hers.

"Just for takeoff. Once we cruise, we can walk around."

She nodded, gaze riveted on the window.

"You good, Cora?"

A glazed look filled her eyes when she swung back around to face me. Her body molded into the seat as she nodded.

"I'm good."

"Because—"

Her hand slid over mine. "I'm good, Hawk. I'm just new at being swept away."

"That speaks poorly to the men in your life."

She giggled. "Literally."

I threaded my fingers through hers.

"Really?"

Cora smiled. Her fingers lifted, touched my cheek. "You and me," she murmured. "We get through it all together. It's what Cade has always said."

My stomach flopped around, and it had nothing to do with the end of the runway as the plane flung itself into the sky. Cora leaned forward, pressed a slow, soft kiss to my lips, and pulled back.

Moments later, we were airborne. By the time we hit 10,000 feet, Cora was curled up around a notepad and pencil. I grabbed my phone and connected to Wi-Fi. Chaos downloaded.

I closed my eyes, took a deep breath, and turned to Cora. "I need to be busy for most of this flight back, and for the next twenty-four hours. It's . . . all about positioning the company and Nicola and our cardiac centers for success. Once the day is over, I'll be able to disengage a bit more."

"Okay."

Her bright response, so unfrazzled, gave me a moment of pause.

"I'll try to communicate as much as I can, but it may not be much right after we arrive. Diego and Tim will take care of you at my penthouse."

"Yep. I'll be fine."

"I know." My hand cupped her jaw. "That's what's so startling about all of this. You don't need me."

"I don't." Her eyes twinkled. "But I think I want you."

Her easily stated words were the closest admission of what lay between us that we'd shared yet. They scrubbed the bubbling uncertainty deep inside away. The question of *what am I doing?* ebbed like a waning tide.

Fears quieted. When Cora sat at my side, doubt ceased. We gripped something special—like lightning—between us.

I pulled her close, crashed our lips together. She tilted her head, deepening the kiss. The moment her tongue touched mine, fever ripped through me. I held her close. Felt her fingertips dig into the back of my neck, her breath hitch.

Ragged, I pulled away.

She closed her eyes, pressed her forehead to mine.

"As soon as we land, Diego will drop me off at the corporate building, then take you to my penthouse. You can stay there. It'll be safer, just in case you're seen, than a hotel. There could be questions."

"Seen? Questions?"

"Media." A grimace crossed my face. "I'm sorry. Tate. And the media. They're a reality I live with from time to time."

"Tate is your father?"

"Unfortunately."

"Obviously, you aren't close."

"No. We never will be. He . . . likes to make beautiful things fall apart. That's all we need to say about him. You wanted to see my life, right?"

"All of it."

"Then you will get a full glimpse of the media, hopefully not Tate, with the gala coming up. I'd rather you be safe before then, just in case."

"I understand. Thank you."

"Sometimes they stake me out, just because I'm an eligible bachelor that has a lot of money and an unfortunately famous father. With the rising headlines around the South American virus, we may get lucky and no one will pay attention to us. I doubt we'll see reporters today. We're more likely to draw attention during the gala."

"I haven't seen headlines on the virus you told me about. I've been scrolling through the news out of curiosity. No one on my social media outlets has said anything."

"Oh," I breathed, bracing myself, "the headlines are coming. Just you wait."

* * *

Nicola waited in the elevator.

Millions of pounds of steel, dry wall, marble, and untold numbers of supplies built the behemoth structure at my feet. Tonight, all of it felt fragile as dust. A saccharine world constructed by sheer tenacity about to hit an earthquake.

"Nicola."

Her dry response, utterly void of stress, soothed me. "Hawk."

"Have a good day?"

"Oh, I love being glued to my phone in a chaotic environment."

Not a hint of sarcasm existed in her tone.

"I know you do."

"The chaos is my life's elixir. Speaking of."

As we passed James' empty desk, Nicola reached over, scooped up a lidded, to-go coffee cup, and handed it my way.

"I had that delivered all the way to this floor five minutes ago, and it cost me fifty dollars, and that better be the best cup of coffee you've ever had, Hawk."

"Liar. You bought this at Starbucks on the way in and popped it into the microwave when the driver notified you we'd arrived."

She grunted.

"Fine. You win."

I laughed.

"James was out sick today," she said.

"Tell me it's not a South American virus."

This time, she laughed. "It's too early for that to be funny. Now drink your coffee and focus. We have a lot to get through and ten minutes to do it. Also, is that all you have to wear? Jeans and a baseball hat? The *entire* board is gathering to discuss the next steps."

"Yes."

Delight riddled her tone. "Excellent."

We pressed through the double doors that led into my

office while Nicola calmly sped through a list of developments since I'd arrived at the airport.

"Caravan Healthcare out of the Baltimore area contacted us requesting any pre-programmed protocols we might have regarding surges in people calling to ask questions. They want servers or something?" Her brow ruffled. "Is that a thing?"

"Set them up with IT. Contact their sales rep to hold their hand through the process."

"You insult me, you know that?" She scoffed, flipped through a stack of folders in her arms. "Of course I've been in touch with Shanessa and she's already been the intermediary. Caravan Healthcare thinks Shanessa has been speaking directly with you, and Shanessa thinks she's been working with you, but really, it's me. I'd like to maintain that for now, if possible."

"Excellent," I hissed through my teeth. "Caravan has been waffling on the customer service support lines through their hospital systems. That potential deal was about to go stale."

"Speaking of deals. The deal," Nicola dropped a heavy folder on my desk, "with St. Mary's in the Northwest has been closed. It lacks only your signature at the bottom. They desire to get ready and start the user interface training immediately. Our teams are ready."

A scribble, a flip of the folder, and she cleared the desk for the next case. Ten minutes passed with her quick updates, my scrawls, and more closures than expected. Implications sprouted through my mind that I stacked into neat lists to tackle later, when I had a chance to silence the chaos of my mind and think through this situation rationally.

With a casual toss of her wrist, the final folder landed in front of me. Her arrogant hip cock alone told me what this would say.

"It is?"

"The unfolding of brilliance. Also, the stages of the plan

that will complete repurposing of three of our ten warehouses to sterile instrument facilities—gloves, surgery equipment, pacemakers. Separated in there is the plan that dedicates four warehouses to cardiac equipment support. I decided what went where based on my interviews yesterday."

Elegantly woven plans lay out in a simple array on the page. I skimmed through the schematics of each warehouse, anticipated output of product, and timelines. How she finalized this so fast, I'd never understand.

My eyes stopped at the bottom of the page, then lifted to hers.

"You're insane."

Her grin widened.

"Nicola, there's no way we will meet this deadline. Repurposing an entire warehouse facility for sterile product creation in *three weeks*?"

"Some of the machinery is already in place. It lacks audits, checks, and final finishing touches."

"With what staff?"

"Existing." Her eyebrows crashed together. "They had an HR nightmare that our teams have been on site dealing with. The workers are already available that can help us repurpose, certify, and pass inspection. We're incentivizing with bonuses."

I shut the envelope.

"You'll hit that in six, not three, weeks, and only because we stand near the potential of a pandemic. Redistribute resources differently. I'll put the idea in front of the board, but not on that timeline."

Her jaw hardened.

"Forgive me, but you're not COO. The call is mine. I manage operations, and I'm making it happen, Hawk. And it will show the entire board that I am the next best CEO because of my natural flair, decisive nature, and ability to predict market outcomes."

I stood. "You're being a fool, Nicola. Allow me to step in as your CEO, not your brother, and advise you against this course of action. You're setting yourself an unrealistic deadline that's doomed to fail. Do you really want that to be your first act in front of the board?"

"It won't be."

A rush of brotherly annoyance, yet pride, followed. I couldn't decide whether I wanted to lock her in a closet until all this passed, or congratulate her on standing up to me. Nicola lacked fear over impossible circumstances.

As insufferable as she could be, I couldn't deny her natural prowess. She'd predicted an additional income stream that I hadn't seen, and a way to positively affect a country in need, well before any other company. Like a good CEO, she read signs of the marketplace and pivoted accordingly.

She just took too many risks, too fast, for an empire.

"We're a cruise ship, Nic. Not a speed racer."

She smirked.

"Don't give me that bullcrap Hawk. Tug boats yank those massive giants out of tight spots. I'm doing it. You won't stop me."

"Fine. Proceed with your three week deadline. Tell the board tonight. I'll give you time to present at the end. Just know the perilous path you take."

"I'm aware."

I hesitated, warring between my place as her older brother and her boss. As always, I took the family route.

"Nic—"

She held up a staying hand, though her tone softened. "Just once, Hawk. Trust me. I'm going to follow my gut on this, no matter what you say."

With great hesitation, I nodded. "Then let's get this over

with. I have a beautiful girl at my penthouse waiting to see me, and this is not where I want to be."

Nicola grinned.

"I can't wait to hear more about that."

"Later. For now, let's talk about a potential pandemic."

Thoughts of Cora dissipated away.

She'd be just fine on her own.

Chapter Nineteen

CORA

A childlike curiosity propelled me into Hawk's world.

Big cities weren't new to me. After I graduated high school, Cade threw as much of his hard earned money into a bank account as he could afford, and patted me on the back. I scuttled into adulthood with two hundred dollars and a bevy of government funds and scholarships paving the way for my artistic career.

"Go to school," Cade said whenever I tried to argue. He'd shake his head in a firm back and forth. "I've always got the animals."

Internships, opportunities, and friends sent me all over the US, from coast to coast, in various capacities. I might have submerged myself into a mountain tapestry for my biggest commission ever, but the world of art galleries and city life had once been mine.

Eventually, my ranch girl heart had wandered back home to Cade. To the smell of mountains and manure.

For repayment.

The funds that Cade had kept me steadily supplied with— while he lived above a garage on a ranch and tamed horses and milked cows and herded bulls—would soon be back in his pocket to give him freedom.

He'd hate me for it.

With the smell of sewage and street tacos in the air, I inhaled deeply. Let memories of friends and art exhibits and obnoxious professors filter through me before I leaned back in the seat.

Flickering street lights, whistles, shouts, the thump of a bar down the road, and the telltale honks of traffic wove a comforting tapestry as Hawk's driver, Diego, sped away from a corporate building.

Dropping Hawk off created a steeper adventure, one more fraught with uncertainty.

Also exhilaration.

"We'll arrive soon, Miss," Diego called.

"Thank you."

A nod followed. Next to me, a round container of ice offered water bottles, a small bottle of champagne. Upside-down glasses hung from a spot off to the left. Were those gold-foil hearts? Oh, wrapped chocolate.

I snuck four.

A bemused chuckle rolled through me as I ran a hand down the leather chair. What was this life? No wonder Hawk observed me for signs of . . . .something.

Being overwhelmed, perhaps. Terrified, too. Neither happened to me yet. Underneath all these new experiences lay a humming sort of panic, stirred by thoughts of viruses and health systems.

Pandemic.

Hospital needs.

Such terrible words, set against the backdrop of a vibrant city, made no sense.

What did a *pandemic* mean, anyway? While the smells and

textures of city-life pressed on each other, I could more easily shuck the fears away. Diego pulled up to a building, then stepped out. I gathered my backpack more tightly as the door opened.

"Miss Cora." He grinned in a toothy way. "Sleep well."

"Thank you."

"Your bags will follow you up shortly."

This part of uptown had an entirely different vibe. Soaring towers of metal and glass. Glimmering surfaces. Women in pencil skirts and heels. Men in ties. As graciously as possible, I headed toward the main doors, where a doorman smiled brightly.

"Miss Cora?"

"That's me. You are?"

He bowed at the waist. "Tim. Mr. Hawk has asked us to take extra special care of you while you're here. Only the best treatment for his guests."

He winked.

I laughed, charmed. "Oh, well, thank you. If you could show me to his room, that would be—"

"We're already on it."

Like a synchronized dance, Hawk's bag and mine appeared at his side. Tim, and an unparalleled sense of wonder, led me from one place to another. Through a sparkling interior, complete with reception desk, bellhops, people milling near a fireplace with crackling flames, and flutes of champagne. Mirrors magnified the burgundy-and-gold tones that overlaid everything, making the foyer feel as large as a football field.

Tim led me to an elevator that didn't even whisper as we raced to the top. Finally, a night skyline sprawled at my feet as we stepped through a doorway and into a penthouse apartment, accessed by a special key.

With a wave, Tim disappeared behind the gentle creak of

the elevator door sliding closed. An elegant world waited inside.

I stood in the middle of it, mouth half open.

Hawk lived in a penthouse apartment at the top of the world. City lights speckled below a soaring two-floor ceiling cut in wide windows. A few faint stars peeped through the light pollution.

An interior designer had clearly put this room together. Pillows, blankets, a plush rug over expertly stained hardwood floors. They fit like pieces of a puzzle perfectly aligned. The ideal environment to entertain guests.

Empty of life, though.

My fingertips trailed along the back of a couch as I set my bag down, wandering to the side wall where a bookshelf waited. Leather hardcovers littered the shelves in organized synchronicity. Five here. Seven there, set around small oriental pots for an uptown feel. On the bottom shelf, worn paperback books clustered together.

I perused them with deepening interest.

You're In Your Own Way.

Money In, Money Out.

The End Game.

Self help. Naturally. I edged away to wander into a pristine kitchen, swept with open windows and glittering chrome.

Outside, a balcony with well-maintained greenery awaited, providing a screen to prevent others from peering inside. Trellises crawled with vines. A wooden picnic table held fat pillows along the benches, orchestrated by matching color. Empty flower boxes lay open to the sky.

Finally, a bedroom.

I knew it was Hawk's by the smell the moment I passed by. Aftershave. Spice. Subtle and tantalizing. A glimpse of a perfectly made bed appeared from the hallway. A rack of baseball hats. Mirrors that tossed around light and made every-thing bigger.

I pressed on.

Two spare bedrooms boasted different themes. Black-and-white for one, accented by lilac purples that faded to aubergine. Earth tones for another. I chose the latter. The smallest, but the closest to Hawk.

Privacy abounded in this room. Skylights gave way to dark stars, but not so many windows cluttered the walls. Less open and encompassing. Safer, with firmer structures in place. I sank to the edge of the bed.

Ten minutes in his penthouse, and already so much of Hawk made sense. I laughed, shaking my head.

What more would he reveal?

Well, with this beautiful-but-bony home, nothing. It held no beating heart in the hollow spaces.

Back in the kitchen, I leaned against an opaque marble bar, my backpack set on the swivel chair to my right. The half-open zipper spilled a pencil and the edge of a paper. I zipped it open the rest of the way, eager to get my hands on some charcoal.

In moments, I leaned over the notebook. My fingers worked steadily as I recalled the city, the foyer, the glimmer outside. In the car, Hawk's gaze turned away, out the window, while we hustled through the city. I tried to capture the feeling of tons of metal pressed overhead, the bated breath of Hawk.

After an hour of sketching and ten pages later, I closed the book, wandered back to the main area of the penthouse. Low lighting guided me to windows, where the view soared.

I grabbed a pillow, a blanket, and snuggled into a sprawling couch. The lights of the city became a blur.

With all of humanity below, I fell into a deep sleep.

Chapter Twenty

HAWK

Concerns plagued me, ticker-tape style, while I worked.

CORA IS ALONE IN YOUR PENTHOUSE.
NICOLA'S PLAN WILL FAIL.
YOU'LL NEVER LEAVE M. VENTURES.

Which only made the unexpected news Nicola delivered seem fuzzy. Unbelievable.

I stared at her.

"You're kidding."

With a burdened sigh that would have impressed the greatest of martyrs, she dropped her head back on her neck.

"*Not* kidding. Adelaide asked if you could have dinner with her and Trent tonight."

"She's CEO of the largest string of hospitals on the West Coast."

"Uh huh."

"I haven't seen them in years."

"Yep."

The pop of her *p* would have been irritating with any other news. Nicola glanced at her tablet, then back to me.

"Her husband just retired," I continued, speaking more to myself. "Trent had one of the greatest exits from his C-suite office that I've ever heard of."

Nicola nodded, a stifled yawn making her lips thin.

The thrill of excitement at seeing them—in addition to the potential for landing a massive new prospect—rippled through me. Normally, this level of acquisition funneled to different members of my team, but like the hospital outside of Pineville that I had visited, Adelaide and her husband were a special case.

Trent had exited from a multi-billion dollar cargo company three years ago, sculpting out not only the smoothest transition I'd ever seen, but an ideal life on the other side. Not only could meeting with Adelaide cement M. Ventures success this upcoming quarter across the company, but also my own life.

On a far different trajectory.

"I already told her you would be open to it," Nicola said, "but she's waiting for confirmation."

"Send it."

Nicola's brow lifted. "Will you be bringing a date?"

Her singsong tone meant she already knew what I would say. I opened my phone and started a text message for Cora.

"You know I will."

Hawk: You busy?

Nicola turned to go. I shoved the phone back into my pocket as I called out to her.

"Wait, Nic."

She glared at me through lowered eyebrows. She'd been patient with me all day, letting me boss her around like an assistant, with orders ranging from the trivial to utmost importance, but clearly the line of tolerance thinned.

"We're almost there," I said.

"I know, Hawk. I get it. But I need you to stop telling me like I don't know and sign the papers already."

I set aside a bolt of brotherly annoyance and grabbed my pen. My signature scrawled across the bottom of four different pages.

"Fine." I tossed the pen aside. "Authorizations are done. We'll discuss the recruitment process for the new CTO in the morning. Plan on hiring from within."

"Duh."

"We need to get them into place before . . ."

I trailed away. The words *before I get out of here* flopped from my lips. There was no actual plan for that. Promises. Wisps. Nothing but vague ideas and hopes I hadn't bothered to manifest. Now that a certain large-eyed painter sat at my penthouse . . .

"Anything else?" Nicola asked.

My gaze darted to the clock. 3:15 pm. I'd been at the office for twenty-four hours. An all-nighter was nothing new— except I hadn't really needed one for the past couple of years.

They weren't all I cracked them up to be.

Now, a social dinner awaited, except this one offered a remote hope of future liberation.

Then Cora time.

A metaphorical breath slid out of me. Damn, but I had asked too much of her. Brought her here, ditched her at my penthouse.

Had she been alone all day?

Going up the wall?

Nicola set her hands on her hips.

"Do it, Hawk. You must go to dinner with Adelaide. You can firm up the potential contract we've been discussing with her, and you can talk to Trent about getting out of here already."

The eye roll I wanted to release paused, but only because Nicola had been unobtrusively patient with me. Together, we'd created a plan to prepare the company, the sales force, and the rest of the management team about the plan to prepare our hospitals with necessary resources. The forward-facing leadership it gave her would benefit M. Ventures in the long run.

Still.

It came at Cora's expense.

I didn't like that.

Nicola tossed a hand in the air. "I know you don't want this potential pandemic to be real. I know you think you'd leave the company at a bad time if you moved your exit to the end of Q2, but it's just . . . not true. I've got this. Your team has got this. It's time to let it go."

A sour taste filled my mouth. The flavor of unfiltered honesty.

"I know."

She deflated. "So what? Why are you hesitating? You should make a list of questions to ask Trent, not stare at the desk like I just took your candy. What is it? You don't want to leave the company?"

"I do, but it's a lot to ask."

"It's Tate, isn't it?"

The need to guard myself around that name resurrected with sudden pain. Yep. Tate. Our father. The man we didn't even bother to call by an affectionate name but had to answer to for . . . just about everything.

Even my own company.

She softened. "I'm sorry if I'm frustrated, I'm just . . . tired. We've set the team up for success through the storm that's coming and at least that's firmly established now. The final big contracts that you're closing will ensure a successful quarter, and potential growth through the storm."

"If it's a true pandemic, there's no knowing what's coming, Nic."

"I know. Now, we have to just lean into the plan and you have to trust me." She nailed me with a punch on the shoulder. "The first step of that is for you to go to dinner, reassure Adelaide until she signs that bloody contract, and ask Trent everything you can think about for exiting. In the meantime, try to involve Cora? I'd love for you to have someone to go home to, for once."

I reached out, squeezed her shoulder.

"Thanks. Pep up session received. I'll get out of your hair now while you do the job of running this company."

"Call me after dinner? At least text me and let me know that you've cemented the contract."

"I will."

After Nic left, I spun around. A slow glance of the office didn't give me the expected pang of sadness. Leaving M. Ventures while at the pinnacle of my career was the right thing, but I had nothing to leave *for*.

Until now.

Cora gave me a taste of what the other side of corporate life might look like. The future came down to two distinct possibilities. Life with a woman like Cora.

Or . . . my empty penthouse.

No *wonder* I hadn't moved forward.

The insecurities and doubts that swelled up every time I contemplated my exit strategy, particularly now of all moments, had a paralyzing touch. Not so when Cora entered my mental picture.

My phone rattled in my pocket.

Cora: Yes, I am busy tonight, but no. I am not.

Hawk: What does that mean?

A picture accompanied her response. At least ten canvases cluttered my penthouse table. Three new sketch books and so many tubes of oil paint she'd need fresh luggage just to take them back.

Hawk: Oh, you met the resident art fairy.

Cora: I drew her a picture and won her favor.

Hawk: I'll bet it was beautiful, but not as beautiful as you.

I burst out laughing when a picture of her replied, with one cocked eyebrow in a decidedly half-annoyed, half-flabbergasted expression.

Cora: Do you pick up girls like that all the time? No wonder this penthouse is empty as old bones.

My hilarity faded. Did she feel it there too? It could be a hundred degrees in the summer and that place still felt like the cold brush of death held it in its palms.

Hawk: I have an offer for you if you want to get out of there.

Cora: Establish the terms, sir.

Hawk: One intimate dinner with another couple—whom I highly admire—at The Rosewood Mansion. It's a Michelin restaurant. Good place.

Cora: How long do I have to get ready?

My sleeve peeled away from my wrist as I checked my watch.

Hawk: An hour.

Another image popped up. Her hands, coated in charcoal-colored paint. A slash across her wrist, another on the tip of her nose, only drew my curiosity out further.

I hooted, slipping closer to my desk.

Hawk: What have YOU been working on?

Cora: Me to know, you to find out.

Hawk: Cruel.

Cora: The anticipation is worth it. I'll be ready in twenty minutes.

Hawk: Really? Twenty minutes?

Cora: Hawk, you puppy. Most women don't take six hours to get ready for a meal, even one at the most expensive restaurant in the city. I came prepared.

Hawk: Efficient turnaround times? Super hot.

Cora: I'm just getting started.

My mouth watered at the thought.

Hawk: I have a few things to complete. Mind if we meet there? It'll reduce the chance of cameras finding

us unexpectedly. I'll make sure you're brought in a
back door, if you want.

A few seconds passed.

Cora: Front door is fine. Is all that really necessary?

Hawk: To keep you safe? I'll do anything.

Determination filled me. With me, she'd always be safe.
Now that I messaged with her, I hungered to see her again.

The idea of taking her out to two people that I deeply
admired and needed shared wisdom from felt intimate. For the
first time in my adult life, I wanted Adelaide and Trent to meet
someone I dated.

Cora: Then I guess I'll see you in an hour! Again, the
front door is fine.

The anxiety in my stomach melted away. I closed my eyes,
exhaled the storm that built up over the last day, and sent the
final text.

Hawk: It's not soon enough.

With a hand dragged through my hair, I spun to my desk
to pull together a list of talking points with Adelaide and
Trent. The ball of anticipation at seeing Cora again smoothed
away.

This life?

Wasn't so bad.

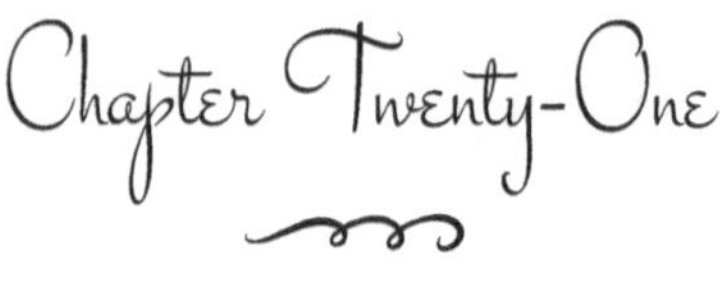

Chapter Twenty-One

CORA

Downtown, big city Texas moved slowly as Diego inched us through traffic.

I ran my thumb over the side of my phone, checked my dress for the tenth time. The long-sleeved piece fell down my torso, stretched across my hips and over my legs in perfectly straight lines. The muted turquoise fabric was the same throughout, but a bangled necklace splashed white and evergreen at the top.

The ensemble wasn't necessarily high-class, but it looked a lot more ritzy than the coveralls, tank top, and painted arms I'd ditched to come here. A last-minute grab as we left Pineville nudged me to retrieve it from my closet. A flake of oil paint still lingered on my pinky finger. I rubbed it away.

"Oh!" Diego let out a giddy screech. "I found one!"

A gleeful laugh followed. He waggled a finger out the front window. I groaned in a dramatic attempt at acting deflated. A little girl in a bike helmet crossed the street behind her father, who towed a cart.

"Who lets their children ride bikes at nine o'clock at night in downtown Texas?" I cried.

He shook his head, still chuckling.

"You underestimate Texans, miss. Weird things happen down here. Much, much weirder than that. I won that round!"

"You won, fair and square. Now, it's your turn."

"Okay." He readjusted, hand lifted. His fingers twiddled back and forth as he deepened in thought. All at once, his expression illuminated. "Ah ha! I have a good one. Find a taco stand."

"Those are on every other corner!"

"No, no, my friend!" he cried, twirling his hand in the air more dramatically. The light turned green. He carefully eased onto the gas, carrying us into the intersection like a sailboat on glassy water. "This taco stand must have the words Juan, Yucatan, and million."

"That's awfully specific."

He giggled.

My eyes darted around as we sped past busy sidewalks. No taco stands with those words emerged from this high-class district of the city, though packed sidewalks clustered at each interchange of grid-like streets.

Pictures of Texas longhorns, flautas, and Bible verses littered most bus stop benches.

"How long have you lived here, Diego?" I asked.

"Twenty years."

"So you know that there's probably no taco stand with *Juan, Yucatan,* and *million* in the same sentence? If that's the case—fair. You definitely deserve to win, sneaky driver."

A dopey smile pasted his face. He hummed a mariachi song under his breath, fingers drumming to the beat. I searched harder to distract myself from the knot of nerves in my stomach.

One could have mistaken it for anticipation.

Felt more like fear.

Hawk and I hadn't seen each other in a full day. He had locked himself up in his corporate tower, utterly silent. The urge to text *Rapunzel, Rapunzel, let down your hair,* had been difficult to overcome.

I had spent the time well by purchasing a rush of new art supplies that would set me up for months. I'd visited art galleries, sketched an old couple in the park, then gave them the drawing. For lunch, I had tea with an art store owner that had stories for days.

Yet, here I stood, at the base of his metaphorical Rapunzel tower, waiting to see the man himself.

Because this world . . .

"Oh!" I shrieked. "There, there!"

Bright red and green lights flashed as we flew past a taco stand with a sign that said *Juan's Million-Dollar Yucatan Taco Stand.*

"You knew!" I said, laughing.

"The lady always wins!" he cried, finger in the air. "The lady always wins."

"Maybe I should bring you as my date tonight."

He clucked under his breath as he spun the wheel with a palm, slowing as we turned out of busy traffic. A half circle admitted us to the door of an upscale restaurant with subdued lighting, pristine servers, and a low soundtrack in the background.

A fluttering feeling stole my stomach when I realized Hawk waited inside.

"No, no Miss," Diego sang. "Hawk, he's a good one. Much better for you. I'm too old."

"Thanks Diego."

"You have a good night. I'll be here when you finish."

For some reason, that comforted me.

He shook that long, skinny finger. "And then I will win!"

Laughing, I stepped out of the car. I'd brought a smashing

dress . . . but not great shoes. The cream-colored flats weren't glaringly off, though an outfit like this really needed strappy heels.

With a breath for courage, I headed inside.

A woman at the door met me with a warm smile as I approached. Words fled from my brain, and I realized too late that I didn't know whether I should ask for Hawk—and draw attention to the fact that I would be here with him—or give her my name.

What were the rules?

Would paparazzi jump out of the walls? The windows? Flashing lights, angry bellows, like in the movies?

Uncertainty froze me into place. I stared at her like I didn't know what she was doing there. Before I could muster a word, a strong hand slipped around my waist.

"She's with me," Hawk said.

The woman smiled.

"Very good, Mr. Mercedy. This way, please."

The sound of his name, *Mr. Mercedy,* weakened my knees. Relief followed. I almost sank into it—he would have held me up—but I didn't dare. If I gave him my weight, I knew he'd take it, then I'd never gain my own two feet again.

"You," he murmured with a friendly kiss to my cheek, "are exquisite."

The caress of his breath on my skin was a wordless reassurance. I closed my eyes, momentarily suspended in Hawk, before he tightened his hold and swept me away.

My breath struggled to recover as we followed behind the woman. A passing glimpse of him appeared in a mirror. Elegant suit, perfectly crisp. White shirt, gray tie. A ridge between his brow showed deep thought, even fatigue. The smell of aftershave wafted off of him.

When had he changed?

Moments later, we entered a far corner, strategically

stacked away from the rest of the open floor. The section screened off by elegant partitions with flowing, rippled fabric in water-like patterns, lay in a much deeper quiet.

The hostess motioned us to our chairs. "Your server will be right with you. I'll escort the Shaws here as soon as they arrive."

I stepped forward, but Hawk's tight hold on my wrist stopped me. My breath caught. I glanced up, heart in my throat. Hawk pulled me closer until I felt the rise and fall of his chest against mine.

"Not so fast, Cora."

"What?"

"Let me look at you."

A smile found me. "After living a full day in your world instead of my own, you don't seem real." I reached up to brush a wayward fluff off his slightly stubbled chin. He wound his fingers through mine. My bones turned to water under his hungry stare.

"I feel the same way." The edge of his thumb touched my bottom lip. "I'm sorry I was gone all day. Literally all day."

"I missed you, but I understand."

"I missed you, too. I'd prefer we eat alone, in our pajamas, on my couch with takeout, but this is the second best option."

"These people mean that much to you?"

He nodded. In a flash, he looked for all the world like a lost little boy. I couldn't imagine what put that expression on his face, but I'd do anything to get rid of it.

"Then this is where I want to be."

A kiss caught me by surprise, starting at the corner of my lips. My eyes fluttered closed. I leaned into him, opened my mouth to deepen it. Hawk made a noise in his throat, hand on my chin, when a voice called out behind us.

"Well, we should have stalled a few more minutes, Trent."

Hawk jerked away.

I gasped.

A deep, rolling laugh from Hawk's chest should have reassured me, but it only sent heat through my cheeks. He released me from his tight grip, but didn't let me go far. I lifted my chin, braced myself for the deepest embarrassment of my life, and turned to face his friends.

Instead, I encountered the warmth of a middle-aged woman with crow's feet and a sparkling set of teeth. Her sharp features belied a genuine smile. Hawk embraced her, laughing with a man that walked just behind.

"Hello, Hawk," she said. "It's been far too long."

While they embraced, I stole the chance to catch my breath again, still tangled in Hawk's spinning web. She released him. Her friendly, but assessing, gaze fell to me.

"You must be Cora."

"Yes, it's good to meet you . . ."

Panic bolted through me. Oh, no! Hawk hadn't told me their names. I stumbled to remember the last name the hostess had mentioned, but Hawk's kiss scattered my thoughts.

"Adelaide," she said with a laugh. "And don't worry about it. I'm not surprised Hawk didn't mention who you'd be eating with. He's brilliant, but details aren't his forte in social situations."

"No, he did. Sort of. We just—"

Adelaide lifted a hand. "When a guy like Hawk is around, there are other things to think about." She winked. "Trent and I aren't as frightening as some might assume."

As if commanded, a man with dark features and close-cropped hair stepped behind her. He extended a hand toward me, smiling warmly.

"Cora, it's good to meet you."

"You, as well."

Hawk returned to my side, as if drawn by string. He put a hand on my shoulder. Joy still danced in his gaze, lingering from a laugh at something Trent had said. His unrestrained joy thrilled my whole body.

Happy Hawk?

I loved them already.

"Let's have a seat," Hawk said.

He took my arm, led me to the other side of the sparkling table. One edge butted up against the window, peering out on the street. Cars and people whizzed by. The thick windows muted most noise, leaving the room buzzing with a quiet incoherence.

"So," Adelaide drawled as Trent tucked her seat in. "You two are recent lovers?"

The word *lovers* startled me out of the hazy kiss with a firm jerk. Hawk reached down, hand on my knee. Not an ounce of hesitation appeared when he said, "Yes, mostly recent. We met a month ago."

And didn't speak for that month, I silently added, but held the words in because they didn't matter.

Time meant little when this felt so right.

Adelaide's eyes bounced between us as she snapped her cloth napkin open with a shake.

"How very sweet."

Trent reached over, draped an arm over the back of her chair. His hand rested idly on the space between her shoulder blades. They had a lazy, sweet energy with stolen winks, quick smiles, and constant touch. Hawk's hand weighed on my knee with a steady, reassuring reminder.

"A month," Trent drawled, right across from me. His gaze found Adelaide. "That's how long it took me to propose to you."

She laughed. "Three weeks. That's it."

"Stupid sucker, should have gone for it sooner."

Trent winked when I laughed, eyes dancing as Adelaide pressed a quick kiss to his cheek, then accepted a wine menu from a server. By the time we had placed wine and appetizer orders, Adelaide folded her hands in front of her.

She peered at Hawk.

"So, Hawk, talk to me. We have a potential pandemic on the way and I run a lot of hospitals. I believe we could help each other out."

Hawk grinned. "Adelaide, if I'd known it would take a pandemic for you to come over to the efficient side of patient documentation, billing, and customer support, I would have taken a totally different tack in my approach."

The way he held his body changed ever-so-slightly. His smile became a bit more rote, his words more fixated. He held his shoulders tighter through the back, as if bracing for something. He kept an easy arm at his side, but the other one had found my fingers and laced us together. The pressure of his fingertips pressed into my finger bones.

Steady, not painful.

While Hawk and Adelaide tossed around questions like *customer service portals* and *billing cycles* and *strategic placement over transactional leadership*, Trent reached for his water and met my gaze.

"Insufferable, isn't it?"

I grinned. "Fascinating when you consider it."

He half shrugged, folded his arms, and placed them on the table. The carefree way he sat made me want to laugh. What had I been frightened about? Powerful people they might be, but they didn't differ from my dorkier friends.

The thought eased my concerns.

"They won't do this for long," he said with a touch of reassurance that made it clear this had happened before.

"You already know?"

"Adelaide wanted Hawk here to discuss a few things, yes. They've been dangling a potential contract for over a year. With what's coming up, it's the best time to clench it down."

The casual way he mentioned *what's coming up* made my stomach churn. The reduction of so much unknown potential descending on the world startled me.

"Hawk was very excited to meet with both of you."

"Hawk worked with Adelaide before she left Mercedy, Inc. She trained him on the sales team when he was eighteen."

"Eighteen?"

"You didn't know?"

I shook my head, struck by the realization of how *little* I knew. What was Mercedy, Inc?

"No."

Trent studied me for a moment, then moved on, as if he wasn't all that surprised. "After he graduated high school, Hawk flipped the bird to college, started right into his father's company at eighteen."

"That's Mercedy, Inc? Not M. Ventures."

"Correct. Hawk told Adelaide during his interview that he wanted to sell, not go to college. She became his supervisor."

Shock forced me to reconsider all the articles I'd read about him after he left The Frolicking Moose—when I felt hungry for the slightest brush of his life in mine—none of them had mentioned earlier years of his life. He wasn't much older than my twenty-nine years at thirty-six.

"No college," I murmured. "Very interesting."

"Eventually, he went." He rubbed his lips together, tangled in a different thought, then shook himself out of it. "But he did it at night and worked during the day. It was more obligation than desire, from the way he tells it. Finished an MBA before it should have been possible. He's intelligent to a fault."

"I've noticed."

"The boy sold like a natural. Worked through the ranks until Tate couldn't justify not promoting him."

"Tate, as in his father?"

Trent's voice pitched higher. "Yes. Hasn't he told you about him?"

"Very little."

Trent only whistled, eyes wide, as if to say *dodged a bullet there.*

The word *father* wavered strangely. Suddenly, I remembered there was a whole other angle to Hawk's life I hadn't considered much.

His family.

And all that meant.

Trent drew me back to the present as he leaned away, still speaking casually, but with a more fixed cadence, like treading carefully.

"Hawk refused the promotion Tate offered at Mercedy Inc. and formed his own company."

My mouth dropped open.

"M. Ventures is Hawk's?"

Trent's gaze tapered, suspicion thickening his tone. "What *do* you know about him?"

"Not enough, apparently."

Amusement filled Trent's eyes. My quick response, as baffled as it sounded, must have engendered some trust. He ducked closer, casting a quick glance at Hawk.

Adelaide had him trapped in deep thoughts. Hawk listened intently as she spoke, like an animal about to make a move. His fingers had slipped away from my thigh in the intervening minutes and pressed to his mouth in a fist now.

"Hawk doesn't like to talk about himself," Trent murmured. "Drives you mad, I bet."

With a sigh, I shook my head. "Not if it saved his own life."

A laugh followed. "He'll open up. Just give him some time. I know his old man. It's . . . a bitter family situation they have over there. The Mercedys might be powerful. They might have a name that carries a lot of power, but I couldn't say that any of them are joyful people."

"You seem to know Hawk well."

"Better than most. Adelaide has been a soft spot for him to land when he needed it. She's a networking wonder."

My voice lowered, but not enough to obscure my words. If Hawk turned any sort of attention our way, he'd instantly know we spoke about him. I didn't want to hide the topic—that wouldn't be fair—but I didn't want to lose the thread, either.

"I only know about his sister, Nicola."

"Nicola," Trent drawled, perfectly at ease where I felt stressed. "Now there's a young Adelaide. She's in line to take over M. Ventures when Hawk exits. Has he told you that?"

"No."

"Not surprising. I haven't heard details of his plans for it, anyway, just that he wants to. Much to Tate's chagrin, of course, he'll probably put Nicola in as CEO."

"Tate doesn't want her in that position?"

"He had different ideas for her at Mercedy, Inc. Lower ideas, nothing as illustrious as CEO. Still, in Tate's eyes, she's not as big of a disappointment as Noah."

He flicked the name out like a discarded poker card.

"Noah?" I cried.

Did he have a flowchart available?

"The youngest sibling. The proverbial lost sheep, so to speak. No one has heard from him in years. Not since Tate and Noah argued. Tate punched him, and Noah punched back. He put the old man in the hospital, and hasn't been seen since."

My eyes widened.

"No."

Trent grimaced, nodded.

What a willing fount of information. "Anything else I should know?" I asked drily.

Trent deepened in thought. I hadn't expected him to take me seriously. He tsked under his breath, and it only made me more nervous that he had to think so long.

"Hawk is the best of the best, no matter what his family does. Be patient with him." A wry smile stretched across his face. "He's trainable. Nicola would be an excellent ally, just don't get in her way. And do whatever you can to avoid Tate. He has a history of . . . exposing people he doesn't like."

The warning sent an ominous shiver through me. Hawk's fear of the media made a little more sense, though I doubted I'd ever truly understand this world.

"Got it."

"Not that you have to worry about it. I doubt Hawk will ever introduce you. Hell, you're the first one we've met, and he actually likes us."

The first one.

Something about the categorization gave little comfort. Neither did the lonely truth behind it. Did Hawk have *anyone* in his life not attached to the business web?

"Thanks, Trent."

"Hang in there. Hawk will figure out life. Eventually."

A dozen questions surged through me. What did Hawk have to figure out in life? Was his family a big part of it?

What had I gotten myself into?

The inquiries clammed up, lost in a fog of uncertainty. Ugly as the truths were, I couldn't help but feel grateful. I didn't realize how much I needed the Hawk details—the context—until it came.

A full day in Hawk's world had given the barest hints of insight. He kept his home abrasively clean, near sterile. Used the same toothpaste as me, stocked mostly water and protein drinks and take out leftovers in his fridge, and leaned toward tile and wood over carpet.

In five minutes, Trent had dropped more than I'd been able to glean online or gather from Hawk himself. For the areas that mattered.

"How long have you and Adelaide been married?" I asked, hopeful to turn the topic to something less concerning.

Unmistakable warmth returned to his expression. He brightened.

"Five years."

"Practically newlyweds."

"Every day."

While the server swooped in with wine glasses and trays of elegant appetizers that looked too delicious to eat—cranberry brie pockets, stuffed baguettes, and crystalline bowls of cold blueberry soup—Adelaide's steady questions lowered in energy.

Trent regaled me with hilarious stories of retired life, a pool boy that didn't know how to swim, and attempting to fix lights on a cabana and nearly electrocuting himself.

By the time the business conversation wound down between Adelaide and Hawk, dinner had arrived. Trent placed his hand on Adelaide's shoulder, gave a squeeze. She pulled in a breath, cast him a wry glance, and held up two hands.

"All right." She laughed. "That's his sign that it's time to close business. I'm all done, I swear."

Hawk tilted an eyebrow. "Let's work it out together over breakfast tomorrow, with Nicola and my managing director. Stop by the suite. James will have it all laid out on my desk. He'll forward the paperwork to your lawyers tonight so we can move to closing stages tomorrow. It'll have to speed through the approval process, but I think we can make it happen."

A note of inflection entered her voice. "We don't have a lot of time to get this started, Hawk. Are you sure your company can implement and train my people in three weeks? They're expecting the virus will arrive here by then."

"If you sign tomorrow, yes."

The confidence in his tone sent a shiver all the way down my back. Hawk's sexy side slipped out with his sureness.

Adelaide studied him, as if taking his measure, and nodded.

"Then you have a deal."

Hawk grinned slowly as he reached out, accepted her hand. A wide smile split Adelaide's face. The corporate tension drained out of Hawk all at once. He glanced at a plate full of appetizers, as if surprised to see them there.

"Well now, Cora and I know each other better than I knew Adelaide when I married her," Trent said with a laugh.

"That's your fault," Adelaide said quickly. "You were the insufferable one that wouldn't stop talking about himself."

He laughed harder, rubbed his chest in a fake wound, and reached for a fork.

"Touche, my dear."

Hawk glanced over, an apology in his expression. I smiled, squeezed the fingers that had already found mine again.

"The brie is delicious," I whispered.

A silent, but hungry, gaze responded. If the look in his eyes meant anything, these appetizers weren't what Hawk wanted most tonight.

Chapter Twenty-Two

HAWK

Cora's fingers laced through mine like a braid.

I stared at them, resting on top of my thigh, while Diego gently drove through downtown, penthouse bound. Cora's head leaned on my shoulder, eyes closed. Steady, even breaths caressed my jacket. I thought through the evening with her at my side.

The puzzle of guiding Adelaide through the next steps of our contractual process cluttered my head. Adelaide's terms —stiff, but not unyielding—would be doable on the large scale she might need. Our ability to pivot quickly sold the contract.

I processed these bullet points quickly. I had long ago established them, and completed them now by rote memory.

Cora returned to my mind.

Her delighted laugh replayed throughout the dinner. Those glowing smiles and her quick wit made it the best evening I'd had with Adelaide and Trent. Normally, dinners with the Shaw's went well.

Today, it was phenomenal.

Trent's follow up advice on high-level exit strategies filled my head with other avenues and possibilities. Options, like roads, populated in curving, complicated ways.

All of them led to Cora.

How could they not?

The feel of her soft body at my side, keeping me close, anchored me in the whirlwind. A high level of anxiety hummed above it.

Could this be real?

Diego glanced back more often than usual, a soft smile on his face. When we stopped at the building, he held up a finger.

"Tell Miss that I won."

"Won?"

He grinned gleefully, waved a hand. "She will know, she will know."

Carefully, I reached up, touched her face.

"Cora?"

Stirring, her eyes blinked awake. She stared at me, registered my face, and smiled. Unable to help myself, totally besotted by her still-sleepy eyes, I whispered, "We're back."

"Back?"

"Home."

"Home?"

She straightened, gazed around, then her eyes widened.

"Oh, right. Penthouse."

Whatever dream worlds she frolicked in, I wanted to join her. I tightened my hold.

"Let's go."

She resisted when I tugged her out. A beaming smile to Diego stalled her as I stepped onto the ground.

"Thank you, Diego."

"I win, Miss."

He pointed to something across the road. Laughing, she climbed free. Once extracted, she bobbled on her feet. I wrapped an arm around her waist, catching her.

"Thanks." She yawned, then smiled. "I guess I'm still tired."

The little girl in her eyes as she peered around made me want to hold her all the closer. With an arm at her waist, I guided her to the building, reassured by the quiet street. No sign of lurkers, cameras.

At the revolving doors, a doorman waved.

"Evening, Miss Cora!"

She brightened, beaming. "Tim, did you have a good lunch date?"

He blushed. "You were right. She liked the flowers better than the chocolates."

"It was the color scheme. Always color, and you really can't go wrong with daisies. They're the friendliest flower, without being too romantic, like a rose. You did good, Tim."

"Thanks again, Miss Cora."

She waved to someone else that called to her near the other door, then followed me inside. In the sprawling foyer, I chuckled.

"You've been here one day, right?"

A befuddled expression crossed her face. "So?"

"Do you know everyone?"

"Only a handful. Seven?"

"In a day?"

"Well, someone was *working* all that time."

I laughed, unable to help it. A woman behind the desk waved at her. She responded, happy as a shooting star, as we slipped across the open space and toward the elevator. She leaned against me while waiting. I tucked her into my side like melted butter. Her loose body weight made my breath uneven. I could stand like this forever.

The tips of my fingers ran over the soft skin along her forearm. Goosebumps rose on her skin, but she didn't shake me off.

"So, what did you think of Trent and Adelaide?" I asked.

"Loved them both. Trent, he's . . . full of surprises."

"Oh, yeah?"

"He seems very well informed."

An elevator arrived, interrupting her loaded statement. Before I could ask what she meant, the doors beeped open. We stepped inside, alone, and sped higher. Wrinkles formed on her brow when she tilted her head back to look into my eyes.

"Is it really going to be that bad, Hawk? With the virus, I mean." She swallowed. "What does it mean?"

"I'm not sure yet. We're preparing in case the worst comes."

"What's the worst?"

"That we don't figure out how it's spread, how to stop it. If there isn't enough cardiac equipment to save lives."

Her eyes widened. Alarm registered in their depths.

"Cora, you'll be safe."

"I'm not worried about me. I'm worried about you."

"Me?"

"You live in the city, Hawk. Surrounded by people. If there's going to be some sort of problem, can you think of any worse place?"

I hesitated. In fact, I hadn't thought through the personal ramifications. If it closed in, I'd deal with them then. For now, we had hospitals to stabilize and secure, which meant a lot of work with Nicola and in private meetings, like this dinner.

"Don't worry about me."

"I will."

The elevator beeped. I pressed my thumb to a biometric pad. The doors slid open. Cora followed me into the small foyer, then through the next locked door. Lights glimmered from outside as we stepped inside, like puddles of light pooling on a black velvet scene.

"Put on something comfy." I nudged her toward the spare room. "Let's chat on the couch."

Twenty minutes later, Cora stood at the window in a frumpy pair of sweats, a paint-stained t-shirt, a pair of socks filled with Bob Ross's face, and her hair in a messy bun at the top of her head. Her arms folded across her middle as she peered out. The juxtaposition of her as this untethered creative set against the immaculately dressed date almost made me laugh.

I approached from behind.

"Mesmerizing, isn't it?"

She leaned into me as I stood behind her, hands on her hips. "So many people, lights. It's . . . fascinating."

Not as fascinating as her lovely neck, but I couldn't let myself go there. After a full day apart, I wanted to hear what she thought of this world.

My world.

For now.

With a tug, I pulled her onto the couch. She molded into my arms with a quiet sigh, two pieces carved to fit together. I reached up, played with her hair, while my body relaxed from the day. I tipped my head back, closed my eyes.

All at once, twenty-four hours at the office, constant calls, and the list of initiatives and measures we drove to stabilize and prepare our staff melted away.

Cora.

She's really all I wanted.

She shifted to look up at me through dark lashes. "Trent mentioned how much he and Adelaide love you."

I chuckled. Trent, the motor mouth. Once he started, the engine didn't cut off.

"They're good people. Adelaide has long been a mentor of mine."

"Are you planning on leaving M. Ventures?"

Too late, I realized I hadn't given her much context behind the meeting tonight. She'd swum uncertain waters and strange conversations with unfettered elegance. Until this moment, I hadn't realized how much she'd smiled and laughed her way through without expecting a full explanation.

"I'm sorry, Cora. I didn't do a great job of helping you understand myself or my life, did I?"

A moment of pause confirmed. Then she said, "It's okay, Hawk. We're both figuring this out."

"I've been toying with the idea of leaving M. Ventures for a while. Transitioning Nicola to CEO, maybe starting another company, take a year off, who knows? I haven't known what would follow the exit, which has . . . stalled the decision."

Her gaze flickered around the penthouse. Did she see the same thing I did? Empty brilliance. The penthouse had a bland feel. However, I required little more than a quiet space to crash. Not a refuge.

Cora's loft stirred to mind with her messy palettes and turpentine in the mountains. *That* felt far more like home, but so did this couch when she sat with me on it. Home had little to do with location and more to do with Cora.

"Are you happy with your job?" she asked.

The question startled me. "Ah . . . I don't know that happiness ever entered the equation, to be honest."

"No?"

"No. I mean . . . it's my job."

She'd gone oddly still in my arms. I rubbed her shoulder and reached for a blanket. When I draped the soft material over her, she snuggled closer. The waves of calm that coursed through me turned my legs to jelly.

Soon, I wouldn't be able to fight the sleep. Though I longed for rest, I wanted to savor each moment with her.

"Trent told me about your brother, Noah."

My drowsy eyes shot open again. A rush of unexpected

energy ripped like a zinger through me. Cora pushed away, hand on my chest, and studied my face. My arms stiffened. It happened too unexpectedly to stop it.

"Sorry." I reached up, ran my thumb over her cheek. "Didn't mean to startle you. I didn't expect to hear Noah's name from your lips."

"I'm sorry."

"Me too."

Pain ripped through my chest. Noah, who thought he hid so well. A private detective had found him easy enough years ago and helped me keep track of him. When Noah moved, I knew.

Tate might not know or care where Noah disappeared to, but I did.

"Noah," I said slowly, "is a special guy. I haven't seen him in years, but we talk on the phone now and then. He's . . . softer inside than he acts, so he takes emotional moments hard. A veritable tough guy with an insecure edge. When he was younger, Tate used to rough him up a bit, trying to *beat the sissy feelings* out of him. One day, when he was sixteen, Noah fought back. He won. Tate went into the hospital and . . . changed after that. Noah disappeared."

"At sixteen?"

"Yes."

"How did he survive? Where did he go?"

"Well, I may have helped him disappear with some of our family on the other side of the country. Mav helped him, too."

Shock glazed over her eyes. Regret that I had to betray such horrendous realities welled up inside of me, but so did relief. If the ugly history of the Mercedy family had to shake free at some point, better to do it now.

"Did Tate hit you?" she asked.

I almost laughed at the bubbling indignation in her petite

voice. Cora would be a kitten against a tiger if pitted against a man like Tate. Still, kitties had claws.

"No, he never dared to touch me."

"Why not?"

"I would have destroyed him."

The ice in my voice should have frightened her, but she didn't go anywhere. She fell quiet for several minutes before asking, "You're not trying to hide your family from me, are you?"

"I won't hide anything from you."

"Do you ever see Noah?"

"I try. He hasn't been interested. I set things up, but he doesn't come. Every now and then, he'll answer my phone calls when I try to check in."

"Does he blame you for something?"

Pain seized my chest at the thought. "I don't know. I won't guess at his purposes, but I always keep tabs on him. When he's ready to reconnect, he knows I'm here. Tate keeps a close eye on me, as his most prosperous child. I think Noah is trying to stay off Tate's radar."

Her fingers played with the collar of my shirt, smoothing it out, tucking it higher. The touch of her hand erased my shock from the mention of Noah.

"One last question?" she whispered.

"Anything."

"Do you plan to introduce me to Tate?"

"Absolutely not."

The hard-spoken words sent a shiver through her. She started to say something, then stopped.

Time to change the subject.

"In the morning, I need to meet with Adelaide and my managing director to complete details for this contract, get the qualification and procurement process started, and then I'll leave. How about we meet somewhere for lunch?"

"Sounds perfect."

She yawned. Her eyes drifted closed.

We fell into silence while I played with her hair, enjoying the way her scalp felt on the tips of my fingers as I ran my hand through the strands. Grogginess overcame me. I pressed a kiss to the top of her head. She sighed, a sleepy little thing.

"Stay with me tonight, Cora?"

Her nod reassured me.

Without a squawk of protest, she allowed me to scoop her into my arms. In the dim light of my bedroom, her hair sprawled across my pillow. She scooted down, spine pressed to my chest. I drew her closer with an arm around her waist.

We dropped into dreamless sleep.

Chapter Twenty-Three

CORA

"Hawk likes baseball?"

The question flew out of me in a shocked whisper. Tim, working again, nodded emphatically.

"Very much."

"Playing or watching?"

He shrugged. "Both? He has so many hats!"

Astonishment robbed my speech at first. What a normal thing for Hawk to love. It shouldn't have been that surprising. So far, all I knew about Hawk was his company, a few family secrets, and the delicate feel of his touch dancing over the top of my skin.

Why did I have to keep learning about him from everyone else?

"Thanks, Tim. That is good to know. Do you have any recommendations for a place to get brunch?"

Sunshine warmed the sidewalk as I stood outside Hawk's building, peering at the city. When I'd woken up to the silent penthouse, I'd quickly dressed, grabbed my purse, and headed down with absolutely no plans.

Eventually, I'd have to return to the isolation of snowy

mountains and a canvas to finish, so I didn't want to waste the adventure while I had it. Sleep still lingered in my thoughts while Tim rambled about a few areas to try eating. When he offered to call Diego, I waved him off.

"I'd rather walk, but thank you."

"Wait, no. I can't let you."

I paused. "What?"

Tim croaked, "Hawk told me not to let you walk anywhere by yourself, just in case."

"Hawk is a little paranoid, don't you think? He went to dinner with me last night."

He shrugged. "He asked, Miss Cora."

I cocked a hip, finger tapping my chin. "What would happen if you didn't see me leave?"

His gaze tapered. "Are you trying to be very sneaky?"

"I am," I said, laughing. "Tim, please, I'm a grown woman. You won't get into trouble because no one will know I left. Downtown Texas isn't out to get me. They don't even know who I am."

"But they might do something," he said quietly, "if they knew who you were."

The solemness in his eyes gave me pause.

"Is it really that dangerous?"

He shrugged.

A wash of uncertainty flowed through me. Sure, magazines, tabloids, online blogs stalked Hawk, to some extent. Articles populated about him all the time, but there were dozens of other millionaires that . . .

. . . he wasn't them, though.

Hawk was handsome, single, thirty-something, and a billionaire. The profile created its own celebrity. Tate loomed as an uncertain figure in the background, but with an almost-warm day and sunshine spinning over head?

He seemed so far away.

"Hawk has made sure they won't know who I am," I said with finality. "Assuming you keep our secret?"

"Always!"

"Then thank you for your concern, Tim, but we have nothing to worry about. I'll check in with you when I return, all right?"

His brows knitted together when he nodded, resignation in his slumped shoulders. "Yes, Miss Cora."

"See you soon!"

I winked, headed toward the place he claimed made a wicked caramel macchiato. My stomach buzzed with anticipation. The bustle of city life, rush of cars, beep of horns, made it feel as if Cade, canvas, real life, lurked ages away.

Part of me never wanted to go back.

Halfway to the little shop, my phone rang. Elated to see Hawk's name, I picked it up.

"Hey!"

"Hey pretty lady. How's the day going?"

His tone was a low drawl. It lacked some of the resonance from him in close proximity, as if he were in a room with someone else. Knowing what little I did of his business, I assumed people must always surround him.

"Just heading out. Where do you want to meet for lunch?"

"About that."

The drop of his tone made my stomach curl.

"You can't make it?"

"I'm so sorry. I'm wrapped up with a few other things that I pushed off to meet with Adelaide today. It would be better for the company if I stayed and finished them, particularly with . . ."

He trailed away, but didn't need to finish the sentence. *Hospital systems in need,* I thought. Try as I might, I couldn't entirely suppress the disappointment in my voice.

"Oh. Right, I get it."

"I'll make it up to you."

"With dinner?"

"The best nachos in the city."

Delighted for a tidbit of Hawk to come through this evening, I said, "Then it's a date. I'm not sure where I'll be tonight. Can you just text me when you're ordering?"

A pause filled the air.

"Where are you now?"

Too late, I realized my mistake. *Not sure where I'll be tonight* wouldn't sit well with a man who feared for my safety at every turn. I slipped into the coffee shop and kept my tone intentionally light.

"Grabbing some caffeine."

"With Diego?"

"Nope, just walking."

My nonchalance sounded forced, but I doubt he even noticed. The edge in his voice hardened.

"Look, I know it seems safe, but I'd be more comfortable if you let Diego drive you wherever you want to go."

An open booth near the front window boasted a small pot of flowers and plenty of privacy in the corner. I sat on the far side, facing the door, and set my purse in front of me. "Why are you so paranoid about it, Hawk?"

He paused.

"I just want you to be safe."

"From your adoring public? No one knows about us. I have my doubts that photographers go around taking random pictures of women on their own, then accusing them of dating wealthy people."

No amusement appeared in his voice when he said, "Not exactly."

"Why don't you just tell me?"

He sighed. "Look, I can't right now, but I'm happy to later. It's not just paparazzi. It's . . . Tate. I need to start a meeting. Please, let Diego escort you? I'll worry about you less and I'll explain more tonight, all right?"

"Oh."

"Promise?"

"Okay. I promise I'll be safe."

"Cora."

His growl didn't bother me. Cade spent most of my teenage years in a half snarl at any boy that *looked* at me.

"Hawk, a little trust?"

"Fine." He blew a dramatic raspberry. "But for the record, I don't like this *at all*. Check in with me via text, all right?"

I rolled my eyes.

"Yes, Mom."

"Be safe, babe. You mean a lot to me."

My insides melted at his sublime use of the word *babe*. A nickname that had never made me feel this way before. I smiled, unable to help myself.

"I will."

The call ended, but my heart fluttered on as if his voice never stopped.

* * *

The gentle purr of the elevator vibrated all the way into the small bones of my feet when I rode it back up to the penthouse later that afternoon. Beeps sounded as we passed each floor. It moved effortlessly. A perfect counter to the breathy, stressed voice in my ear.

"I'm not trying to be a bother, you understand," said Carlotta Milo in my ear. "I just wanted to call and check on your timeline to finish the painting. Are we still on track?"

"Yes, Carlotta, I totally understand. You can ask me for updates whenever you want. We are still on track."

"Just this morning, I confirmed that the Mountain Silver

Gallery has a slot in April. You're certain we'll be done by then? It's creeping toward the end of February now."

Calendar math quickly sprinted through my brain. If I stayed in Texas for only four more days with Hawk, that would give me the chance to attend the gala. I'd return in time to finish with several days to spare. Assuming she wanted no major corrections or changes, we'd be finished well ahead of time, with March for framing.

The thought of leaving already made my stomach curl, but business was business.

Hawk would understand.

"More than done," I said confidently. "I'll have it finished by the end of the month."

"Oh, how lovely! I'll be glad to confirm it with them. I think we'll be able to convince Sergio to take the masterpiece and show it off a bit. This timeline allows for me to provide revisions, if any?"

"Yes, but that's a rare occurrence for a nature painting of this type."

"Of course," she said soothingly. "Of course. Well, I think you should plan on the showing at Mountain Silver the first week of April. With any luck, we can extend through the month. It should do both of us some good."

My stomach nearly flipped at the finality in her tone.

The Mountain Silver Gallery was the most renowned art gallery in the Pineville mountain area. Wealthy tourists that flocked to Jackson City during the ski season often shopped there. A successful display at Mountain Silver created an undeniable branching square of success. More galleries, more showings, and more income.

Which meant more opportunity to help Cade.

"Of course, Carlotta. I'm excited to get to that stage."

"I haven't had a progress photo in a week. Any chance you could send me one?"

I clutched the phone a bit more tightly. "I had to leave town for a bit, but I should return soon. You can expect one with plenty of progress in ten days."

A few breathy start-stops followed. She had always been a worrier, but lately she'd taken it to the next level. Her anxiety was palpable through the phone, reaching for me. Not even my most placating voice had stemmed her worry.

"All right," she finally said. "I'll trust you."

"That is most appreciated."

The elevator beeped as it slowed, accepted the keycard Hawk had given me for access, and rolled the doors open. I gratefully stepped off the elevator, into the penthouse lobby area, as Carlotta wound through the last of her distressed spiral.

"Well, thanks for taking my call, Cora. I hope you stay safe during your vacation. There are rumors of a plague coming. Did you hear that?"

"A plague?"

"Out of Russia."

I blinked. "Oh, no. I believe there's a virus that started in South America that they are tracking, though."

"Yes, well. Let's hope it passes through quickly. Goodbye, dear."

Empty-handed after a restless day in the city, I unlocked the penthouse door and stepped inside. A bouquet of fresh flowers drew my gaze immediately. Cream-colored roses tipped in light pink stood on the table, sprawling with majesty into the room. I smiled, stepped up to them, and buried my nose in their silky folds.

Delicious.

A card waited in the middle.

Thanks for being here.

The tented card propped on the table as I set it aside, plucked a single rose, and strolled over to the skyline. Darkness settled on the far horizon. Lights clustered below, cluttering the world like fireflies gathered in a dark bowl. They flickered on and off, silent from so high.

My fingers itched to paint it, but how to capture the city? The movement. The interplay of shadow, life, and light. You saw it for one second, then it morphed. An ever-changing world that never settled.

My musings drifted to the Mountain Silver Gallery, then back to Hawk and my time here, finally to the virus that hovered in Florida with potential to spread. My phone buzzed in my pocket. I pulled it out, surprised to find it was already five thirty-four in the evening.

Hawk: Nachos are on the way. Diego is grabbing them.

I frowned. Something in those words left an ominous feeling.

Cora: Are you on your way also?
Hawk: Soon.

My teeth sank into my bottom lip as I regarded the message. An inkling told me something might have come up, and he was about to let me down gently for our dinner date.

Cora: The flowers are beautiful.

Hawk: I'm glad you like them.

Cora: I love pink flowers.

The simple words felt too childlike to send. Too uncomplicated against the complexity of emotion he stirred in my chest. *They're beautiful, but I don't want them,* I thought. *I want you.*

The words stalled at my fingertips. Could I make that request when he prepared for a potential pandemic?

When the next message came through, the sinking in my stomach didn't surprise me.

Hawk: Care to video chat when Diego arrives with the nachos?

Cora: Because you won't be able to make it for dinner?

Hawk: I'm sorry, Cora. I'm trying, but with the potential for the virus coming, our company is scrambling to support hospital preparation.

Guilt warred within. I felt selfish for wanting all his time and attention when the world hovered on the brink of something huge. It felt petulant to ask for dinner with him when his company could work for the betterment of the world.

But I didn't come all the way to Texas to eat nachos with him over video chat. Same city, yet worlds away.

Cora: I understand.

Hawk: This isn't fair to you. I'm sorry, Cora. I'd call, but I'm texting you during a meeting.

Cora: Go to your meeting. Call me when you can.

I set the phone aside and propped my chin in my hands. Is this what it felt like to date a man like Hawk? Or was this truly a special circumstance?

The tips of my fingers ran over the end of the petals, where the pink-tipped edges faded to cream. Lines of color bled into the white parts, and I studied the veins, the flow of artistry in a single leaf.

Then I reached for my sketch pad, yanked a pencil closer, and let the lonely penthouse flow through my busy hand.

* * *

"Have you always drawn people from across the room without telling them?"

A deep voice reverberated next to my left shoulder. I jumped, poorly suppressed a squeak, and glanced at the padded chair next to me.

A dark-haired man lowered into the empty seat. A scruffy beard covered his tawny face, and broad shoulders hid beneath a plain white shirt. He wore jeans, sneakers. All together too casual for the foyer of Hawk's apartment building that I sat in, where wealthy people mulled in an overbearing elegance.

His gaze focused past me, to the paper on the table, and then to my eyes. A slight smile lingered there. He leaned far enough away, and slightly to the left, that I felt no panic at his proximity. Still, the approach of a total stranger set me on edge.

Heat bloomed through my cheeks as I comprehended what he said. *Have you always drawn people from across the room without telling them?*

Oh.

Awkward.

Too late, I realized that my model for the sketch now sat next to me. I swallowed hard. Had he noticed me alternately staring at him, then dropping my gaze?

Probably.

This bungled situation had happened before. I'd find

someone who caught my interest by their stance. The way they held their arms. A casual pose lined with tension. I would stop, draw them. The process made me oblivious to the person I drew, who often noticed my attention.

Men, especially, approached.

I fought the urge to shuffle the paper away. There was nothing to apologize for. Nothing in the image was anything to be embarrassed about. The way he'd been sitting on the chair, his ankle propped on a knee, hand resting out, charmed me.

Effortless, if I had to put a word to it. Natural beauty brightened the male form.

Interest lifted his eyebrows a little higher.

"You're an artist?"

"Yes."

A slow smile crossed his face. "And you draw random people in a lobby?"

I laughed, startled by the amusement he had captured. He had an easy way of smiling that put me at ease.

"Ah . . . apparently, I do."

He chuckled. "Who doesn't?"

"Plenty of normal people, I'm sure."

"Normal people are boring."

"Maybe it's normal for artists?"

He conceded with a tilt of his head. "Just the good ones, though. If you'll find anything in a place like this," his hand swept around to encompass the room, "it's real life art."

Quietly, I nodded. A vague definition of art didn't interest me as much as people, however. Not knowing this person—at least, I didn't think so—I kept my lips sealed. He continued grilling me with questions.

"Why are you drawing random strangers in a lobby, by the way?"

A shrug followed. "The penthouse was empty and there's no inspiration in loneliness."

"Penthouse, huh?"

I blew a raspberry. "Don't judge me."

Laughing, he held up two hands. "No judgment here. Money is just money, especially in a world like this."

"It's not my penthouse." I picked at the edge of my sketchbook. "It's my . . ."

Words stalled. Boyfriend? Friend? What were Hawk and I? *Impossible*, I thought, startled by the word. His drawling question jerked me back into life.

"Your what?"

Too late, I realized I'd been staring at the floor for an awkward length of time.

"Right, sorry. It's my friend's place. He's caught at work and I've already had too much coffee. So I came down here and . . . anyway, I was walking through and saw you and wanted to capture the ease in how you sat. I like poses. There is something really powerful about them."

Another quick perusal dropped to the paper. He nodded, lips pressed upward in a half smile.

"You captured it. I look powerful."

With another laugh, I slipped the paper over to him, grateful to have it off my lap. For some reason, it felt too heavy. Something familiar in his face drew me closer. The dark eyes, simmering intelligence. It all felt . . . familiar.

"You can have it."

"Really?"

"Yeah. Take it."

"Cool!" He accepted, held it out to regard it from a distance. "I'll put this up at my place. Thanks."

With a smile, I closed my sketch book. He leaned forward. His shirt sleeve shifted, drawing my gaze. Warbling tattoos stretched from sleeve bottom to wrist on his left arm. The beginnings of the same had already started on his right arm, just behind his bicep. His dark beard hid what appeared to be a handsome face.

But those eyes.

"So," he said crisply, "you're waiting for your friend. Can you wait for your friend while you go to dinner with me?"

Heat bloomed across my cheeks.

"I don't think that would be a good idea."

"Ah." Understanding flooded his features. "Is your *friend* a really rich guy that owns a penthouse and is so busy at work he can't make it back to take you on the date you deserve?"

Shock rendered me almost mute.

"Ah . . ."

White teeth flashed in a quick smile. "I've heard this type of thing before. Well, I'm sorry. He's a blind fool. Oh, I didn't catch your name?"

I stuck out a hand. "Cora."

He accepted, slipping his warm grip into mine. His firm handshake communicated worlds about him.

"Cora. I'm Noah. It's good to meet you, and thanks for the picture."

"Good to meet you as well."

A glimmer of familiarity slipped through me. Dark eyes. Noah. Something just on the verge of knowing hovered at the edge of my mind. All at once, knowing snapped into place.

Noah.

He stood, holding the paper carefully. Before I could conjure my question, he waved and walked toward the front doors. Moments later, he left. I stared after the man that could be Hawk's brother in mute shock.

Had that just happened?

Chapter Twenty-Four

HAWK

Two bells on a door jangled as I slipped inside a small building on the north side of town, close to my corporate office, the next evening. A smell like lavender floated into my nose, reminding me of Cora.

A little squeal issued off to the side. I spun to find her racing toward me, arms outstretched. The stress from the day melted as I caught her in my arms, gratified to have her chest pressed to mine.

"Cora."

"You came!"

I hid a wince as I set her down. "I definitely deserved that."

She beamed. "You deserve it, but you're forgiven. Look where you've brought me!"

The shining light in her eyes deepened my guilt. Last night, I hadn't returned until midnight. Cora had been asleep on the couch, a pink rose in front of her. I'd carried her to bed and curled around her. When I woke up to leave for work early, she hadn't even stirred.

This was no relationship.

She deserved better.

Soon, I promised myself, though I swam through a metaphorical sea. Amid that sea lurked ugly monsters. Pandemics. Passing off a billion-dollar empire to my sister. My father and his guaranteed issue with Cora, who had no family, money, or power to her name.

None of those other monsters were more terrifying than *that*.

Cora pressed a kiss to my lips—a kiss I hadn't earned. Unable to help myself, I wrapped my arms around her, brought her close. Like a balm, she soothed away all the ruffled agony of the past several days. My overstimulated brain, wired and jumpy from too many decisions and conversations, calmed in the gallery's quiet.

The sound of a clearing throat interrupted my dream. I turned, an arm around Cora, to find the director of the gallery, Magree, standing a few steps away. My dazzled brain came back into focus.

"Magree." I held out a hand. "Thank you so much for letting us have the gallery to ourselves."

She grinned widely. "My pleasure, Mr. Mercedy."

"Ourselves?" Cora whispered.

Magree smiled with a poorly suppressed annoyance. "Yes, all to yourself tonight. Take your time. We'll be by with champagne, if you'd like."

"Please," I said.

Cora's wide eyes expanded further as Magree stepped away, her heels like drums on the wooden floor. Cora spun to me, grabbed my shoulders. Excitement thrummed from her tight grip on my arms.

"Alone?"

I grinned, relieved by her brilliant excitement. I brought my arms around her, loving her natural heat, the easy feel of her in my arms.

"Alone."

"You paid for it?"

"Yes. Totally worth it."

"But—"

"It was nothing, Cora. Let me worry about that?"

Discomfort flickered through her eyes, but a quick glance around distracted her. With a squeal, she grabbed my hand and headed off to the right.

"I love this artist!"

The next two hours faded into Cora. These galleries usually brought me to bored tears, but Cora breathed new life into the experience. Her eyes illuminated. Gentle squeaks came from her throat. Her fingers pressed to her lips when she regarded a piece that touched her.

Several times, she stared for minutes on end. "Beautiful," she'd murmur, then move on.

I trailed behind, lost to the spark of life in her eyes. The quiet gallery and bubbly champagne I sipped relaxed me. Admiration and obsession flowed from her with each minute that passed. Cora ignored an offered glass of champagne, hors d'oeuvres, and water. Piece after piece wrapped around her in a stunning show of attention.

Paintings, sculptures, and sketches captured her.

She captured me.

After days of meetings, bottom lines, sales force negotiations, supporting our managers, one-on-one discussions with Nicola, and lining up a company to prepare for an inevitable disaster dissipated.

Into Cora.

With stunning force, I realized the depths of my investment. She illuminated the dark spots in my life. Released the built-up stress and pain. Cora revealed the real side of life. The part that hid from the daily grind I disappeared into. Life existed outside of work, apparently.

Which meant it was time.

Time to pull the plug on my job. To tell Nicola that she was ready to take over as CEO—of course she was ready—and start my step back. The only way I could do that was to force my hand.

I pulled out my phone while Cora crouched near a sculpture of three small cats, stretched to thin towers, that leaned on a father cat with glasses. She tilted her head, cooing over the details of fur in the sculpture work, while I navigated to my text messages.

Hawk: You're ready. I'm ready. Let's pull the plug.

An immediate response came.

Nicola: Is this an alternate reality?

Hawk: Prep a press release. We'll launch it the day after the gala.

Indicator dots popped up, then stopped. They appeared again, then dropped. I almost laughed. Rarely did I catch Nicola by surprise.

Finally, her response came through.

Nicola: It'll be ready for approval in the morning. I'll call my decorator and prepare to redesign your office.

I tilted my head back and laughed. Cora peered up at me. Her shock eased into a girlish delight that thrilled me all the way to my toes. I'd pay anything to see her raw enjoyment again.

"What is it?" she asked. A half-smile lingered in her gaze. She reached up, pressed a fingertip to the corner of my mouth. "You look so happy."

I wrapped my arm around her and buried myself in her neck. Silky strands of auburn hair drifted across the bridge of my nose, tickling the skin. Now that I had sent the message, I tested the weight on my chest. Would panic rise? Would I scramble to undo the decision?

So far?

Only freedom. The feeling of flying. Euphoria.

Cora slipped into my life like a quiet snowfall, but triggered a raging blizzard. Everything I once thought whirled in dizzying bursts.

Yet, I saw so clearly.

I pulled back, tucked a strand of hair out of her eyes. She mirrored my adoring smile. Her quiet voice, more breath than not, roiled me up.

"What is it, Hawk?"

"I love you."

A sharp intake of breath followed. Her eyes widened. My fingers trembled when I touched her cheek. Questions filled her shocked expression.

"I do, Cora. It makes no sense." A breathy laugh escaped. "It's too fast. It's *so* fast. We don't even know if our lives can merge. I don't know your favorite colors or who your great aunt is that you never see except at Christmas, but all of that is inconsequential, anyway. I know you. I know how I feel around you. And . . . I love you."

Her lips parted. I pulled her closer.

"You don't have to say it back," I blurted out. "You have no obligation to feel whatever I feel. I just had to say it. I've never felt this way. Like everything will be all right. That there's something to fight for. A reason to extract myself from the octopus of corporate life. If you asked me to leave everything behind, to burn it down, to forsake all the billions . . . I would do it right now. For you. For us. Ask it, and I'll give. You have me, heart and soul."

She'd frozen rigid under my hands. Unable to read the unmoving expression on her face, I paused. Held my breath.

She cradled my cheeks and pulled me into a kiss. Her touch, so toasty and solid and certain, rocked me. Stars exploded somewhere. Heat popped under my skin, crackling like dry paper. While my body felt like it would explode, silence rippled around the room.

When Cora pulled away, tears sparkled on the edge of her eyelashes.

"Thank you, Hawk."

I grabbed her, twirled us. Bright colors whirled in a tornado as I focused on Cora, giggling and happy. Her hair billowed as we spun, laughing.

Cora.

The love of my life.

* * *

The towering lights of a park close to the gallery kept nighttime at bay. Cold settled, our breath almost visible, as Cora insisted we stop for ice cream.

"It's winter," I drawled. "You realize that, right? Wouldn't hot chocolate be more appropriate?"

She rolled her eyes. "You know what Cade calls this sort of winter? A joke. He's back at the ranch battling five feet of snow and sub-zero temperatures while I can walk in sandals. Now is always a good time for ice cream, Hawk! When was the last time you went out for a treat or an actual date?"

My reply stalled on frozen lips.

Far, far too long.

"Fine." I held up both hands. "You win. We'll buy ice cream."

Twenty minutes later, we strolled along the sidewalk, treat in hand. Cora hummed under her breath.

"Can we go to your office?" she asked. "I'd love to see your workplace! I have so many questions. Do you decorate it? Is it at the top of the building? Do you have an incredible view?"

The barrage startled me out of pleasant thoughts about the gallery, her sweet reception to my shocking words.

Sputtering a little, I said, "M-my office?"

"I'd love to see where you work! It would sort of help me put the puzzle of Hawk together." She gave me an innocent-enough look. "It's one more part of you I haven't really seen yet."

"Uh, no. No office."

"Why not?" She threw up a hand. "You saw *my* office."

I cut her a fake-perturbed glare, which only deepened her hilarity. How Cora was so happy about everything, I would never understand.

"You work in a loft, Cora. That's vastly different from a corporate office."

"A lovely loft and office it is, too. We aren't doing anything else tonight, are we?" Her voice dropped, smaller in tone. "I'd love to see that side of your life, Hawk. So much of it is vague. Unavailable to me."

"I have firm boundaries around my office. I don't let real life intermix there. No woman has ever come to my place of work before."

"But why?"

Panic streaked through in a bright stream. How could I explain to her that my office wasn't safe?

Tate wouldn't approve of you, would never cross my lips, despite being true. Neither would the other macabre reality of: *Tate likes to sabotage the happiness of others, particularly when he can't control it, by leaking information to tabloids.*

M. Ventures was mine, but Tate strolled up to my office whenever he wanted. Try as I might, I couldn't entirely rid my life of his presence. Despite my departure from Tate and his overlord ways at Mercedy, Inc, he had methods of snaking into everything. Tate might see her there, then play a stupid stunt that I'd never forgive. He would expose her. Test her mettle, certainly.

The blessed future I could finally grasp might crumble, right when it all felt so possible. If I lost my chance with Cora because of Tate, nothing would recover.

"Do you miss your painting?" I asked.

She paused, thinking through the answer as we stopped at a corner intersection. If she noticed my diversionary attempt, she didn't call it out. Cars streamed past. People congregated around us in a growing circle, and the bustling noise comforted me.

Busy streets almost always let me fade into the shadows of life.

"I do," she said. "I'm about to start a really challenging portion of it, and I'm eager to get started. Sometimes, it's boring and routine and rote, but I miss the structure in my day. There's only so much I can do in downtown Texas by myself," she added as a wry aside.

Easy censure riddled that comment, and I didn't blame her. My following question almost made me sick, but I had to ask.

"Do you need to go back soon?"

"Yes, after the gala."

The commotion nearly drowned out her response. Her whisper resonated down my body. Her expression betrayed the same truth. Cora stopped at a chain-link fence and peered through. Another lick of her ice cream cone made me insanely jealous. What would cherry ice cream taste like on her lips?

I'd love to find out.

"Hawk, look!" she cried, giddy as she pointed down the road. "Baseball!"

"You're right. Looks like a small league. Certainly isn't the time of year for it."

"We should go play."

"What?"

"Really! Let's see if they'll let us play."

"No! That's crazy."

Cora tilted her head to the side, regarding me like I'd lost my mind. A drop of cherry ice cream lingered at the corner of her mouth. I leaned in, kissed it free. She laughed, planted a hand on my chest, and shoved me off.

"You love baseball," she said, unwilling to let go of her shock, "yet you never go to the park and play? It looks like a good time!"

"How would I play baseball by myself?" I asked, laughing.

She leaned over, stole a lick of my maple nut ice cream. "Don't play by yourself," she concluded. "You go join the game."

"Doesn't work like that."

She scoffed. "Bet it does. See that team?"

I hesitated, following her gaze. The four baseball diamonds that filled up the middle of the park lay scattered with people. Hats, mitts, bats. The ring of a ball hitting aluminum sang through the air, followed by the noise from a wildly cheering crowd.

"Those are private leagues," I said. "You have to pay and sign up and it's all very organized. A bunch of people that want to play in the off season, I'd bet. Look how many people are watching?"

"So join the league!"

I laughed, "You're impossible. There's no time for a league."

"Why do you like baseball so much?" She met my gaze as she slurped at ice cream that threatened to trickle down her cone. "You wear the hats. Tim says you love the games. So what about it do you love?"

The fact that the doorman gave her that information should have shocked me. It didn't. Cora was entirely too friendly for her own good.

"I don't know. Baseball is . . . an escape. I think it had something to do with my team as a kid. Baseball was the only place Tate had no power, so I escaped to it as often as possible."

She sobered. "You escaped your father with baseball?"

"My team was my family. The coach was like a father to me, always made sure I was there, and ready. I miss that. When I watch the games? I remember Coach Jones."

She grinned, replacing the melancholy that only Tate could cause with a mere mention of his name.

"I'm glad you had someone. Maybe you should have gone into professional baseball instead?"

I snorted. "I might have loved it, but I wasn't that good. They always called me butterfingers. I let go of the game after high school. I had . . . things to prove about myself, I guess."

"Have you proven them?"

My chest locked up. I answered as honestly as I was able.

"I don't know."

"How sad."

The note of sincere mourning in her tone surprised me. I canted my head, regarding the baseball crowd. A familiar zing of life slipped through me at the sight of players running bases, balls flying, and the sound of people cheering.

Sad, indeed.

With a tug, she led me onto the sidewalk that led to the baseball diamonds.

"Let's watch! It'll be so fun."

"But—"

"No buts. We're going to be spontaneous."

"Cora—"

She silenced me, turned her attention back to her cone, and strode closer with all the confidence of someone supposed to be there. Three minutes later, we sat on a metallic bleacher to watch. Cora cheered the moment she sat down. I tried not to look as awkward as I felt.

Cora blended right in. She leaned close to a white-haired woman on her left and whispered, "Who are you here for?"

"That tall drink of water on first base is my grandson," the woman said in a shaky voice. "He's the best player out there!"

Five minutes later, the two of them were giggling like hens.

Cora cheered for a home run, shouted against a bad call from the umpire at home plate, and cackled when a burly man from the other team glared at her. The grandma at her side flipped him the bird. Cora dissolved into happy tears.

With forced attention, I made myself look at the diamond. I didn't stare at the surrounding faces. Did they recognize me? Did they see me?

No one knows you're here, I reminded myself.

Five minutes passed.

Cora clasped hands with the grandma, laughing at something her adult grandson did as he crossed home plate. The old lady waved, and he waved back. Cora melted, her hand on my knee. The quick touch sent something hot and protective and almost feral through me.

A relaxing sensation followed.

No one here knew me. No one jumped out to ask questions. To spring an interview. Nothing like that.

Anonymity.

It felt good. The thought of doing this more often with Cora solidified the new move forward, out of corporate life. Now, I had to find a time to tell her. I'd inadvertently bowled over her question earlier by telling her I loved her.

Didn't regret it yet.

Cone finished, I turned to my buzzing phone. A quick glance at the screen dropped me into a bath of fire and ice. A text message from an unidentified number with a picture. Stomach twisted, I turned my body so Cora wouldn't see and accessed the image.

Cora.

Me.

Walking outside the gallery.

The words beneath the image sent further ice through my veins. From Tate, as expected.

Tate: New girlfriend? Weren't you going to tell your father?

I turned off the screen, shoved it back into my pockets.

Creepy old man.

Cora's delighted cry drew me back to the game. She squeezed my leg, drawing my attention as another home run came through. I gave her a wide smile and hoped she didn't notice the fake energy behind it.

An errant foul ball loomed overhead. She stood to protect her friend, but the ball bounced several feet away and rolled to the side.

With her distraction, I sent a reply to Tate.

Hawk: Let's talk about this one-on-one. Saturday, lunch. I'll come to you.

Tate: See you then.

I leaned my elbows onto my knees and stared out.

My new can of worms had just begun.

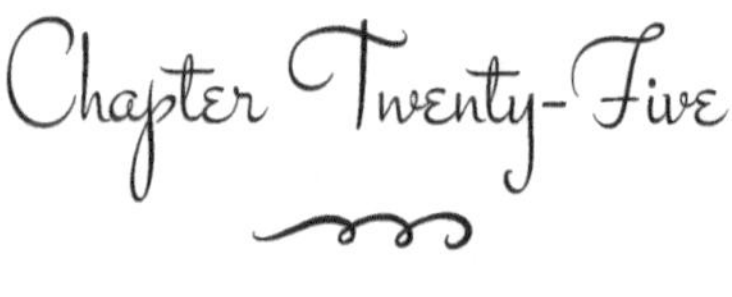

Chapter Twenty-Five

CORA

Frustration boiled like a tea kettle inside of me.

I shoved away from Hawk's table and paced behind it. It was day four in Texas. We had a lovely evening together last night, now another full day alone. No promise of Hawk on the horizon.

Brutal ups and downs.

My painting called from across the great distance. I itched to work on it again. Ease the canvas away under the power of color. Layers awaited me. I couldn't linger here too much longer.

Thankfully, the gala approached. Once I attended that with him, I'd be able to go home. Have a better perspective on his whole life. The gala might be my only chance to glimpse his work.

Rain drizzled outside, streaking down the giant windows. The gray-coated room felt like a shiver. My phone flashed with another text message. Probably from Cade, asking when I'd be home.

A great question.

Resigned, I grabbed my phone and looked at it.

Cade: I miss you. Wanted to see what you're up to. Old man Morgan died and we're trying to sort out what happens next.

Alarm ripped through me.

Cora: Died? Cade, I'm sorry.

Cade: He wanted to go, and he was at home, safe, and warm. His granddaughter is coming to settle the ranch and house. There's a will somewhere, I hear.

Cora: What will happen to the ranch?

Cade: Auction, probably.

Cora: Can you buy it?

Cade: I wish.

Hope elevated my heart with a bright flutter. This was my chance. I *had* to finish that commission so I could get the money to help fund Cade. I had almost twenty thousand dollars in a savings account I'd earmarked for him for the last four years.

The urge to flee back home and get to work almost consumed me. I lowered to the couch, forced myself to slow down.

No, I couldn't be rash. Abandoning Hawk wouldn't feel good either. Not after he just told me he loved me. He'd exchanged the most powerful words. He *loved* me. Instinct told me that a man like Hawk didn't use idle words.

For certain, I didn't.

In fact, I'd never given those words away. If I gave them to Hawk, they would mean something.

Love or not, however, I couldn't stay here, waiting for his attention. I had a life and goals back in Pineville to achieve. Those goals had deadlines. After I helped Cade with the ranch, and this virus passed over, there would be more time to spend at Hawk's penthouse.

But . . . a pandemic could mean difficulties. Time apart, perhaps?

What *did* it mean, anyway?

Rock, meet hard place.

Another buzz drew my trailing thoughts back to the moment. A text from Hawk waited.

Hawk: If you're interested, Magree would like to meet with you. Remember her from the art gallery? Bring your sketches and those paintings propped against my wall. They're interested in your portfolio.

A cold tremor slipped through me. By the time my brain wrapped around what he meant, my hands shook. My artwork in *that* gallery? It would be . . . surreal. A lifelong dream. Elation and disbelief and a hint of suspicion followed.

Recollections of Magree moved back through my mind. She hadn't been warm or welcoming when I arrived, though she clearly had a soft spot for Hawk.

Irritated.

That's how I would have described her.

Cora: You're kidding.

Hawk: Nope. Twelve o'clock. Better get moving.
Diego will pull the car up any moment now.

With a squeal, I vaulted off the couch and headed for my bags.

* * *

Magree welcomed me with an icy smile.

A billowy skirt sashayed around her legs as she swept closer. Her high heels lifted her several inches above me. Without them, we might have seen eye-to-eye.

"Welcome," she said. "I'm glad to meet with you. Please, come this way."

Without a moment of eye contact, we wound through the displays toward a hallway at the back, on the right. The shadowed place housed several rooms. We slipped by to the far room and stepped inside.

Her office had a funky eclectic vibe littered with small sculptures, splashy paintings, and a bookshelf stacked with book spines and nicknacks. A broad desk swept an entire wall. When she lowered into a padded chair, it made a *whoosh* sound.

She waved me into a chair, gaze on stacks of paperwork in front of her.

"Have a seat."

"Thank you."

The sound of my voice did nothing to engage her attention. She lifted some papers, stacked them together, moved them to a different spot. Picked up a pen, placed it elsewhere.

With bold disapproval in her tone, she finally said, "Hawk tells me you're an artist that would be interested in gallery representation?"

"Yes. Like any artist, I'm always interested in more opportunities to have my work seen."

"What mediums do you work in?"

"Oils, mostly, and charcoal."

"Hmm. And have you taken any classes?"

A disbelieving laugh came from me. "Yes, of course. I graduated from the Newton School of Design with a BA in painting."

Her right eyebrow flicked up a bit.

"Oh."

"I've had representation in other smaller galleries across the eastern coast," I continued, sensing a gradual warming. "Small town ones, mostly, but they've been successful. I have a modest income from commissions. Currently, I'm working on my biggest commission yet. Depending on our current negotiations, it should also display at the Mountain Silver Gallery in April."

Magree's tightly held shoulders dropped back a bit. Unlikely that she'd know the gallery, despite its local fame, but a firm name appeared to build a little trust.

"I see," she murmured, hitting me with her full gaze. Assessment lingered in the cold depths. "At least you have some experience. Let me see some of your work."

My stomach curdled.

Did I want to hand it over?

No.

Despite my reservations, however, I slipped the folder with sketches to her side. Printed images of paintings that I'd sold stacked beneath them. Intense works that revealed the ferocity and warmth of nature.

A close up on a brightly colored bird, water beaded on one tense wing as it watched for a predator. Winds tearing at the sea, flinging foam into the air like a warrior.

Magree studied them, lips pursed. Her carefully controlled expression moved from a heavy frown to something more perplexed. The silence in the room grew almost unbearable until she finally lifted her head.

With one tilted eyebrow, she passed it back to me. I tucked it into my bag.

"You have natural talent," she said with slightly less hostility than our greeting. "I could find a spot for you . . ."

Her gaze drifted to a boxed-out chart in front of her.

I froze.

I could find a spot for you.

The trailing reluctance immediately set me on edge.

Oh, no.

This is *not* what I signed up for.

The hesitation in her comment led me to realize that something *else* had happened here. My hands gripped the chair arms more tightly as I hesitated.

Hawk.

Hawk had forced this meeting on Magree. Undoubtedly a patron, he had likely asked Magree to see me. She must be under prodigious pressure to represent my work, lest they lose an important benefactor. No wonder she eyed me warily.

In her eyes, I must be a desperate power-grabber. Did she think I slept with Hawk to finagle this opportunity? She must have assumed that I was a novice. A hobbyist that dated one of the most powerful men in the city, therefore able to get whatever I wanted.

Ah, that idiotic man.

Despite the sweetness of the gesture, I couldn't help my frustration. Why didn't he understand? I didn't want *this*. He didn't need to save me, to pave the path for my success. He needed to be at my side.

"Cora?"

Blinking, I slipped out of my daze and let out a long, controlled breath. The flow of air calmed my initial outrage just enough that I'd be able to get through this without exploding.

"Magree, can we be honest with each other?"

Magree's shoulders jammed back. Her eyes widened. I held up a hand to allay her fears. "Did Hawk arrange this meeting?"

Stiffly, she nodded once. I held her in a tight gaze, though I could sense her discomfort.

"Are you looking for more artists?"

An equally-tense no.

"Do you typically represent naturalistic oil paintings or charcoal sketches of people?"

Another awkward negative.

I lowered my hand to my lap.

"I see. Magree, I must apologize. Hawk doesn't know how the art world works, and he meant well by trying to give me an opportunity into an art gallery that I highly admire. Your collections are beautiful and impressive, but they aren't the style that I work within. Thank you for your time and considering me, but I must let you off the hook."

She opened her mouth to protest, but I stalled her.

"Please, don't worry. I won't say a word to Hawk. He'll know that you were gracious enough to invite me in, let me know there could be a slot, but that I refused. Truly, this would be an honor, but my work wouldn't fit here. I'd like to help you maintain the integrity of your reputation."

Her tense cheeks loosened. The wrinkles between her brows smoothed away as she regarded me. A gentle sigh lifted, then relaxed her thin shoulders.

"Thank you, Cora. I . . . appreciate all that Hawk does for us, and I will help him when it's possible. You are talented, there's no doubt. Your use of color is impressive, and I enjoy the moods of your paintings. As you said, however, this isn't the type of work we're known for."

Relieved to have salvaged the situation—and my pride—I stood up.

"We agree. Thank you, Magree, and best of luck. I hope to visit your gallery again soon."

* * *

The *thud* of my feet hitting the sidewalk grounded me as I fast-walked down the street, my folder of sketches and images tucked under the wing of my arm. I sent a text message to Diego.

Cora: I'll be back in a minute. I need to walk off some frustration.

Diego: It went badly?

Cora: Magree was professional and lovely.

Diego: Ah, you did not answer my question.

I left it at that. More messages followed, asking where I had gone, when I would be back. Reminders that Mother Hen Hawk wouldn't like me being in the city by myself. I set aside concerns Hawk would be angry at Diego on my behalf. He wouldn't.

Hawk would be angry with me.

Good.

Same-same.

The call of a doughy, salty pretzel drew me to a small street food vendor. I whipped out a ten-dollar bill, accepted the buttery carb heaven, and let the woman behind the counter keep all the change. A small park, nestled between buildings, called to me.

With a *humph*, I sat on a painted bench, the sound of laughing children filling the air as I chewed through the tangy dough. Delicious. Better company than thinking about the embarrassing event at the gallery, anyway.

Despite my rage, I couldn't help but understand that

Hawk meant well. He didn't understand the subterranean machinations of the art gallery world. Reputation was king. Feel and cohesiveness and respect for the other artists were paramount. He'd simply tried to help me fill my time while here and advance a budding career with greater networking opportunities.

Which brought us back to the original problem.

His lack of presence.

My mind spiraled around the conundrum when an old man settled onto the bench at my side. He propped an arm on the back and stared out. Streaks of dark illuminated mostly white hair. A clean-shaven face, troubled with wrinkles, stared out.

I turned back to my pretzel.

"Beautiful day," he said in a rumbly voice. "Isn't it?"

The rain had cleared, giving way to a chill in the air. Only two kids tumbled around the slides, near a tired mother that texted on her phone. They wore long pants and zipped up jackets, their wrists and pant bottoms saturated from the earlier downfall.

"Yes," I said, for lack of anything else. The bag for my half eaten pretzel crinkled as I set it on the bench to my right.

He cast a sidelong glance that I met. For a moment, our gazes held. Hazel eyes, pale skin that hung off his bones loosely. Sallow, too. A man with health problems, I'd wager. An underlying intensity in his eyes startled me.

"You're not from here, are you?" he asked.

I shook my head.

"Where are you from?"

Something about him didn't sit quite right. A too-concentrated depth to his gaze. Stark appearance in his eyes. Behind us, Diego pulled up to the curb, peering around. I almost lifted my arm to wave, but something stopped me. A heaviness in the air, perhaps. The hair on the back of my neck prickled.

"Farther north." I gazed away. "This is my first trip to Texas."

"Do you like it?"

"Yes. It's a big, fun city."

He made a noise in his throat. Quiet swelled between us for several moments. My phone buzzed in my pocket. Diego, probably. He remained at the curb, but looked this way. Just as I almost gathered up my pretzel to leave, the old man spoke again.

"Big cities are all I've ever known," he said conversationally. Some of my suspicion ebbed. "I've always wanted to try living somewhere a bit more wild, you know? Mountains, maybe."

The chill returned. I swallowed hard.

"Mountains are lovely." My hand lowered to my phone. A darting glance to the side revealed Diego standing just outside his car. A phone pressed to his ear, a look of distress on his face. He waved toward me.

I froze.

Something wasn't right.

"What do you do for a living?" he asked.

"I'm a . . . preschool teacher."

He lifted his brow, as if he sensed my lie.

As if he knew.

"What did you say your name was?" I asked.

"I didn't say my name, Cora."

The sound of my name on his lips sent ice-cold fear through me. I leaped to my feet, abandoning the pretzel. Before I could go far, a familiar figure appeared to my right. Broad shoulders. Arm full of tattoos.

Noah, from the lobby.

"Get back to Diego, Cora," Noah said with a hand on my arm. "I'll be there in just a second."

I hesitated. The old man stared up at Noah through

rheumy eyes, muttering a shocked swear word under his breath. Undisguised hate simmered between them.

Noah stepped forward, putting himself between us. Laughable, that such a wiry old man could have any strength against a towering beast like Noah. There must have been something to fear, however, because Diego ran over, calling my name. He waved his phone.

"Miss Cora!"

Noah is a special guy, Hawk had said. *I haven't seen him in years.*

My uncertainty around meeting Noah the other day faded. I meant to ask Hawk, but had fallen asleep before he returned, then lost myself in the art gallery, the ice cream, and the baseball game.

Definitely Hawk's brother. Their undeniable similarities in their facial structure confirmed it. The firm reply of Hawk's voice after I'd asked him if he'd ever introduce me to Tate resurrected next.

Absolutely not.

Even Trent had warned me. *And do whatever you can to avoid Tate.*

Apparently, Tate wanted to find me, because he had.

Horror filled me, though I didn't know why. Something in the old man's slimy presence sent a shudder down my spine. The bruised rage in his glare, the downward tuck of his lips. His pale skin, so different from the cozy brown of both Noah and Hawk, shocked me.

Diego arrived at my side, puffing slightly.

"Miss Cora!"

My phone buzzed in my pocket. Hawk calling, perhaps? Diego held his phone in his hand, the screen black. I left my phone tucked away, too stunned by these developments to answer.

What did Tate want?

Why was Noah here?

The questions swirled like a storm.

"I'm coming," I murmured as Diego reached for me. "I'm coming. I just . . ."

Noah hadn't said another word, but seemed to occupy all of Tate's narrowed, snakelike attention. According to Trent's tale, the last time Noah had seen his father involved a punching match that didn't end well for Tate, and almost a decade of separation after.

Instinct compelled me more than anything else. I touched Noah's arm, not surprised when he jerked away out of surprise. Seeing me, his face softened.

"Sorry. Noah? Will you come with us?"

Wordlessly, he nodded. Noah shuffled closer to me. Watching him, I couldn't imagine how I hadn't immediately seen Hawk in his profile, the way he held his shoulders, the lithe ease of his movements.

Where Hawk wore baseball caps and carried confidence, Noah teemed with coiled tension.

Diego's wide gaze bounced between the three of us before he shuffled back, plucking at my sleeve.

"Please, Miss Cora," he pleaded. "Please come?"

I turned to go. Noah followed. His eyes didn't leave Tate the entire time, not even as Diego pulled away. The last glimpse I saw of Tate was an old man, sitting on a bench, staring out at nothing.

Chapter Twenty-Six

HAWK

Nicola dropped a stack of paperwork on my desk that made me roll my eyes.

"I don't want that."

"I know." She sank into a chair and suppressed a yawn. "They're just authorization signatures. Standard, boiler-plate stuff. Latesha posted the job opening for the new CTO. We have internals moving up, and a few outside applicants."

"Think you can squeeze them in before the virus? New CTO and CEO? Could be interesting."

"We will."

Her confidence helped. Nicola always took firm charge, but with a sense of amusement about it, as if life were a great cosmic joke. She leaned back, propped her head on her fingertips, and closed her eyes. A blissful smile stretched across her face.

"Ah," she breathed. "Silence."

"Not for long," I muttered. "Talk to me about moving our workforce home in case the pandemic closes offices down. Are we outfitted?"

Nicola ignored me for five more seconds, two more deep inhales, then opened her eyes and met my gaze.

"Yes."

We dissolved into a discussion until the clock chimed on the wall. I straightened, reached for my wallet in the top drawer. "Gotta go. I promised to meet Cora for lunch after her meeting with Magree."

Nicola followed suit.

"Cases confirmed in Seattle, by the way. A few in LA. None so far in Houston or Dallas, but it's only a matter of time. No deaths, so far."

"Moving closer, certainly."

"One of the warehouses I acquired is almost ready to go. The other two are only a few days behind it. A fourth is lagging. We're receiving questions from lab and manufacturing companies about space, should we need it." A triumphant grin spread across her lips. "Let's just say that M. Ventures is perfectly positioned."

"Never doubted you, Nic. The announcement about you becoming CEO?"

"The morning after the gala. The gala is tomorrow night, in case you needed a reminder."

Gala.

Right.

I'd completely forgotten.

Lunch with Cora would provide plenty of opportunity to discuss it. I tossed my baseball cap on, eager to see her. To leave all this behind. Nicola would have another cup of coffee, recharge, and plow into all that needed to be done while I lived my life.

What a novelty.

Meanwhile, I'd find the girl of my dreams, discuss her rise to artistic power through Magree's gallery, and live life. I could get used to this split in responsibilities.

My phone rang. Diego. I answered, putting it on speakerphone.

"Hey Diego."

"Mr. Hawk, ah . . . I think something is happening."

"What do you mean?"

"Miss Cora was upset after her gallery appointment. She didn't come back to the car, but walked down the road, bought a pretzel, and sat on a bench. I stayed with her, as I promised you. But then . . . an old man was with her."

I closed my eyes.

Nicola swore.

"Is it Tate?"

Diego had worked for Tate for years before Tate fired him for something inane and untrue. I immediately picked Diego up afterward. He hadn't often seen Tate since that time. He knew that avoiding him at all costs was the best strategy.

Something I'd made abundantly clear.

Diego became frantic. "Yes! I didn't realize it at first, until he turned and I saw his profile. He's with Cora on a bench. What do you want me to do? Tate doesn't seem . . . healthy."

"Where are you?"

"South street and fifth, that little park."

I reached for my coat. "What's happening now?"

The sound of a car door opening and shuffling followed. Cars whizzing past and louder sounds occluded the background.

"She's . . . talking to him, I guess."

"Can he reach her?"

"Yes?"

"Go over there right now, Diego. Tell her to come back."

"Ah . . ."

Hesitation followed.

"What?" I snapped.

"Someone else has shown up. I think . . . no, it can't be. I'm going, Mr. Hawk. I'm going now."

"Dieg—"

My shout fell on empty ears. Diego had already ended the call. I looked at Nicola in fury. She stood back, her jaw tight. She peered out the window, one leg half bent and pressed against the wall. Only the sink of her teeth into her bottom lip gave her away.

"Tate texted me about Cora," I said. "We're supposed to meet for lunch tomorrow, before the gala."

Apology lined her tone when Nicola said, "You know he likes to engineer his own situations, Hawk. Apparently, you didn't move fast enough for him."

I headed for the door, but Nicola stopped me.

"Wait. Let Diego call you back."

"I need to—"

"Trust me."

Something in her eyes gave me pause. My fists clenched as I forced myself to stay, to wait for the ring. What felt like an eternity later, my phone rang. Only half of it sounded before I answered it, put it back on speakerphone.

"Where is she?"

Instead of Diego, a deeper voice replied. "Cora is safe with me."

My heart leaped out of my chest. I stilled. A hint of a smile appeared on Nicola's face, then faded.

"Noah?" I gasped.

"There's some explaining to do," Noah continued, as if it hadn't been months since we'd spoken on the phone, and years since I'd seen him in person. "She's fine, Tate didn't touch her. We're on the way back to your penthouse. Meet us there?"

"I'll leave now."

"Nic?" Noah called as if he knew she listened.

"Yeah?"

"Stay there and run the company, all right? I'll take you to dinner."

She laughed. "You're bossy for being the younger brother."

His deep chuckle followed.

"Hawk? See you there."

Just before I left, propelled by utter astonishment, I stopped at the doorway and turned around. Nicola stood at the window now, peering out. The CEO's office towered above the city, almost as high as the penthouse that she would also inherit from me . . . eventually.

"Nic?"

She turned around with a, "Hmm?"

"You knew Noah was there, didn't you?"

She hesitated, then nodded. "You weren't the only one keeping track of Noah all those years. I knew he'd come back because of something with Tate. I figured he'd be there. He said he met Cora the other day and really liked her."

"Thanks."

She waved me off, eyes compassing the room.

"My decorator mentioned a new color for here, you know," she murmured, trailing off. "She titled it *cold blueberries.*"

I dodged free, her laugh trailing at my back.

* * *

Noah slammed into me like a boulder.

His giant arms wrapped me in a tight hug, nearly lifting my feet off the ground. I returned the embrace, to let him know he might be strong, but he'd never be stronger than his big brother.

Once he let go, I shoved him into the wall. He'd muscled

out over the last several years, sprawling like a broad-shoul-dered fighter, but I still held prowess on him.

"Two years?" I barked. "You couldn't even meet me for lunch in two years?"

He laughed. "C'mon, I texted."

I glared.

Two hands up, he said, "I'm sorry, Hawk. I'm sorry that I didn't respond a lot. I just . . . needed time. Nic kept track of me, too. I know you had an investigator on me."

"I did."

He chuckled. "Thanks. I think."

Moisture gathered in my eyes as I stared at him. Memories of our time as boys. We'd been happy at home with Mom and our other siblings, particularly when Tate left for business ventures. Red beans and rice. Jambalaya. Mom had a southern palette that fed our growing bodies. When I saw Noah, my mind filled with the scent of gumbo.

"Good to see you," I murmured huskily.

Noah smiled with a softness that I didn't forget. "You too, Hawk."

Cora stood, drawing my gaze. She wore a long-sleeved shirt with a high collar and a pair of jeans. Her hair fluttered around her shoulders, slightly damp from the wet day. Relief swelled through me as I crossed the room and brought her into my arms. She melted, tucked herself close. Minutes passed while I soaked her in.

I pulled away, gazed into her eyes. No fear lurked there. Only questions.

Wariness.

"I'll explain."

She nodded, curled her hand in mine. Relieved to see she'd made it out unscathed, I pulled her to the couch with me. Noah took a chair, sprawling his long legs out. He rested his arms on the side.

"You know Tate is dying?"

Reluctantly, I nodded. "Yes. At least, I've assumed so. I have some friends that . . . keep me apprised of his situation. I don't have details, though."

Noah barked a laugh. "Spies, like you had for me."

I shrugged.

"I only know because Tate's lawyers called me." Noah's brow furrowed into a serious stare. He leaned forward, elbow propped on his knees. "They said that Tate wanted to meet with me to discuss my inheritance in the will. I didn't trust it, to be honest, so I dug deeper. Turns out to be true. The old man is dying."

Dig deeper was a simple code for *hacked into secure systems that should have no access.* Noah had always been a whiz at the computer.

"So you came back?"

Noah shrugged. "Figured it was worth seeing you and Nic again, then meeting with whoever wanted to speak with me about the will."

"I've received no such call."

"Neither has Nic."

Curious, but not surprising. Tate played head games all the time. He had extensive wealth. Much of it locked up in holdings and stock options. Liquid assets were easy enough to find in all he had.

Because of the violent relationship between Tate and Noah, the most likely scenario would mean that when Tate died, all his wealth would go to some stupid, miserable person we all hated just so Tate could make us angry forever. A horrific political candidate, or something.

"I'm talking to Tate tomorrow," I said and tightened my hold on Cora. "You want in?"

Noah's gaze gleamed.

"You know I'll be there."

Chapter Twenty-Seven

CORA

Later that night, the darkness of Hawk's room felt like a fuzzy envelope. It wrapped around the room, closing down distractions. A heavy blanket lay over me. The weight pressed me into his mattress, anchored me against the tempestuous feeling of being in Hawk's life.

A single question haunted me.

Did I really want this life?

This up and down?

His lack of understanding, communication, presence? Hawk had mentioned leaving his company, but gave no other information after. We lightly discussed his brother, but I had known almost nothing until Noah appeared on his own.

Would Hawk leave? If he did, what would that mean for us?

I sank farther into the pillow.

Hawk and Noah's voices purred from outside the bedroom, their low, rolling sounds as comforting as the pattern of rain. More than Tate's creepy presence, the shock of Noah showing up at my side, or Hawk's teary expression as he embraced his brother, and the text messages from Cade haunted me.

The ranch.

My opportunity to surprise and assist my brother had come. What if I missed it because I lingered here for too long? Life called. I had a world to return to—one that made sense. The security of the paints, the loft, called to me.

I wanted everything to make sense again.

Stability. Even-keeled events. Knowing what would come next.

Cade.

Hawk slipped into the room, breaking through my thoughts. The sound of him shuffling around, slipping to the bathroom and brushing his teeth, created a calm soundtrack. The smell of him lingered in my nose, soothing me.

He padded over to the bed.

"Cora?"

"Yeah."

"You're awake?"

"Mm hmm."

A stir of cooler air came as he slipped between the sheets and settled next to me. We didn't touch. I turned onto my side to face him, able to see the bumps of his profile, but little else. It gave me the courage I needed to say, "I want to go back home after the gala tomorrow."

He sighed. His fingertips found my cheek through the darkness.

"That's fair."

"The news reports are finally discussing the virus, and I want to get back to prepare, just in case. I haven't seen Cade and I need to get that painting done, too. I've been getting calls about the gallery in Jackson City and Cade's ranch owner died and—"

"You have a life."

A yawning chasm of questions stretched between us.

Would this work?

Could we make it?

If the virus spread as much destruction here as it had in other places, would it force us apart? No, no virus could stand in the way of love. Hawk could, however. His obsession with work, love for challenge. Could Hawk be satisfied with a distinctly emotional relationship? The answer wasn't apparent.

"I'll have the company jet fly you back."

"I can take a regular flight, Hawk."

"I'd feel better if you didn't."

"You can buy me a first-class seat."

Weariness infused his voice. "We'll talk about it later."

Unwilling to argue, I simply nodded. Both of us had a trying day. The story of Tate and Noah, set against the backdrop of the escalating virus, pressed a heavy weight on his shoulders. I understood.

And hated it.

The warm touch of his fingers fell away. I wanted to call them back, but the mention of me going home yanked a wall up between us. Or, perhaps, just for me. I needed to find my footing again. To ground myself in the security of what I knew, set against what I didn't.

"We have the gala in the evening tomorrow," Hawk said, stiff with that business-like tone, "so I'll send James out with you to help find a dress. He knows what to look for in style. Noah and I are going to meet with Tate before the gala, so that will all be taken care of before we attend."

The words drifted through my sleepy mind.

James.

Dress.

Gala.

Should be fine.

"Mmmkay," I heard myself mumble.

Sleep beckoned.

My experience with Magree at the gallery had long since faded into the back of my mind. Hawk and I needed to talk about it. If we were going to be in a relationship—if love was truly what thrummed between us so vividly—then he had to appreciate and accept my boundaries.

Sleep called to me now, though. Too tired to bring it up, I let myself drift into the fluid darkness.

I dropped to rest, Hawk at my side.

* * *

"Miss Cora?"

An attractive, youthful face peered at me from behind tilted sunglasses the next afternoon.

Tall, with a broad sweep of shoulders, a tailored shirt, and an impeccably arranged tie. Hawk's assistant, James, was a handsome pillar of business.

Also, an unnecessary imposition.

"James?"

He smiled with teeth white as the fallen snow—nothing on earth could be *that* naturally white—and pushed his sunglasses into perfectly sculpted blonde hair. A recent trim left it clipped close to his head, but long enough to wave on top.

His hand shot out, clasping mine.

"Good to meet you. I'm here to help you find something to wear for the gala tonight."

A twist of nerves reminded me. Ah, yes. The bustle of city life never seemed to quit. Exhilarating, in some ways. Encompassing and overwhelming in others. After a night curled up in Hawk's arms, then waking to a note on the pillow next to me, I wanted *less* social time.

More Hawk time.

"Actually, I've been here for about an hour already and found a few great candidates." I held up a couple of hangers. "I was just putting them back because I decided on the one I want. Sorry that you came all this way—Hawk didn't give me your number—but I should be fine on my own."

James' gaze skated past me, to the racks at our back, as if I hadn't spoken. "A dress will be necessary, particularly for this event. Something sophisticated and understated."

"I just—"

"You appear to be an eight?"

"Um, yes."

"Definitely no yellow tones."

"What?"

"Black will have some elegance, but we can't overdo it against his tuxedo. I told him to go slate, but he didn't listen to me."

An exasperated, if not affectionate, eye roll followed. James made a noise in his throat, stepped to the other side of the store. I followed, dresses rustling at my side.

"Thank you, James," I said a little more loudly, "but I believe I've already found something to wear. There's this dress that I really loved. In terms of color, it's just right with—"

He paused, held out a hand.

"May I see it?"

Suddenly, his attractive facade didn't seem so appealing. I lifted a golden dress that draped along the front in rouched layers. A bold curvature around the hips dropped into a split near the knees. Daring, but lovely. More subtle than one might expect, yet still breathtaking.

James' brow ruffled.

"Not quite it, I think. Too yellowish in tone, you see? Feisty, yes, but not firm enough for this gala. Besides, the event is for women's heart health. We should keep it on theme and look for something red."

I gritted my teeth, trailed behind him.

"Red isn't a good color for me. It combines too much with my hair sometimes and looks—"

"I doubt that."

He shoved past an ochre dress with a long train. I suppressed the urge to ignore him, buy my dress, and leave him in the dust. As Hawk's assistant, however, I'd probably have to deal with James again. No need to put a sour taste over any relationships.

In case I ever *saw* Hawk again, at this rate.

James let out a cry. "Like this!" He whirled around a few racks away. A sparkly crimson dress, deeply red and slightly shiny, fell to about his knee. The high skirt would barely hit mid-thigh on me, and I looked at the backless dive with a little shudder.

"That looks cold."

He scoffed. "It's Texas."

I stared pointedly at him.

James replaced the dress with an aggravated sigh. "Fine. Forget that one. Here's another. It's more mauve-toned than red."

I eyed the next one.

"Any bolder and it won't be a dinner dress."

He dropped it back into the rack with an exaggerated eye roll, flittered away. I stood firm.

Nope.

Not doing this.

This is where I wouldn't allow Hawk's world to intrude on mine.

"James, stop."

Something in my firm tone must have caught his attention. His steps slowed. Reluctantly, he gazed back.

"Thank you for your time, your suggestions, and your offered help. I truly appreciate it. However, I've found the dress I want—I won't change my mind. I appreciate your insights with color, but that's something I understand well."

Something shuffled through his features, momentarily sharpening them. He stood there as if I were . . . competition. Something to defeat.

"Let's save both of us time, because I'm sure Hawk keeps you busy. I'll purchase the dress and be on my way to get ready."

"You have a hair appointment in an hour."

"No, I have a lunch appointment with Hawk."

"Not anymore. Something came up. I'll have lunch delivered to the hair salon, if you need it. I booked you at a place uptown, close to the penthouse. You'll love them. They work well with inexperienced cases."

My jaw tightened.

"Excuse me?"

"After that," he said through a long breath, "we'll get you back to the penthouse to change, then Diego will take you to the gala this evening. It'll just be best if you meet Hawk there."

"But—"

"He'll call you later." A pandering note filled his tone. "He's busy."

Rage bubbled under my skin. I drew in a deep breath through my nose, strove for patience, and tried not to snap the hanger in half with my clenched fist.

"No."

James blinked.

"Excuse me?"

"No. I'm going to pick my dress, do my hair, and find Hawk before the gala. I'm not . . . that's not how this is happening."

James paused, peered at me with a tapered gaze. "What world do you think you've entered, Cinderella?"

His question caught me off guard. Startled, I could only blink.

"What?"

"This is the world of Hawk Mercedy. You might *think* you know what you've aligned yourself with, but you don't. If you want to survive—or not burn Hawk to the ground with you—you will trust those that understand this world better than you.

"We are not in the mountains. We are not an artists' alley. This is a dinner with financial tycoons and famous socialites that some folks only dream of seeing in person or speaking with at a gala. Hawk is a pillar amongst *those* people, not your people."

All my hackles rose. If, in the depths of James' eyes, I had seen something like sincerity or concern, I might have heeded the warning. If anything except disdain or annoyance had been present, I might have backed down.

As it stood, I saw nothing except resentment.

"Are you dismissing me because you're threatened by me, James? I don't understand why we're clashing."

He turned away, jaw tight and released a barely controlled breath. Awkwardness swelled between us for several passing moments.

Unable to stand the burdened silence, I said, "I'm sorry, James, that you don't like me. I imagine you care about Hawk to stand up for him like this. How could you not? He's a wonderful man. I'm sure that you work hard to watch out for him. But this is not how I will let you treat me. I have my dress. You executed your orders. Please leave me alone."

James studied me out of the corner of his eye. A protest formed on his lips, however weak it appeared at first.

"I'm—"

"No," I said firmly. "I'm done here. Please cancel the hair appointment and leave me alone."

The barely controlled tone seemed to deflate his displeasure. He hesitated, mouth open, for only a moment before his fingers locked into fists. His teeth clenched as he spoke.

"Hawk will fire me if I leave you here. I'm supposed to pay for the dress, take you to lunch, get your hair done, and make sure you're ready for Diego at 4:30."

His response set my instincts on edge. No *wonder* James looked at me with such disdain. Hawk set him on babysitting duty.

I rolled my eyes.

"Absolutely not. I'm not twelve and I don't need someone to manage my schedule. Thank you, but he and I will have words over this. I'll let him know that I chose to leave you, and you did your job."

James said nothing.

"Are you going to leave me alone?"

He shook his head.

"Fine." I set the beloved dress on the closest rack. "Then I will leave you."

He called out to me as I charged out of the store. I felt him hustling at my back, chasing after me. As the front of the store closed in, a black-uniformed security guard caught my gaze. I hurried faster, called over my shoulder, "Leave me alone. Don't follow me. You're making me uncomfortable!"

The security guard intervened, detaining James with a growl.

I rushed to freedom.

* * *

Tears burned my eyes as I darted through downtown.

The guard would detain James, but for how long, I

couldn't be sure. I slipped away as fast as I could, dodged into a few populated crowds walking down the road, then ducked into an unobtrusive and sleepy coffee shop. The smell of espresso swamped me, reminding me of the Frolicking Moose.

My painting.

Cade.

The familiar scents eased my initial rush of fear. No, James wouldn't follow. I'd made my point clear enough.

Now, something had to be done.

Grim with resolve, I sat at a table and dug my phone out of my pocket. Furious tears remained in check while I searched for Hawk's number, then pressed *call*. Two rings later, his voicemail picked up.

I shot him a quick text.

Cora: Do you have a minute? James mentioned you couldn't make it for lunch.

No immediate reply came. I waited a minute, gazed around. Two women sat next to each other, shoulder-to-shoulder, in a booth across the way. Textbooks and notebooks sprawled in front of them. A barista yawned behind the register.

Still no reply.

A minute passed.

Four.

I called again.

No answer.

Frustrated, I searched for Cade's number, realizing with a growl that I'd need to go back and buy that dress. My hasty departure hadn't accommodated the need for elegant clothing. A shudder slipped through me at the thought of running into James again.

No. I didn't want to go back there. So, I'd have to find another one.

Two hours wasted this morning. I tapped on Cade's phone number, then pressed the phone to my ear, seeking stabilization and calm amidst the fury of questions. The same firm footing I had all of my childhood.

Cade's voice filled my head. "There's my favorite sister. Where have you been?"

The tears loosed, tightening my throat, making it almost impossible to speak. I swallowed hard, the motion painful, and sank lower into the chair. My shoulders hunched as I tried to curl away from the shop.

When no sound came, concern filled his voice.

"Cora?"

"Sorry," I croaked. "Sorry, I'm just . . . having a bad day."

His voice hardened. "What happened?"

"Nothing horrendous. I'm just . . . just a difficult day, I think. I hadn't talked to you in a while and . . ."

I need to remember who I am.

Swept up in Hawk, in glittery lights, expensive wines, lush dresses, in the whirlwind romance that side-swiped me twice. I realized just how knocked around I felt. The dizzying sensation of Hawk was safe, easy, *right* when we were together.

So far?

We hadn't been together much.

"Do I need to kick someone's ass?"

I laughed, unable to help myself. He chuckled, and I sensed a loosening in the sound.

"No. Not that."

"I came over this morning. They said you were visiting a friend."

Trust Cade not to text or call. He always had to be in person. *Gotta see your face,* he said. *Or else it doesn't mean as much.* Getting the man on a video chat was next-level miraculous. Loaves and fishes. Cade on a video call. The same, in my book.

"Sorry. I meant to text you, but things have been . . . moving sort of fast."

"Doesn't sound good."

"It's not bad."

"Then why are you crying?"

"I was just chased out of a store and I didn't get the dress that I wanted."

Attempting to make something comical out of the confrontation with James halved the tension. One day, it might be funny. For now? It was not.

"Chased out of a store? Where *are* you, Cora?"

"Texas."

He sputtered. I pictured him drinking hot, black coffee while he warmed up and ate lunch. Not for long, though. If it was noon, he'd be out with the livestock again shortly. Checking fences in the deep drifts with his favorite horse, hat perched on top of his head and cowboy boots on.

"Why are you in Texas?"

"Here with a friend."

A pause clued me into his suspicions, but before I could head them off, he asked in a tone like ice.

"Is that friend a man?"

I froze.

"Uh . . ."

Warning added a dangerous drawl to his voice. "Cora." The elongation of the vowels spoke to his intense, brotherly protectiveness. The thought of being back on the ranch with Cade sent thoughts of safety through me.

For all my life, I'd been able to run back to him. His calloused hands would hold me tight.

This time?

I wanted Hawk's sinewy arms.

Never in my life had I felt more protected by a man who was not my brother. Why did that man have to be so . . . absent? A tear dribbled down my cheek. I swiped it impatiently away, a careful eye out on the sidewalk as people rushed past.

"Who is it? What is his name? Are you safe?"

"Yes, I'm safe."

He muttered something unintelligible.

"I'm fine. There's an event he invited me to go to with him. A gala. It's why I came to Texas. The gala is tonight."

"What's his name?"

"Hawk."

"Huh."

Not in any world would Cade ever think to Google the name, nor would he draw a parallel between Hawk and Maverick. At least I had that much in my favor. Cade would *not* be happy about Hawk's elite status.

"What event is this gala for?"

"A gala for women's heart health. It's . . . rather public, with lots of cameras and people and we'll be around lots of security guards."

Not by much, but at least a little, Cade's ruffled annoyance unwound.

"That's . . . something."

Conveniently setting aside the fact that I had slept curled in Hawk's arms and bed the previous night, and I hardly knew him at all, I continued.

"I just had a bad day, Cade. Talking to you has made me feel better. I wanted to hear how you were?"

The edge had faded almost entirely when he said, "I'm glad you called. I've missed you and wanted to invite you over for dinner, but funeral preparations have kept things busy here. I'm doing fine. The old man wanted to go."

Old man Morgan, the owner of the ranch that Cade ran,

had been a sweet, wizened old guy that couldn't manage the livestock. He had spent most of his time in his house, snoring in a hard rocking chair. Applesauce cans and old coffee mugs always littered the table next to him because he refused to eat much else.

"I'm sorry, Cade."

"Ah, it's fine." The dismissive note of his voice gave a little reassurance. "Cycle of life. Anyway, when will you be back home?"

My throat tightened with another wave of tears. *There's a virus out there,* I thought of saying. *It might reach home in weeks. Could be a pandemic. This is scary. You need to prepare.*

But I didn't.

Because we didn't know that for sure, though indicators—and Hawk's breakneck pace at work—pointed that direction. A clock with a gangly, wide-eyed cat that had arms pointing to noon drew my attention. When I pulled away to glance at my screen, no text awaited.

For all intents and purposes, I had been stood up.

"Hello?"

"Oh! Sorry, Cade. I got lost in thought." I ran a hand over my face, blushing. Boy, I needed to get it together.

"When are you coming home?"

"Home? Tomorrow."

The thought sent a depressing spiral through my gut that I had to ignore, despite how much I longed for it.

Couldn't I have the life I wanted with Cade, and Hawk?

Not yet.

"Let me know. I'll come grab you at the airport."

"Thanks. I'll do that. And I appreciate the call. I need to go find a dress for the gala tonight and make a few more calls. Be safe out there."

"Always am."

"Love you."

"Love you too, squirt."

Long after the call ended, I stared out into the city. The indistinct murmur of life was a comforting melody, not to mention the steady voices of the patrons, the clink of cup against plate.

Reassured by the sound of Cade's voice, I slowly wound down from the clash with James. I clutched my phone, willing it to buzz.

When five minutes passed without a response from Hawk, I turned to a map, looked for department stores. Eventually, I'd find a dress that would more than suffice for the gala. Then I'd return to the penthouse, get ready. Ignore the sketchbook that called to me. My fingers longed to draw this rage out on the page.

Everything would be fine.

Yet, I wondered if *I* would suffice.

People didn't scare me much. Mortal position and power really meant nothing in the grand scheme of things. Whatever billionaire I spoke to at the gala would just be another person who saw things and believed things and held access to things in different ways. Like Adelaide and Trent.

Not all that different from myself.

Money is just money, Cora, Cade would say. *It's energy, that's all.*

There had been too many days of my childhood where I had been left to wonder if I was enough. Long after Mom disappeared, I'd promised myself I'd never question my value again.

Today, it had all been resurrected.

When no response to my queries for Hawk arose fifteen minutes later, I shoved the phone back into my pocket. Renewed energy filled me. I banished the wallowing feeling, grabbed my purse, tucked it under my arm, and stood.

If *this* was the life I should expect with Hawk, then I'd

need to set my own boundaries. Whether he realized it or not, he'd done it again. Attempted to placate me with stuff, throwing money and glamor and an experience at me, instead of just being there himself.

I had a dress to buy.

Then a statement to make.

Chapter Twenty-Eight

HAWK

Tate sat like a king at his own kitchen table.

His irascible brow glowered at Noah and me over the top of the gleaming cherry wood surface. A folder with documents lay across the table, set in front of him like soldiers marching to battle. Each one even with the next, perfectly spaced, like a photo opportunity instead of a last will and testament.

Without coordinating beforehand, both Noah and I wore our best suits, freshly pressed into perfect lines. Habit, really. Tate expected perfection. His voice was a startling rasp when he spoke directly to Noah.

"You came."

Noah inclined his head.

"I didn't think you would."

"I almost didn't."

"What changed your mind?"

"Curiosity."

Tate snorted. With a tilt of his head, he motioned to two chairs flanking the other side of the table. Silently, we sat, but not in the place he pointed. Tate shoved two of the papers in our direction. Seeing their identical nature, I slipped one farther down the table to Noah.

The words across the top startled me. I expected *Last Will and Testament.* What I saw was *Requirements for Inheritance.*

A dark feeling sank in my gut.

"As you know," Tate said, with a clearing of his throat. His voice lightened with the sound. "I have extensive wealth and holdings. Beyond what you're aware of or what you've been told. There's so much money it's incomprehensible. In order to bequeath it to you, I have requirements."

I skimmed the following bullet points with a sinking feeling in my chest. His top lip curled back, jaw tightened.

- *Work for Mercedy, Inc as a Board Member or Executive Team Member until retirement age.*
- *Refuse donations to the organizations listed in section 4D.*
- *Marry a woman within approved families listed in section 2.*
- *Have two heirs, at least. More if the first two are females. You must have children until a male child is born. If infertility is an issue, please see subsection 2A.*

I barked a laugh, awash with disbelief. And, in some large part, no surprise at all.

Tate.

Always invoking the most ridiculous ideas. Noah remained silent, astonished. His years apart had jaded him to Tate's malevolence and thwarted worldviews.

Tate waited patiently.

I set the paper down, turned to face Tate more fully. He should have been a wretched old man by now. Wrinkled as a raisin, perhaps coughing up blood or unable to walk or some other equally horrendous, painful experience.

None of those happened.

Dying, he might be. Dead, he was not. Either he played a solid game or he wasn't feeling the effects of whatever would kill him. Hatred bubbled inside, but I forced myself to quell it. Wishes of pain and annihilation on Tate were suppressed as well, but with greater difficulty.

"That's quite the list of requirements, Tate," I said, for lack of anything else.

"They are what they are. We don't need to draw this out. You either sign the contract or you don't."

"If we don't?" Noah asked.

Tate leaned back. "Then the money goes to Mason."

Mason.

Our cousin, youngest brother to Maverick, and an oily human being. The kind of man that smiled while he shoved a knife into your back. Mason would take the money and destroy the world with it. Buy up islands, then sink them. Flaunt his wealth. Amass food, let it spoil. Something equally horrendous.

I held few attachments to physical things in life, but the vast estates, the ability to do good in the world, momentarily arrested me. Once Tate died, assuming his contract wasn't completely ironclad, I could change the world for so many people with that wealth.

"Mason," Noah hissed.

Tate inclined his head. His laissez-faire attitude didn't fool me at all. Tate's gaze darted to me too sharply, too often. He was attempting to read my response.

Tate had always tied himself into the idea of the familial succession of his wealth. He wanted me to want it as much as him. Eldest son, leading in his footsteps. Continuation of company and culture beyond his death.

Did Tate fear death?

I hoped so. I hoped he wallowed in something that terrified him. Tate spent his lifetime cruelly amassing all this power, only to die in the end. It must rankle him that he couldn't control death, either.

Noah ripped the paper in half.

"Your contract can go to hell."

He stood up, shoved away, and strode out. The sound of a door closing behind him echoed in the room. Tate leaned to one side of his chair, elbow on the armrest, and regarded me with a curious question.

I met his gaze.

"I figured he'd throw a fit like a child and leave," Tate said evenly. "He was a spoiled brat as a teenager, and he's proven it now as an adult. Well, he had the chance. Now let's really get down to business. Noah might whittle away billions of dollars to go live wherever he's gone, but I know you have better sense in that head of yours.

"You've never been excited about the path that I wanted for you, Hawk. You were hell-bent on proving yourself away from me, and you've done it. M. Ventures is a sprawling success, and it's no secret.

"But now it's time for you to get into an even bigger game, and you're ready. I know you are. You lack a few areas that I can help you with before I die, if you're willing to take help."

The normalcy of Tate's tone startled me. Tate had always spoken to me the way one would a disobedient child. Reprimanding and sharp, as if he could have explained nothing well enough.

Now, there was a cadence of . . . acceptance in the words. Tate was trying to tell me I'd arrived. I was *good enough* to pick up Tate's vast empire and continue on with it.

Or desperation bred a beggar.

The vast size of such a behemoth created an oh-sotempting draw, if only because of all the good I could do with it. In some ways, the world would never be the same.

"There's a small list of organizations that I have requested my legal staff not allow any money to go to—some of them won't surprise you. As long as you agree to my requirements, which ensure a powerful legacy to our family name, you'll always be on top, Hawk. Always. No more fighting or grappling for your position. No more attempting to prove yourself. You've arrived, my boy."

I skimmed the words again. Tate required a signed contract in order for his eldest son to receive the inheritance. No doubt he had a legal team that would monitor the financial transactions, withhold certain amounts, and hold authority to remove all access to holdings and credit them toward Mason if I didn't listen.

Without Tate, I'd have an overly comfortable life. My holdings and assets would support me for lifetimes.

But all the rest of this . . .

My gaze was arrested on one line at the front of the page. *Marry a woman within approved families listed in section 2.*

Cora wouldn't be on that list. I didn't need to look to know that. Tate's meddling with her, his texts, the photos of us outside the gallery, made a lot more sense in light of these requirements. Sick old man had been scoping out who I had an interest in.

Though tempted to ask for a copy of the contract, I slipped the paper back toward Tate.

"You already know I won't do this."

"Oh?"

"You know about Cora. You did your own investigations. I have a feeling that bullet point appeared on this paper *after* you saw me with her. Were you staking me out to see if I was dating anyone?"

A damning silence followed.

Finally, a sigh.

"I always have eyes on you, Hawk."

I frowned. Well, that was an ominous idea.

"She's not used to this kind of wealth, Hawk. It's not very kind of you to ask her to join this world when she has no idea what—"

"You'll never convince me of that."

"It's not my job to convince you," Tate immediately countered. His voice heated. He leaned closer, as if he looked forward to arguing. "I will see this wealth and property through to the end. *That* is my job, and that's what I'm doing here."

"This is insane."

"This is business."

"We're family."

"You claim that now."

"I've always claimed that."

"Family doesn't abandon each other," Tate cried with rising fury. His hazel eyes snapped. "Family doesn't go off on their own, support an abusive brother, forget their father is alive while they create their own empire. That is *not* family."

I pressed my lips together. Desperately, I wanted to believe that none of this was true. That Tate wasn't such a demoralized old man that he wrote up something as ridiculous as this contract.

Deep inside, though, I couldn't lie.

None of this surprised me.

"Noah has already walked out," I said. "You're bastard enough not to give Nicola the inheritance just because she's a woman. So what are you going to do, Tate, when I refuse you again? You'll really give this to Mason, just like that? I have my doubts it would be so simple."

Tate blinked once, twice. Without tearing his eyes from

me, he pressed his fingertips onto a folder to his right and slid it across the table. I accepted it.

When it opened, I almost vomited.

Images, words, headlines, bold fonted, assaulted me all at once. Cora in the art gallery, smiling at me. The park. Walking into my building. An image with my arm around her shoulders as we walked into the ice cream parlor. Snapshots in which we looked happy together. Below those lay paragraphs, typed in article fashion. Headlines sprawled around.

Baseball cap billionaire romance?

Mercedy money loves a pauper.

Girlfriend of billionaire comes from drug-infested home.

I closed my eyes, sucked in a stabilizing breath.

"Tell me you haven't—"

"Already with the editors."

I clenched the end of the table with one hand, opened my gaze back onto Tate. A bright light filled his rheumy eyes now. The light of someone who had just won. Maybe that's all Tate wanted all along.

Maybe this was just a ploy for revenge. A way to get back at me for having the courage to make my own life.

Or a manipulative ploy.

"Let me guess," I murmured. "If I sign the contract, all of them go away."

Tate snapped two fingers. "You got it." His gaze flickered to the clock. "You have two minutes."

"You wily old bastard."

Tate said nothing.

My mind streamed with harried thoughts. The quick formation of pros and cons. What would Cora say?

We'll get through it together, I imagined.

Would she forgive me for this publicity? The breach of privacy into her and Cade's life? Pictures of a broad-shouldered man on a horse lay amongst all the others, with a mountainous backdrop that appeared just like Pineville. Dirty old man. Tate hadn't held back.

There was only one way to win. And in doing so, I might lose Cora. No matter how ugly it would get in the papers and for her, it would be worse to walk away.

Cora, I silently pleaded, *please forgive me.*

I grabbed the contract and tore it in half. When I stood, shoving the chair back, it clattered.

"Tell Mason to be happy with his billions."

Tate stared, lips parted, hollow cheeks half open as I turned and strode out the door. Halfway out, I grabbed my phone to call Cora. She didn't answer.

I called again.

Noah met me outside.

Wordlessly, we fell into stride toward the waiting car.

* * *

James didn't quite meet my gaze when he repeated the words.

"I don't know where Cora is."

I stood, arms folded across my chest, legs braced. A glimmering skyline lay at my back with a sun that sank ever-closer to setting. The office windows radiated a slight chill that kept me grounded.

Noah waited behind me. Nicola was in her own office, cruising the headlines for whenever Cora's life would spill. Knowing Tate, he'd have convinced the scandal sheets to post it as soon as possible.

My gaze flickered to the clock.

Four o'clock.

The gala started in an hour and I stood in my office, tangled in half a tuxedo. I undid the last button, my wary gaze frozen on James. He squirmed under the intense stare. The stink of being around Tate, his hideous offer, still hung around me. I wanted to shower, but there wasn't time.

"What does that mean, James?"

His jaw tightened.

"She left the store because she didn't agree with my suggestions." A twitch rippled over his cheek. "I haven't been able to find her since. She didn't answer her phone when I tried to call her."

"The penthouse?"

"Empty."

"Has she returned to it?"

"I couldn't be sure when I stopped to check. The staff had nothing to say about it. Not that doorman, anyway, but he seemed like he might be covering for her."

Behind me, Noah whistled. "Lost her," he muttered. "Bad deal, my dude."

James paled. He had to know he'd get fired over this if I discovered nefarious treatment on his part. Fear, more than irritation, consumed me now. Why would Cora leave the store when James suggested something? That didn't sound like her. A missing piece existed in this story.

The thought of all the things that could happen to her, alone in downtown, sent a spasm of terror through me. Someone could hurt her.

Should I call hospitals?

The police?

The frantic thought knocked me off the downward trajectory. No, this had gotten out of hand. What would I say to the police? *I can't find my girlfriend.*

No.

Was she even my girlfriend? Such a reductive phrase wasn't

big enough. The term was insulting compared to how I felt about her. Cora was so much more than that.

I loved her in a way I had never loved another woman. In a panicked, rushed, unable to deny it sort of way that had its own magnetic pull. A train I couldn't stop.

Too much lay undecided and unknown between us for me to answer that question, and that irritated me further.

"Hawk, can I be frank?" James asked.

"About what?" I reached for my phone. Cora hadn't answered my calls earlier, but I figured she was busy getting her makeup done or something.

Isn't that what most of my dates did?

Cora wasn't anything like them, though. With James assigned to taking care of her, I thought nothing of her lack of presence until now.

When he showed up without her.

"About Cora." James swallowed hard. "I just . . ."

I paused halfway through unlocking my phone screen, glanced up. James hesitated again, his hands opening and closing at his side. A sheen of sweat popped up on his forehead.

"What about her?"

"I don't think . . . she doesn't really fit, you know? She's not like the women you normally date. They're more practiced with this lifestyle. They know the drill. How to show up, how to entertain, that sort of thing. Cora doesn't know what she's getting into with this gala. She doesn't know anyone there, who they are, why they're important. What will she say to people there?"

My already bubbling irritation nearly sloshed over. With careful control, I said, "That's the whole point, James. She's different."

In frustration, he spit out, "It's not fair to her."

Doubts sprinted through me at the words. Tate said something similar, but held ulterior motives.

"I'll find her, James. Thank you."

With a wave, I dismissed him.

When James made a move toward the door, a knock came.

"Come in."

The handle clicked, then opened slowly. Eventually, it widened all the way. My breath caught.

Cora stood there, resplendent in a glimmering blue dress that swept over one shoulder and left the other bare. It tucked in around her waist in a swoop, accenting the roundness of her hips. Shimmering folds dropped to the ground.

Subtle.

Exquisite.

Her hair lay in strands around her shoulders, the slightly auburn color bright. A necklace that sparkled—matching an elegant set of earrings in her ears—drew my gaze to her lovely shoulders.

Doesn't really fit?

She would *own* that gala.

Behind her, the chaos of my outer office had calmed. Three people stared at her from behind, mouths open. Never had a woman that I dated come to my office. Certainly not a gala date, and not someone I actually cared about. The only person who had any connection to my personal life that had graced these halls was Nicola.

Panic filled me.

Cora.

In my office.

The crossover of my life. This could *not* happen. I sped to the door, grabbed the handle, and closed it most of the way.

"What are you doing here?"

She opened her mouth to reply, but paused as James and

Noah shuffled out around her. James stopped. "You look lovely, Cora."

Surprise bubbled up in her bright gaze. With a half smile, she nodded. James continued on his way out. Once Noah quietly closed the door behind them, I breathed easier.

Cora slid away, blithely stepping out of my reach. The defiant tilt of her chin caught my attention. So did her smoky eyes, darkened lashes. For a moment, I couldn't look away.

I knew this Cora, but I didn't. Her breathtaking appearance made it hard to breathe. Being in her presence again reminded me how stupid all this other stuff really was.

"Hawk, we need to talk."

"We do. You left James at the store. Why? I've been worried about you. He just said that you didn't like his suggestions. And you can't come here. It's . . ."

It's not safe.

I almost ran a hand through my hair, but stopped myself in time. The headlines would land any moment and she didn't even know.

Tate had eyes everywhere, and Tate loved any opportunity to gain some upper hand. Publicity. Pictures. Whatever put Cora into the public eye would give him the chance to act. He'd already lashed out against me, and lost. Now he'd become truly wild and fight me through Cora.

But . . . hadn't he already done that? What more damage could he do to Cora than what was about to land?

I couldn't bear this agony.

"I'm sorry," I said quickly. "I'm sorry. This isn't fair. You don't have all the information."

Cora's wild edge calmed slightly.

"Same for you."

Before this moment, I'd never realized that my fear over the world seeing Cora, knowing her value, was actually more about Tate than anything else. Now, Tate knew. He played his cards and lost. The pressure loosened across my chest. The worst had come, and I'd survived.

We'd get through the rest together.

Cora's brow wrinkled. She licked her lips, glossy but not painted. Like an invitation that made me want to yank her into my arms and lay a heartfelt kiss on her.

"What did James tell you?" she asked calmly.

I repeated his quick explanation, without the *not good enough* part. She sighed, shaking her head.

"Hawk, I left that store because I don't require a babysitter."

"Babysitter?"

"I wanted *you*. Not . . . a credit card and hairdressers and . . ."

"You paid for the dress?"

That piece had to cost hundreds. Did she have that working as an artist and paying her own rent? I didn't even know.

Should I know that?

Her nostrils flared. "Yes. Dammit, Hawk. Are you listening?"

"I'm sorry, I'm trying to understand, Cora."

"Are you?"

Frustration sparked through her like firecrackers.

"You stood me up for our lunch date without explanation. I understand unprecedented events are on the way, but you can send me a text. You can answer a phone. Instead, you sent an assistant and basically ordered him to babysit me. Believe it or not, I don't need someone to dress me."

Astonishment filled me with a cloudy-headed feeling. Irritation followed. Why did she over-analyze everything I did? A kind gesture was a kind gesture. Who cared if I spent money on her? I wanted her to have a great experience.

"I wasn't trying to have you babysat, Cora. I was trying to be nice."

"When you ignored my calls, my texts?"

"I was—"

I paused, unable to complete that. *In a meeting with Tate that is going to change your life forever, and you might hate me.*

I'd created this whole mess. I hadn't been up front with her from the beginning, and now she had no idea what really was going on.

How could I possibly unload the truth on her now?

"You were what, Hawk?" Cora cried. Tears sparkled in her eyes. "Work is all you've done since I arrived, unless it benefits you. We went to dinner—because you could close a deal. You took me to the art gallery, because you needed time off. You never let me in, Hawk. The walls around your work life are too high for me to scale, and I won't be shut out. For all I know, you sell hot dogs on a corner stand."

A dark feeling welled up inside me. It moved fast as lightning, spurred on by the rage and frustration Tate inspired just hours ago. One I didn't quite know how to handle. It filled all the empty spaces, brought shadows to the bright places. The sinews and rage and simmering angst that feared losing Cora above all else.

Beneath it, the truth stung.

She wasn't entirely wrong, though my motivations hadn't been so macabre. I didn't tell Cora anything. Not about my impending exit strategy and desire to form a life with her. Tate and his machinations. She knew about Noah only because he showed up.

I'd messed up.

Yet, I'd tried so hard.

"This is how you see it?" I asked quietly.

Cora softened for a moment. Her lips pulled down into a contemplative expression before they became firm again.

"Honestly? Yes. But I don't think it's that simple. I think you're afraid of something, Hawk, and you won't tell me what it is. You don't trust me, and I won't be in a relationship that has no trust."

"I see."

"Do you?"

"Yes," I snapped. "I see."

I stepped back, bobbling with the words that I wanted to say. None of them would come out. What was there to say?

Wouldn't this be better, anyway?

If Cora hated me, we could break up. Tate's power over her life would dissipate. There would be headlines, but I'd be able to tell them they were false. Tate fed them a lie, and Cora would fade into history as a fluke. Perhaps, with the right wording and influence, I could inspire a retraction in the paper.

To live without Cora, though?

The worst.

A bright and burning question hummed beneath all of this.

Was James—even Tate—correct?

Was Cora ready for my life?

"This is who I am, Cora."

"I know. I know, Hawk. That's what worries me, because I can't live with it."

"What do you want? I'll give you anything you desire. The world can be yours. You want an island? It's yours. You want a car? I'll have it tonight."

Tears filled her perfect eyes, shimmering against all the glitter that was Cora.

"I want *you*, Hawk."

"You have me."

"I don't."

Tension tripled in my chest. I couldn't look at her,

meeting her gaze so full of hope. Tate filled my mind. Flashing lights. Paparazzi. Headlines. We were already too late to stop the news—I'd chosen my path.

Perhaps the wrong one, after all.

"I don't want anyone but you, Cora." My breath sped up. "I want to come home to you every night. Want to see your face in the morning and spend the day with you. But it's not that easy."

"It's not that hard."

"Give me time? I can't explain it now, not before the gala. There's too much to dive into and people are expecting me. Tonight, I will lay it all out. I just . . . I need this one more event."

The words brought the depth of her point all the way into my chest.

Her frustration.

Oh. This is exactly what she meant.

The irritation in her features soothed to something else. Pain. Such a quick shift startled me. It couldn't signal anything good.

I stepped closer.

"Please, Cora? Noah will back me up. You'll understand. We'll get through everything that's about to happen together."

Her gaze narrowed.

"What? What's about to happen?"

Something in my tone must have made her realize the urgency behind my words. I let out a deep breath.

"Tate found out about you."

A perplexed expression crossed her face. "Tate? Of course he did. He saw me at the park. No, he *found* me there."

"Yes, he . . . knew who you were when he sat next to you that day at the park, obviously. But he'd already done research into you. He's trying to use you to manipulate me, so he sent photos and information about you to massive news syndicates, no doubt. Gossip columns, those places."

All the color left her face. I wanted to reach for her, but froze. All of this had come out wrong. If I had to explain anything first, it was my real and deep love for her. I needed to convey my willingness to give up everything in this world, but I had to do it safely.

Instead, the compulsion to warn her ran the show.

"He's having the details published tonight, I think. Maybe tomorrow. Nicola is watching for the first ones to hit, and so is Noah. There . . . were images of Cade and us and—"

"Cade!" she cried in horror. "What does that mean?"

"I don't know yet."

Staying calm was a feat I thought beyond myself by now. Somehow, I rallied together, holding her traumatized gaze.

"Who will see it?" she asked.

"Many people who don't matter at all. Please, Cora, we can talk about this tonight. You can stay home from the gala. We'll . . . figure it out. We'll do it together. You and me, right?"

She backed up until her spine hit the door. Tears shimmered in her bright eyes. She shook her head, swallowing. A tear trailed free.

"I'm sorry, Hawk. I can't."

"Cora?"

"I can't do this anymore. I can't pretend to be someone that I'm not. Maybe James is right. Maybe I'm not made for your world."

"Cora, please—"

"Leave me alone, Hawk!"

With a sob, she fled.

Chapter Twenty-Nine

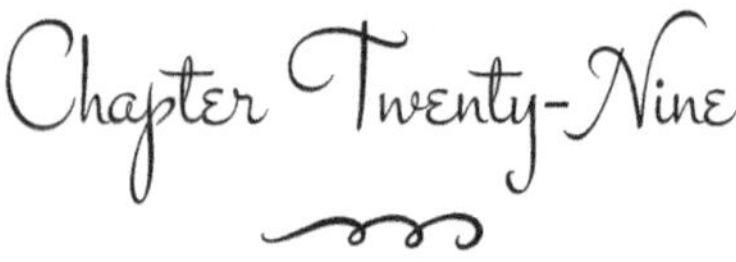

CORA

Tears streamed down my face as I hurried away from the building. My right heel broke. I let out a cry, stumbled, and righted myself by holding onto a stop sign. With a wrench, I jerked the shoes off, then ran.

I didn't know where I wanted to go, I just went. Hawk's stony expression, like ice, shot through my veins. He looked like a totally different person when he talked about Tate.

Dangerous.

Slick and brilliant in a different way.

Doubts followed me down the road, past people staring in shock at my shoeless, elegant attire. I ignored the more lurid gazes—perhaps it hadn't been the most intelligent thing to rush through downtown in this elegant gown.

Certainly not barefoot.

A cheap cafe drew my gaze with a bright neon sign. I hurried inside, slipped into a booth, and crouched down so no one could see me as they passed. Thankfully, I reached into my bra where I'd stashed my phone, my credit card, and my license.

Hawk called.

I ignored it.

A server came up. I ordered a cup of coffee to get rid of her and discreetly wiped my cheeks. My fingers trembled as I dismissed another call from Hawk, then opened my text messages.

Cora: I'm coming home. Can you pick me up?
Cade: You bet. What time?

Great question.

I navigated online, perused flights. A far-too-expensive flight would take me right back to the mountains in less than three hours. I had less than two hours to get to the airport.

On my own, thank you very much, Hawk.

Wiping the tears free again, I thanked the server, purchased the ticket online, and had a sip of coffee. Hawk had to go into a box. Stuff him away. Noah. Tate. The gala.

Later.

Cade wouldn't have looked at headlines, magazines, nothing like that. He wouldn't know. People in Pineville might. Leslie, Dahlia, they might see whatever Tate sent. I could imagine Leslie's welcoming hug and teared up all over again.

I needed to get out of here.

Ten minutes later, my rideshare arrived. I headed to the airport.

Alone.

* * *

Winter skies awoke me.

Twirling snowflakes. Slushy puddles. The smell of linseed oil and turpentine. I savored each scent, luxuriating under heavy down blankets in a comfortable, familiar bed. The pillow lay cold where I didn't touch it.

Home.

My eyes opened to the sound of rhythmic rapping on the door downstairs. With a groan, I rolled over.

The loft remained in the same state it had been when I left. Wide-open windows, freezing cold climes. Mountains in the distance, hovering over a sparkling lake. While I loved the majesty of the city, nothing spoke to my soul quite like the Frolicking Moose.

"Cora?"

Cade's voice called through the doors. I slipped out of bed, grabbed a fleece jacket, and hurried past my table. Printed, online magazine articles splayed across the top. I'd found them last night. No doubt there would be newspapers today, too. So many outlets, which said nothing of the social media chatter about me, Hawk. Sometimes Cade. A few articles featured my mother, but had no photography to back it up.

Seeing images of my radiant gaze riveted on Hawk, our casual encounters splayed for everyone else to witness. Those captured moments should have been ours, and ours alone.

Terrifying that they weren't.

The close walls of the loft lent a false sense of security. Here, I could hide for weeks. Finish the canvas, ignore the press of the world until the tide rolls on. Quell my aching heart that yearned for Hawk.

The cold floor sent shocks through the bottom of my feet as I hustled down the twirling stairs and unlocked the door.

Tears leaped to my eyes at the sight of Cade. He stepped through the door, shaking his big shoulders free of snow. Two cups of to-go coffee, my favorite croissant pastry, and a bag full of other food—all for his voracious appetite—filled his hands.

He grinned a tilted smile that reminded me of a little boy. Snow drifted off his suede brown cowboy hat.

"Hey squirt."

I stepped inside his hold, coffee and all. He staggered back a step, caught himself, and stood there, coffee and pastries and me in his arms.

Tears spilled over my eyes and dripped down my cheek. He smelled like hay and horses and earth and everything that comforted me all the way to the bone. Like homemade soup after a cold, rainy ride.

"Everything all right? Have a good sleep?"

"No."

"Let's sit." He gave a resigned sigh. "We have things to talk about."

* * *

The loft felt bigger, less empty, with Cade occupying so much of it.

The heavy tread of his boots as they crossed the floor, the way he cleared his throat, spoke softly, filled my ravaged heart. Though he'd picked me up from the airport the night before, we said little.

While I had a sip of coffee, he cleared all the magazine articles, dumped them in the trash, and settled into the chair across from me.

At first, I trembled at the thought of telling him about his breached privacy, my broken heart. I thought he wouldn't take it well. He appeared no worse for wear. He spilled a smorgasbord of food in front of him. A giant to-go cup of coffee lay near his right hand. He picked up a melty breakfast sandwich, looked at me, and nodded.

I told him everything.

From the moment Hawk arrived to the embarrassing flight

home last night, where I wore an elegant evening gown, had bloodshot eyes, half-done makeup, a broken heel, and not a bag to my name.

The relief when Cade picked me up had been palpable. He asked no questions, just brought me home to cry myself to sleep.

Now, he listened without interruption until the very end. His expression didn't waver when I mentioned Hawk's flinty gaze and cold mannerisms after he told me.

By the time I finished, stopped only by sips of life-restoring coffee, the taste so familiar to Frolicking Moose it felt like coming home, my voice turned hoarse. Cade leaned back, swirling the dredge of coffee in his to-go cup.

"Wow, Cora."

Tears filled my eyes again.

"It's such a mess."

"Well, yeah." He shrugged. "But we'll get through it."

The Cade-catchphrase I had always loved. The one that I teased him relentlessly over, but desperately clung to at the same time.

Wasn't that what Hawk said?

Deepening love for my brother bottomed me out again. What would I have done without Cade? He was steadfast and calm. The stability in my constant storm. While I went out and made life decisions that would probably make Cade shudder, he remained as steady as the tide.

"I'm sorry, Cade. I never wanted this for us. Or Mom," I tacked on wearily. "A few articles mentioned her."

He snorted. "Well, if Tate is powerful enough to track Mom down, then good luck. It might be good to see her again. I'm not worried about her. Not even sure she's alive, to be honest. I'm more concerned about you."

His piercing gaze met mine. The strength of his jaw, his resoluteness. I drank it all in with relief.

Stable landing.

Questions about what Hawk was doing, how he coped with the headlines, how the gala went, buzzed through my mind. Cade's gaze tapered as he stared across the room at my painting. Seeing it again had almost broken me. I loved it. I hated it.

"I wanted the money to help you buy your own ranch," I blurted out. "That commission will top out an account where I've saved over $20,000 for you."

Cade blinked his long lashes. "What are you talking about, my own ranch?"

"I want to help you buy your own so you don't have to work for someone else. Don't you want the ranch you're working at now?"

He chuckled. "Yes, but that's my business, not yours."

"Cade, you paid for my school."

"I did."

"You didn't go to school so that I could go."

"Nah." He shrugged one shoulder. "I didn't want to go to college, not when I enjoyed working the horses so much. If anything, I would have become a veterinarian, and that was just too much school and not enough outdoor time. Didn't appeal to me all that much."

"And *my* school was tens of thousands of dollars."

He spread his hands. "So? It bought me the end that I wanted. You living a happy life doing what you want. Money is money, Cora. It's energy, right? We use it to represent our time. Sometimes, we use that money to show how much we love people. Me sending you to college was a way for me to show you I love you."

The phrase struck a chord deep inside. Hadn't Noah said something similar? *Money is money.* Was I the only one stressing about money and what it meant?

"But I knew you loved me," I whispered. "You took care of me. Kept me safe. You played games with me."

"Those damn games," he muttered, laughing. "I only played them because I knew it made you feel loved. Honestly." His brow lifted. "I *hate* playing games."

His admission made me giggle, but the hilarity quickly passed.

"Really?"

He nodded. "When I could help you with college, I felt like I'd really taken care of you. Shown you how much I loved you. It's just me though, Cora. You have your own way of giving and receiving love."

A dark pit opened inside of me.

Oh, no.

Sweet heavens, had I totally messed up with Hawk because of an insecurity around people spending money on me? Hawk generously gave me things that I saw more as a debt to be repaid, less a show of love.

All this time, he *had* been showing me he cared, just . . . not the way I wanted. It counted, though I hadn't understood it.

"Ah, crap," I muttered.

Cade smirked, tossed the rest of his coffee back, and swallowed.

"Love sucks, Cora. You'll get through. The two of you will figure it out, I wager. Hopefully, before this virus hits."

"Cade, about the ran—"

He leaned forward, cutting me off. "Cora, I appreciate the kindness in your gesture and your plans, more than you know. But I never wanted you to pay me back for your college and yes, I want the ranch, but I don't need the money."

My eyes widened. "Really?"

"Really. I've been working for the old guy since you left for college. That family loves me. Right before he died, he told me he left the whole thing to me. Whether that's true remains to be seen, as he said some wild things those last few weeks. His granddaughter is coming out to hear the reading of the will in a week or two, so we'll find out then . . ."

He trailed away.

I laughed, unable to help myself. "You're kidding. Someone is just going to give you a ranch?"

"It's a bitty thing, but has lots of room for growth. The old guy just didn't have it in him. I wanted to press it farther, expand more, but the family wasn't excited about that. I think they didn't want bigger problems that they'd have to take care of. Either way, if I get the ranch, I also have some savings. All right?"

I nodded, swallowing.

"Then . . . what can I do to show you how grateful I am?"

"Be happy, Cora. Whatever that means to you. We got ourselves out of the situation with Mom. It's our job to do better. We live happy, healthy, functioning lives and we do it together. That's what we do."

Tears welled back up.

"What about the articles? The reports?"

He scoffed. "Who reads that crap, anyway? It'll blow over."

"But Hawk?"

"If he's a good one, he'll come back." Cade planted his hands on the edge of the table and pushed away. "I'll bet you he does soon enough. If he doesn't? Then he's a damned fool, because there's no woman better than you, Cora."

Chapter Thirty

HAWK

"Well," Nicola drawled. "Let's just say that the gala was a smashing success. The fact that you donated five million dollars instead of showing your pretty face certainly helped."

I fought the urge to kick her out of my office.

Instead, I leaned farther back in the chair, closed my eyes, and fought a groan. Why were mornings so bright?

Why hadn't I returned to the penthouse?

Another night, asleep on my desk, left my neck in a kinked mess. I rubbed it out with a moan.

Right.

Because Cora's presence lingered in the penthouse. I could smell her when I walked in, remember her in my bed, and couldn't stand it.

"Sleep well?" Nicola quipped.

"Shut up."

"I have given the official press release about you stepping down as CEO and me stepping up. For good measure, I had one sent right to Tate through his legal team, just to be sure he received it."

The vindictive pleasure in her voice almost made me

laugh. I forced myself to stand as I rubbed the sleep from my eyes with the heel of my hand.

Coffee, and a high-protein breakfast, would get me going again. It was my go-to for those late nights that Nicola and I stayed at work, helping to push out a new initiative or prepare for a new market.

Caffeine might not touch the depth of my frustration and misery, however. I didn't want any of this. None of it mattered when set against the glittering glamor of my heart. She walked around outside of me, in the world.

Without me.

The discordant note it rang in my chest had no end in sight. Nicola's continuing updates trailed to the back of my mind, where a new idea sprang. A brilliant idea, perhaps.

Or a desperate one.

"You're taking over already, right?" I asked.

"What?"

"Why wait? Let's start today."

"Hawk, there's a month and a quarter left. I—"

"Do you need that long?"

Flummoxed, she could only stare for a full five seconds. The cogs turned in her mind.

"Ah, no."

"What about tomorrow?"

"Tomorrow? Hawk, we just announced it! The release is still hot. Our social media team—"

"Doesn't matter. No one has to know that you're in control. I'll turn things over to you and be available for the next month while maintaining the facade of being here."

"What about the COO?"

"You already have someone picked out and primed."

She grumbled, though it was half hearted. "So?"

"You're ready, Nicola. The company is hitting an

upheaval, anyway, with the virus coming. Might as well do it all at once. Plus, you can start to redecorate!"

"Why?" she asked quietly. "What's with the change in heart?"

"Cora."

"You're giving it up for her?"

"Nah. I'm giving it up for me."

Softness overcame her. Nicola had Tate's intensity of expression—heaven help the board when she came to bat without me there—but none of his harshness. Her vivacious attitude, which only seemed to brighten with pressure, was otherworldly compared to the dull funk Tate presented to the world.

"Is Cora still a player in this game?" she asked with a tart rise of her brow. She pursed her lips in a move so like our mother, I almost laughed.

"I lost Cora because I'm an idiot, but I won't let it stay that way. I'm going after her, and I'd really rather not have a company resting on my shoulders while I do it."

"What are you going to say?"

"Everything." I stacked my hands on my hips. "I've been an idiot, Nic. Such an idiot. I should have told her about Tate, but I didn't want to scare her."

"Scare her or scare her off?"

"Off."

She winced.

"I know, and that was only one of my stupid mistakes. It would be a miracle if she gave me another chance. Almost too much to ask for."

"Almost," she said mildly.

I shot her a glance.

A white-toothed smile wreathed her expression, providing a moment of courage.

"Good for you, Hawk. Also, please leave whenever you

like."

"Now?"

"Yes, now! Go. I'll handle the discussions and questions over the press release. My team is already ready. Tomorrow, we can touch base on a few points I'll need help with, and you'll need to attend the next board meeting, but that's all doable."

"Really?"

She rolled her eyes. "Don't be annoying! Go! You have a woman to chase and a new life to live. Besides, my decorator is ready to do something with these windows, and I'd really rather deal with the transition before the virus hits Texas, if you don't mind."

I paused to feel it out.

Did I mind Nic willingly taking over? We had an entire transition plan mapped out that stretched four months wide, but was it necessary?

No.

People would protest my lack of visibility, but with the virus sweeping the nation, no one would notice a hasty CEO transition. Not while Nicola rocked this. She'd achieve growth for the company and desired outcomes for all our clients and the healthcare systems.

Nicola had been doing this at my side for years. The only person who knew the company better than me. I'd be there to help her through the problems when they cropped up—if she needed me at all.

Time to let it go.

"It's yours, Nic."

Her grin broadened. "Go get your girl, Hawk. It's time that one of us has a happy ever after, you know, because Noah and I keep flopping around like dying fish. James will pack your stuff and I'll have all the rest sent to your penthouse."

"Call the jet for me?"

She scoffed, gaze on her phone. "Already on it, brother."

* * *

Just like last time, I packed only a backpack.

A few changes of clothes, my laptop, charging cord, shave cream. The basics. Cora might want nothing to do with me. She could turn me away, or not come down from the loft, like she'd refused the chopper.

And maybe not.

That tiny hope propelled me through my hasty packing, a quick lunch, and a call to Diego. As I reached for the doorknob to leave, a flash of something caught my eye. I paused, glanced down.

A pad of paper lay on a shelf at the bottom of the coffee table. I strode around the couch to tug it free. Cora set it there. Noah, who had packed and sent her things back to Pineville, must not have seen it.

I flipped it open.

A sensation not unlike guilt crept up on me, as if caught reading my little sister's diary. Sketches filled the interior. Their black-and-white beauty came from the rough edges, undefined background. Cora drew from the grittiness of real life. That was obvious in the strange subjects that stopped her.

A bird on a ledge.

A woman standing tall and rigid near a brick wall. Each brick, carefully shaded, added to the overall effect of the building at her back. Her hat covered her eyes, lined with wrinkles.

Toward the back, I found myself. Portions of me. My neck and shoulder. What must have been my hands twined around her own? A profile as I looked out a window—at the loft's broad windows. No background existed, just white.

Curiosity filled me.

Never my eyes. With every page I turned, it became more clear. Always something else. My stance. My jaw. The back of my shoulders. The lobe of my ear down to the curve of my neck.

Pictures and fractals.

Is this how she saw me?

In pieces, not whole. Part of a man. Regret stewed through me. She was right. I hadn't given her all of me. Not really. I'd thrown money at her to make her want to stay, but Cora wasn't that person. She didn't find security in wealth, like other women.

She found security in *me*.

I should be flattered, but I couldn't imagine what she saw in me as it was. Cora deserved more than I could give. But damn, if I wouldn't try to give her the best every day we had left. With determination, I carefully placed the sketchbook in my backpack, zipped it up, and headed out the door. I reached for my phone to call Diego. He answered breathily.

"Mr. Hawk?"

"Hey Diego, can you meet me downstairs? I need a ride to the airport."

"Ah . . ."

He trailed off.

"Diego?"

"Mr. Hawk, I cannot."

"Why not?"

I stepped outside the penthouse, reached for the elevator down button. The whirring buzz of the elevator ascending was already active.

"Diego?"

"Mr. Hawk, you're cutting out."

"No, I'm not, Diego."

"I can't hear you," he sang, and the scratchy sound of his own attempts to imitate a poor connection followed. I rolled my eyes.

"Diego."

The long drawl did nothing to inspire fear.

"Mr. Hawk, please. I can't hear you say my name."

"Then how do you know I'm saying your name?"

A pause.

"Mr. Hawk, I must go. I'm drowning."

"Diego, you're in a car!"

"A tornado, Mr. Hawk. It's headed right for me."

I gazed back. "Blue sky," I called. "Nice try. Are you drunk, Diego?"

He gasped. "Mr. Hawk, I would never!"

"Thought you couldn't hear me," I said with a smug sense of satisfaction—and deepening confusion. Why was he acting this way?

The elevator beeped.

"Mr. Hawk, I'm . . . I cannot . . . you are breaking up!"

He ended the call.

The elevator doors split open, and my heart leaped into my throat.

Cora stood there, peering at me. She had bloodshot eyes and her hair down round her shoulders the way I loved. A single backpack slung over her shoulder. The charcoal stains on the tips of her fingers meant she'd been drawing again. She wore a pair of jeans and a t-shirt and sandals and I just wanted to feel the curve of her in my arms.

She stared, wide eyed.

"Hawk?"

"Cora?"

The elevator beeped as the doors slid closed. With a squeak, she threw herself forward. They stopped and banged into her arm. She readjusted a backpack strap and hustled free. Hesitation filled her every movement.

I tried to recover my slamming heart.

"Cora," I breathed. "What are you doing here?"

"I'm sorry, I didn't expect you at the penthouse. I-I

thought you'd be at work. I was going to plan my next step then."

The words *there is no more work* lodged in my throat.

"Were you just with Diego, by chance?"

Sheepishly, she nodded. The blunt strands of her hair swayed. "Yes, I asked if he could pick me up."

"That makes a lot more sense."

"I came to apologize," she said hastily. "And get a few things that Noah didn't send. Thank you for the stuff."

Her awkward mannerisms almost made me laugh. Cora! Standing here at my penthouse. She pointed a thumb toward the door that led inside.

"They're, uh, they're saying that airports may not be open much longer, so I wanted to grab the sketchbook I left behind and some toiletries."

"You came all this way for toiletries?"

"Ah, no?"

"I thought you weren't afraid of being straightforward?"

She scowled, and I felt my first moment of hope. Her chin lifted defiantly. "I'm not afraid of being straightforward."

"Then say it."

With a pretty scowl, she muttered, "Fine. I messed up. I came to admit my mistakes and beg you to forgive me and see if you wanted to come spend a pandemic at my loft. It's a dream, I know. You work at a billion-dollar corporation and—"

Blinking, I whispered, "What?"

"I . . ." She rolled her lips together. "I shouldn't have left before the gala, and I apologize. I didn't give you a chance to explain, and that wasn't fair. I'm sorry, Hawk. Truly sorry. You tried to show me love in your way and I threw it back in your face."

The mournful note of her voice almost broke me.

"You have nothing to apologize for, Cora."

Undaunted, she continued. "You and I have different ways of showing love and we need to talk about that. Also, art galleries don't work the way you want them to, and we should discuss that, too. And we will because it's you and me. I'm here for it."

Her brow wrinkled. When I stepped closer, she held up a hand.

"No, don't do that. If you step too close, I'll get all pulled into your magic and forget what I came to say. I *will* be heard."

I suppressed a smile.

"You will."

"I'm sorry, Hawk. I didn't recognize all your effort for what it was. You were giving me gifts to show your affection and love, weren't you?"

I nodded.

"And I thought you were trying to buy me off to avoid spending time with me."

"Cora, the only thing I *want* is you."

She softened. "Thank you. I feel that way as well. I should have tried harder to see your side of it. And, in hindsight, I should have given you the chance to tell me what you wanted to say before the gala. It was . . . just a bad day and then you told me about the headlines and—"

The light mood soured a touch, but I wouldn't let this moment torch. I shuffled forward another step. She didn't tell me off.

I lifted my hands, pressed them to my chest. "Cora, it's me that needs to apologize. When Tate first appeared, I should have been more forward with you. I wanted to spare you the anxiety that he induces in just about everyone, but by doing that, I ended up just isolating you. I'm sorry."

Tears sparkled in her eyes. "It's forgiven, Hawk."

"There are plans for my company I didn't tell you about,

either. Active ones to leave and I became wrapped up in everything and should have communicated better with you."

Her shoulders pulled back.

"Really?"

"Really. I don't deserve you, Cora. But I want you more than anything. Let me tell you everything, please?"

"Over nachos?"

Unable to help it, I laughed.

"Yes, nachos. This will be the best day of my life. Nicola running the company. You in my arms and my favorite nachos in my belly."

Cora reared back.

"Nicola what?"

"We have a *lot* to catch up on."

She hovered close enough to touch. Her hand lifted, reaching for the fuzzy hair at the nape of my neck. The tips of her fingers toyed with it, driving me crazy. I clenched my teeth and tried to bury the urge to lock our lips together and never let go.

"Cora?"

"Yes, Hawk?"

"Come inside and let me explain everything? I'll order nachos, you can sit in your comfy clothes, and we'll watch bad television and make fun of it until we're both too tired to go to bed, and we'll fall asleep together on the couch."

Her lips twitched.

"Hawk, you've never made me want to swoon more than this moment."

I hooked a hand around her waist, pulled her into me. "You and me, Cora," I murmured. "You and me."

Her arms wrapped around my shoulders, lips found mine with a hunger that surprised me. This fierce girl.

She was all mine.

Chapter Thirty-One

CORA

Snow drifted outside as I set my palette on the table, plunked my brush into the glass jar, and stepped back.

Painting?

Complete.

Details scattered the work. Touch-ups for shadow here and there. A splash of white under too much gray. Sprinkles of evergreen where I had bountiful umber. Fussies, I called them. Unimportant details no one but myself would notice.

Satisfaction welled up from deep inside. I'd done it. My largest commission yet. A pair of arms came around me from behind. Hawk's stubble grazed the skin of my neck, sending a chill down my spine.

"It's beautiful," he growled.

I laughed, twirled in his arms, wrapped myself around his waist. Winter fluffed from the sky outside. In the distance, a deepening blue appeared. Winds nudged the clouds to the west, opening a wash of beautiful azure.

In the background, the news channel chattered about virus updates. Hawk insisted on listening as the pandemic advanced.

To me?

Didn't matter.

We cozied up together in the loft. Groceries stocked, toilet paper in the closet, oil paints all around, and a healthy internet connection for when he talked Nicola through unexpected difficulties.

Fortunately, those calls didn't happen all that often.

The shutdown of the country as the virus swept through happened outside of the bubble we commandeered. Chattering voices still filled the Frolicking Moose downstairs, before rumored closures. Meanwhile, I curled up in Hawk's arms.

We had all the time together we wanted.

Hawk pressed a kiss to my temple, stepped back. I wanted to follow him, but cleaned up instead. Ravioli bubbled in a boiling pot on the stove, filling the air with heated steam. A text message from Cade appeared on my phone.

Cade: How are you, sis? Miss you.

Cora: Happy as ever. When are you coming over for dinner? You haven't met Hawk yet, and that's just weird. We've been here for a week.

Cade: Soon, I promise. Morgan's granddaughter just bought a flight and is coming out. I have to fly to Florida before she arrives.

A cold shot of dread pooled in my stomach.

Cora: Mom?

Cade: Nothing confirmed. I want to find her one last

time before they shut the airports down. Maybe we
can convince her to come back.

My heart lurched. Unlike me, Cade had never let go of
hope for Mom. I suspected he went to Florida, looking for her,
more often than not. I chewed on my bottom lip, fidgeting
with the neckline of my shirt.

Cora: Is it safe? Cade, what if you get sick?

Cade: I'll be fine. I'll be gone less than 48 hours. My
flight comes in around the same time as Morgan's
granddaughter anyway, so it's perfect timing. We'll
firm up what the will says and go from there.

Cora: Please, keep me updated.

Cade: I always do.

My anxiety faded when Hawk came back to my side, his
hand under my chin. He lifted my jaw to look at him. I
melted, relieved to have him. What would I have done without
him here?

"Your brother?"

"You'll get to meet him soon."

"It's only been a week," he said with a kindness that
dismissed any worry or frustration he might have felt. "I'm
sure it will be fine."

I released concerns about Cade and viruses and Mom and
inheritances and focused on Hawk, who stared at me with
such depth of passion and power.

"You and me, Hawk Mercedy," I whispered. "It's just you
and me."

He grinned.

"I like the sound of that. You're missing one thing, though."

"What's that?"

"Forever. It's you and me *forever*."

Also by Katie Cross

The Health and Happiness Society

Bon Bons to Yoga Pants (Lexie)

I Am Girl Power (Megan)

You'll Never Know (Rachelle)

Hear Me Roar (Bitsy)

What Was Lost (Mira)

The Health and Happiness Society Collection

Finding Anna

Coffee Shop Series

1. Coffee Shop Girl

2. Lovesick

3. Runaway

4. Fighter

5. Shy Girl

6. Wild Child

7. Smoke and Fire

8. Clean Sweep

9. Protect Me

10. You and Me

About the Author

Katie Cross is ALL ABOUT writing epic love stories and wild places. Creating new books is her jam.

When she's not hiking or chasing her two littles through the Montana mountains, you can find her curled up reading a book or arguing with her husband over the best kind of sushi.

Visit her at www.katiecrossbooks.com for free short stories, extra savings on all her books (and some you can't buy on the retailers), and so much more.